THE
GATEKEEPER'S
PORTAL

THE ELEMENTALS TRILOGY
BOOK TWO

S.W. RAINE

The Gatekeeper's Portal
Copyright © 2026 by S.W. Raine

Contact info: http://www.swraine.com

Cover Design by: Fiona Jayde Media
Editing by: Cassidy Clarke

ISBN: 978-1-969518-04-1

First Edition: January 2026

10 9 8 7 6 5 4 3 2 1

The Gatekeeper's Portal has been rated Moderate+ for:

- Significant substance use
- Some profanity
- Moderate violence
- Mention of child abuse/exploitation

For more information on MBR ratings, visit:
https://mybookcave.com/mybookratings

To Joshua, for always preordering

before anyone—except that one time...

CHAPTER 1
Ferenc

Ferenc never thought he'd be captivated by anyone else after Amy. Yet there he sat beneath the shade of a wide oak in the park, unable to look away from Dormouse.

He took a drag from his cigarette—the only reprieve his aching cheeks received from smiling so much—as she launched a frisbee toward Max, his golden retriever. His beloved dog startled a laugh out of him when she leaped higher than he'd ever seen her leap before just to catch the disk.

Dormouse appeared to be thoroughly enjoying herself too. After spending so much of her life shaped by her natural shyness, she'd finally opened up to him over the last few weeks, and he'd fallen for her hard. As a guardian, he didn't know if he could have a relationship with the elemental he'd sworn to protect, but as he couldn't recall whatever past life they'd lived, well . . . he'd deal with any potential consequences later.

After a few more rounds of fetch, Dormouse and Max returned to Ferenc just as he finished up his cigarette.

1

"Did all that running make enough room for dessert?" he asked.

She grinned, dark blue eyes sparkling. "More food?" She plopped down next to him on his blue quilt while Max lay down nearby, panting through her own grin. "Just how much of it did you bring? What else is in there?"

"I'll never tell."

She crawled over him to get to the basket, but he wrapped his arms around her tiny waist and pulled her back with a chuckle.

"Hey, now. That's my secret. Close your eyes."

Dormouse tilted her head, thick eyebrow quirked. He couldn't blame her for hesitating; though her distrust had faded enough for her to confide in him, even share a home with him, years of past trauma couldn't be undone overnight.

"Come on." Ferenc gently placed a hand over her eyes until her lashes brushed against his palm, notifying him she'd given in.

He pulled his hand away and rummaged through the picnic basket until his fingers brushed hard plastic. He opened the container, and the familiar toasted and nutty aroma wafted from the chocolate truffles to his nose. Even with her eyes closed, Dormouse gasped in delight.

A grin came easily to his face as he opened another container with quartered strawberries. Butterflies and knots of nerves fought for dominance in his stomach as he set them on the blanket. "Okay. You can open them now."

Dormouse opened her eyes, a squeak worthy of her namesake escaping as she reached for the containers, fingers hovering indecisively over which to start with. She made her choice after a few stalled seconds, snatching up a truffle and biting into it. The moan that followed set his mind at ease, and he plopped two strawberry slices into his mouth with a smile.

"Oh my God, these are so good," she said, lying on her back.

Ferenc grinned and leaned on his elbow next to her. "I'm glad you approve."

"Where did you get them?"

"Remember when Betty said she was trying some new recipes?" Dormouse nodded. "I snuck down to the diner to get some while you were napping yesterday."

She raised a brow. "Was that before or after you went grocery shopping?"

"Before, actually. She mentioned they'd be perfect for a picnic, and I just ran with it."

"Well, she was right." She finished off her truffle with a satisfied sigh. "I'm glad she gave you the idea."

He chuckled, tucking a loose strand of black hair that'd escaped her ponytail behind her ear. "Me too."

Her cheeks flushed, and the butterflies won the battle in his stomach, fluttering like mad as his heart pounded. He had to swallow hard before he could get his question out. "Can I kiss you?"

Her breath caught in her throat for a second before she nodded ever so faintly. "I'd like that," she replied, barely above a whisper.

He slowly leaned in, ignoring Max's sudden barking, too caught up in the moment.

He should have known better.

"Max is right, you know," came a woman's voice. "That's total gag material right there."

Ferenc's heart skipped a beat. He instantly jumped to his feet, ready to protect Dormouse, but he found himself face-to-face with Olivia.

"Jesus Chr—put some bells on, for crying out loud!" He grasped his chest, where his heart threatened to escape the confines of his ribcage. He then pulled her into a hug.

Over the brief time they'd gotten to know one another, Olivia had become a great friend. She kept him in check, had taught him how to use his abilities, and had saved him on more than one occasion. She'd spent months searching high and low for the elemental, and he'd been worried for her every day.

"Did I scare you?" She giggled, seemingly content with herself.

"If not him, then definitely me," Dormouse chimed in as she sat up.

Ferenc pulled away from Olivia and helped Dormouse to her feet.

"So, when did you two become a thing?" Olivia asked, wagging her index finger back and forth between him and Dormouse.

Dormouse blushed and shoved a hand in the front pouch of her oversized hoodie while bringing the other to her mouth, chewing on her fingernails.

Ferenc crossed his arms over his chest. "Actually, we haven't become anything because *someone* interrupted the moment."

Olivia brought a hand up to cover an embarrassed laugh. "I'm *so* sorry."

"It's all right," he reassured her, despite the heavy sigh. "I'm happy to see you again. How have you been? Any luck finding the fire elemental?"

Olivia shook her head, her straight platinum-blonde hair dancing from the movement, then inhaled deeply. "No, but I had the pleasure of meeting the lunar princess, the lunar prince's adviser . . . and the solar king's adviser."

"Wait, there's a kingdom on the sun too?" Dormouse asked as she pulled her fingers away.

Olivia nodded. "Despite everything that happened earlier this year, you're both never going to believe this."

He hadn't believed in the elementals and his own abilities for the longest time, no matter how much proof Olivia had shown him. He'd been stubborn, analytical, insisting on researching the hell out of anything he could. Never in his wildest dreams would he have ever imagined he'd face off against a lunar high priest by using air magic.

He couldn't imagine anything less believable than that.

Olivia lowered herself to the blanket, helping herself to the picnic basket and pulling out the container of raw vegetables. He and Dormouse exchanged confused looks before joining her.

"The fire elemental isn't the only one who was taken; the lunar prince has apparently vanished as well," she reported between bites of a bell pepper stick.

"Richard's doing?" Dormouse asked.

Olivia shrugged. "They don't know, but they seemed pretty alarmed by what he'd done."

5

The dislike Ferenc felt for Richard as his ex's lawyer—and boy-friend—had been one thing, but when he'd kidnapped Dormouse, hurt her, and revealed himself as some kind of power-hungry being from the moon, that dislike had shifted to pure loathing. And Ferenc hated that they didn't know if Richard had survived or not after their battle inside the Lunar Temple.

"His moon name is Alican. Oh, and get this—the lunar princess is actually human. And she needs our help to get the prince and the fire elemental back."

Ferenc stroked his chin in thought. Olivia had searched that temple high and low without finding anyone. "How do we do that? We don't even know where they are."

Olivia dug into the basket again, retrieving a box of crackers. "I know. But I think I have an idea. The solar king's adviser suggested we find someone named Anya—she's something called a *Gate-keeper*, and she can take us to someone called the *Keeper of the Realms*. This Keeper can not only answer all my questions, includ-ing why everyone kept calling me *General—*"

"General?" Ferenc and Dormouse repeated in unison.

Olivia shrugged, then continued, "This Keeper can also, appar-ently, fully reawaken all the elementals and guardians. That would cause big problems for whoever took them. They might also know where the prince is."

Ferenc slowly nodded. His mind immediately began reeling over every problem they could potentially encounter while search-ing for this Anya person, but Olivia jabbed a cracker at him.

"Hold on. I see the smoke coming from your brain. Before you get too far in that plan you're making up, just know Anya doesn't want to be found. According to the advisers, her last-known location was 'somewhere in Russia.'" She formed air quotes with her fingers for emphasis before shoving another cracker in her mouth.

Ferenc sighed. Good thing he knew how to research better than anyone. "I need another cigarette." He reached into his breast pocket and pulled out a slim silver case.

"I'm sorry." Her emerald eyes dropped to the truffle container, and she nabbed one before adding, "I didn't want to drag you into this, but I didn't know what else to do. Doing it alone is hard."

Ferenc lit his cigarette. "You're not dragging us into anything. This whole *elemental-and-guardian* thing became a part of our lives the moment I hit you with the jet." She smiled sheepishly, and he flashed a smirk in return. "But I'm glad you came to us. We'll help any way we can . . . within reason. Right?" He shifted his attention to Dormouse. "That's what friends are for."

She didn't reply, but the faint nod of her head told him she agreed.

Dormouse had wanted nothing to do with being an elemental from the start. She'd been running from all the unwanted attention from Richard's masked goons and unearthly creatures—lunanites. Ever silent and reticent, the thought of being an elemental scared her, and he couldn't blame her. He never forced her to do anything she didn't want, and he'd done his best to prevent Olivia from pushing her to that point.

7

When Richard had kidnapped Dormouse, forced her into her sylph form, and drained her energy to use against him, Ferenc had vowed to himself to double down on never forcing her to do anything involving being an elemental or using powers. He'd continued practicing, mastering his own air abilities, and in the meantime, he'd kept his word. He planned to continue to do so.

"Come on," he said, putting the lids back on the containers. "Help me pack this up, then we can go home and figure this out together."

CHAPTER 2
Ferenc

O ver two hundred people in Russia bore the surname Bordyu-kova—but not one of them shared the name Anya. At least, none Ferenc nor Olivia could find.

They'd returned home after the picnic and promptly began their search. Olivia borrowed his laptop while Ferenc scrolled on his cell phone, neither of them stopping until Dormouse's growling stomach reminded him it was past dinnertime. They only stopped long enough to order pizza before diving back in.

Finally, when his eyes burned too badly to keep going, Ferenc set his phone face down on the arm of his recliner as he lay his head back with an exhausted sigh. "Anything?"

"I mean, we can try the *Annas*, since it's apparently the same origin, but other than that . . ." Olivia shut the laptop without finishing her sentence. They'd both clearly had enough for the night.

"I need a cigarette." At his words, Max shot up from the rug, wagging her tail expectantly. "Looks like someone else needs to go outside too."

9

Dormouse stood from her lazy, reclined position on the love seat, stretching her arms over her head with a yawn. "Come on, Max."

"Yeah, I could use some fresh air too," Olivia added.

A knock at the front door interrupted his craving. That had to be Amy, here to take Max for the weekend.

He opened the door and found familiar freckles and a pair of brown eyes glaring up at him on the other side. "Ferenc," Amy greeted coldly. Before he could reply, Max forced the door open wider, whipping his legs with her excited tail. "Baby!" Amy squealed, dropping to Max's level, her brown curls bouncing as she dove for a hug.

Ferenc welcomed the distraction. Things had grown awkward between him and Amy. She'd broken up with him for being distant, and she'd grown colder and meaner ever since, even dragging him to court multiple times. But she'd been under Richard's weird lunar spell then. Since Richard's defeat, Amy had seemed to fight off what remained of the influence, but she hadn't completely escaped it— her hatred for Ferenc ebbed and flowed like the phases of the moon.

He'd loved her. But that love had shifted over the months, and the last of his attachment died out when she'd stayed on Richard's side despite everything the high-priest-turned-lawyer had done— even turning Amy into a monster. A *lunanite.*

He still deeply cared about her, but as a guardian, his full attention belonged on Dormouse . . . even without taking his feelings into account.

Amy twitched in her internal battle as she stood back up. That fake smile she reserved for her coworkers found its way to her lips. "Is she ready to go?"

"Oh, uh, yeah," Ferenc said, running a hand through his hair. That cigarette craving struck with a vengeance. "She just needs to be let out. Come on in."

As Amy stepped inside and followed him down the hall, Dormouse peeked past the wall and called for Max, who trotted over to her.

"Everything okay?" Olivia asked, looking down at them as she leaned against the kitchen railing.

"Oh, your *other* girlfriend's here too?" Amy spat.

"Classy," Olivia countered as she pulled away.

Ferenc turned to her from the stairs. "Amy," he scolded. She'd voiced her dislike for this polyamorous idea she'd suddenly formed in her head before.

She hissed and winced in realization—part of that ebb and flow. "I'm sorry, I didn't—"

He continued up and into the kitchen. "Pay no mind to what she said. She's just taking it out on me."

"It's okay, not everyone has to like me," Olivia replied as she pulled the glass door open. "Not everyone has good taste," she added to Dormouse with a playful wink.

Max's dangerous growl caught his attention first, then Olivia gasped, drawing his eyes to her.

A wide-shouldered figure in a silver filigree mask stood on his balcony, a large hand on Olivia's wrist.

11

Ferenc's stomach dropped. His mind raced back to the chaos of the masked goons relentlessly hunting Dormouse. A symbol of everything Ferenc hated: dark lunar magic. Nightmarish lunanites. Richard.

"You're not the elemental," the masked man said.

Olivia struggled against his hold. "No shit!"

Ferenc grabbed both the frozen Dormouse and Amy by the arms, yanking them behind himself. "Lock yourselves up in the bedroom downstairs."

"What's—" Amy started.

"*Go!*"

Dormouse darted down the stairs in an instant, Max hot on her trail. But Amy stalled, confused, and she ducked and screamed when Olivia crashed into the back wall next to her, collapsing to the floor. The figure's massive shoulders dipped through the door.

"Oh, no, you don't." Ferenc launched cutting gales at him to push him back outside, but the man stood solid, save for his long, wavy blond hair that whipped around his face. Ferenc snarled. "Get out of my house!"

Without a second thought, he snatched the closest kitchen chair and hurled it toward the intruder with all his strength. The masked man raised his hand, palm out. The chair shattered midair, a rain of splinters showering the floor. Ferenc stumbled back, his heart racing.

The man fully stepped inside, unfazed. "Where's the elemental?"

Ferenc scrambled to his feet and shoved a blast of air toward the intruder. The man braced himself as he slid backward, slamming into the frame of the sliding door.

Ferenc glanced over his shoulder. He needed help, and fast. "Liv?"

"I'm okay." Olivia staggered to her feet with help from Amy, only to drop back to one knee as the entire house violently trembled. The cupboards slammed open and shut; the dishes tumbled out, shattering upon contact with the floor. Amy shrieked, wrapping her arms protectively over her head. Olivia waved her arm, creating an air shield to prevent the rest from touching them.

Violent barking and a blood-curdling scream pulled Ferenc away from the unnatural earthquake. He instantly hopped the railing from the kitchen down into the living room, flicking his wrists to slow his fall. He then darted down the hall in three bounds, skidding to a halt as he grabbed the handle to Dormouse's room. He pushed it open only to shove it into a dark, gangly creature.

Ferenc's jaw tightened as he swiftly manipulated the density of the air, creating a javelin-like weapon. He then thrust it into the lunanite's stomach, impaling it into the wall.

Dormouse cowered in the corner atop the bed. Max stood protectively in front of her, teeth bared.

"Good girl." He patted Max on the head before extending his hand to Dormouse.

She launched herself off the bed instead, wrapping her arms around his waist. He hugged her tightly, his heart racing as he glanced at the dead lunanite.

13

He'd been *that* close to losing her again.

"Let go of me!" Amy snarled.

Ferenc froze, instantly releasing Dormouse. The house had stopped shaking, and the edge in Amy's voice hit like a jolt—something must've happened to Olivia. He rushed down the hall and into the wide-open living room. He narrowed his eyes at the blond man up in the kitchen, who held Amy against him by the throat with a muscular arm. Olivia stood nearby, palms cautiously outstretched, as she assessed the new situation.

"Hand over the elemental, and nobody gets hurt," the man demanded.

"Over my dead body," Ferenc replied.

"If you don't want it to be over *her* dead body . . ." He squeezed his arm a little tighter. Amy, struggling to break free, gasped for air. "I suggest you cooperate."

Ferenc's mind raced through every possible option, every escape route or negotiation tactic. Every scenario arrived at a dead end.

He refused to hand Dormouse over to anyone, and despite her hatred for him, Amy didn't deserve to be hurt or killed. The balance of the situation tilted dangerously, and he couldn't see how to restore it.

"Please, let her go." Maybe this time, reason could win out. "She has nothing to do with this. She's not from the Realm of Air."

"All the more reason to hand the elemental over."

"Take me instead," Olivia offered.

Ferenc's stomach dropped. "No." He wouldn't allow Olivia to sacrifice herself. He couldn't afford to lose her.

His mind quickly searched for a solution. The most logical choice. The priority. He needed more time, more information—and no way to get either.

Sirens blared, swiftly approaching. A neighbor must've called the cops about all the commotion. Great—now he needed a cover-up story on top of everything else. Nobody would believe him if he mentioned masked magic users or dark creatures. Another variable to manage.

The masked man hissed in displeasure. "Time's up."

A spiral formed behind him, spinning with swirls of purples and grays. A portal. He took one large step back, vanishing into it, Amy's echoing scream cutting off when they both disappeared.

Without hesitation, Ferenc darted forward, calculation giving way to the need to do something—*anything*—to stop this from spiraling further out of control.

"Ferenc, stop!"

Olivia stepped in front of him, clasping his shoulders to slow him. The portal dissipated until it completely vanished.

"I need to save her!"

"I agree, but we can't go in without a plan. Not like we did with Richard."

"Watch me." He turned to head down the stairs.

"Where are you going?"

"The firm. I'm going to use their portal—"

"The portals are closed," Olivia stated. Her words paused him in his tracks. "The lunar princess had them closed down for safety reasons. I had to travel back to Earth with a moonstone, believe it or not."

He'd put Amy in danger, and he'd never forgive himself if they hurt her or turned her into a lunanite again. And now he had no way of following. If Olivia hadn't stopped him, he could've at least tried.

"I know that look." She stepped in front of him again and shifted her head to make sure he met her gaze. "Don't go down that road. We'll rescue her, okay? But right now, Dormouse needs you."

He clenched his fists, every instinct screaming at him to run after Amy.

"Hey!" Olivia's voice cut through his guilt. "Do you hear me? That guy just tried to kidnap Dormouse, so you can be sure he'll try it again. You can't fulfill your guardian duties with a foot in two separate realms."

He appreciated how she always brought him back to the matter at hand. He let out a breath and spun around to check on Dormouse, only to find her standing at the bottom of the stairs, looking up at him with her arms wrapped around herself. Relief washed through him, and his cigarette craving returned tenfold.

"Are you okay?" he asked her. Dormouse nodded before joining them in the kitchen, Max close behind her. "Is the lunanite still in your room?"

"No, it disappeared shortly after you ran back out."

"Lunanite?" Olivia's green eyes shot back and forth between him and Dormouse. "You don't suppose this proves Richard's still alive, do you? The guy had the same mask . . ."

Ferenc crossed his arms over his chest. "I don't know, but I have a feeling you're not wrong."

Olivia began pacing the kitchen, dodging all the broken dishes. "We need to find Anya. She's gotta be able to help."

"We can't just let them have Amy, can we?" Dormouse asked, nibbling absently at her fingernails.

"No, of course not," Olivia replied, her steps slowing as she shot a glance at Ferenc. "But we can't go after her blind, either. We need to be smart about this."

"What if that guy comes back here looking for me while we're gone?" Dormouse's voice wavered.

Ferenc shook his head. "Something tells me he'll find us no matter where we are."

He thought back to the past few months, when they'd gotten Dormouse an ID card and passport. At least he'd managed that much. After recovering from his broken collarbone, he'd gone back to freelance piloting and suggested she get her passport so she could travel with him if he ever needed to go overseas. Now that time had come.

CHAPTER 3
Deon

Deon's plan to capture the air elemental had gone sideways remarkably fast. The situation had already been unfavorable when he'd accidentally grabbed the other air user instead, but if he'd still been present when the police arrived—with a hostage, no less—it would've only drawn more unwanted attention on him.

He strode down the dim hall, the curly-haired woman struggling to pull her tiny wrist from his hand.

"Let go of me!" she demanded.

He didn't know what to do with her. She hadn't been part of his plan—just an unfortunate, innocent bystander caught in it.

A slim figure stepped out of a room at the end of the hall: his master. Shikki paused and glanced over his shoulder, a raised brow on his features. This wouldn't be easy to explain. Shikki wouldn't be pleased about his failure.

"Help me!" the woman cried. Her voice reverberated annoyingly off the walls.

Shikki's black brows shifted from confusion to annoyance before his pale eyes widened in surprise. He then rushed over.

"Amy!" He lightly placed a frigid hand over Deon's. "Let her go." Deon obeyed.

She snatched her wrist away and rubbed it. "Who the hell are you people? How do you know my name?"

Deon also wanted to know but dared not speak. It wasn't his place to ask.

Shikki's expression softened. "I'm Richard's . . . associate. Sh—" He flicked his attention at Deon for but an instant, the gears in his master's head practically visible in his sharp gaze. "Shane," he finished.

Amy's attitude immediately shifted. "Richard? Is he—"

"He's not faring too well after losing to your ex, I fear," he replied. He then shot Deon a quick warning glance, a silent command to stay quiet and let him handle this. "My friend here was trying to exact revenge for Richard. I apologize for his brutish actions, but it's lucky he found you when he did. I'm sure Richard would feel better if he knew you were safe. Come, let me take you to him."

Shikki walked away with Amy willingly following, leaving Deon behind.

He'd deciphered Alican had used Richard as an alias and that Amy and the air guardian had some kind of past bond, but he didn't understand the connection between Alican and Amy. Still, none of it concerned him.

He removed his mask, resting it atop his head as he strode toward a thick metal door. Mission first, everything else second. That had been the rule as long as he'd been doing this—as long as he could remember . . .

Unfortunately, he couldn't remember much.

Every time he tried, thought itself dissolved into fog. And each time he braved the blind venture, he arrived at what could only be described as a solid brick wall in his mind. He didn't know what it meant, and any attempts to get past it had proven fruitless.

He arrived at the thick metal door and turned the locking wheel with ease. It groaned and squealed before he pulled the door open, casting a faint amount of light into the pitch-black room beyond.

Deon stepped inside, pausing at the smooth bars of a cell. He didn't need light; the faint vibrations in the metals mapped the room for him.

That, and the lunar prince glowed softly like the moon . . . with absolutely none of the celestial body's composure.

"Release us!" demanded the captive prince, his restraints rattling as he rose to grip the bars.

Prince Lomos had been easy to capture. Married to a Gaean woman, he often visited their mansion in Spain. They spent their evenings and nights together, and, like clockwork, the prince would return to the Lunar Palace just as the last rays of moonlight disappeared, making way for a new day. And Deon had used that consistent schedule to his advantage, kidnapping the lunar prince before he even knew what hit him.

Deon ignored the order. "Step back." He placed his hand against the lock, manipulating the element within until the cage unlocked.

"And if I refuse?"

He didn't have time for the prince's games. He batted a hand as if swatting a fly, and Lomos let out a strangled cry as his chains yanked him off his feet. Deon then opened the cell and stepped past Lomos, going straight for the fire elemental curled up in the corner.

The girl cowered against the back wall, shoulder pressed into the metal as if trying to meld into it, but the bars didn't bend for her. He kneeled and touched the thick clasps around her ankles, which clattered to the floor. He then reached for the ones around her delicate wrists, but she pulled away with a whimper.

"Cooperate, phoenix, or it won't end well, I promise you."

"Don't you dare touch her!" Lomos snarled. Deon clenched his jaw and jerked a hand down behind his back. Lomos cried out as he dropped to the ground, the restraints around his ankles, wrists, and neck sticking to the floor like heavy magnets.

Once he removed the girl's shackles, Deon snaked his arms around her and scooped her up with ease. She weighed practically nothing. The elemental flailed her legs and grabbed a fistful of his hair, trying to tear it out of his scalp.

He set her down only to fold her arms across her chest from behind, restraining her further—if she kept writhing like that, she'd hurt herself far more than she'd manage to hurt him.

"It's not me you should be fighting," he murmured. But he understood why she tried. It might not have been his business to say anything to his master, but the pain the girl endured as Shikki drained her energy . . . no child should have been put through that.

He couldn't tell if his draw to this girl—an odd certainty he'd seen her before—meant anything. He couldn't, for the life of him, figure out who she might be. At first, he thought he'd gone soft simply because of her age—no more than twelve, by his guess. Too young to get caught up in this. But the more he followed that line of thinking, the more he found himself face-to-face with the brick wall in his brain.

"Release her!" Lomos ordered, glaring up at him through his long, splayed white hair.

Deon continued to ignore the struggling prince. He stepped right past him—crushing one of the moonstone beads decorating Lomos's hair—and out of the cage once the fire elemental stopped fighting, pulling her along by her bony wrist. Lomos's angry cries echoed down the halls before the thick door trapped the voice within the room—blissful relief to Deon's ears.

He released the girl's wrist and took her hand instead before heading down the dim hall. She followed, her head down, and she sniffled. He cast a sideways glance down at her. She cried behind the filthy orange hair that curtained her face. She must've been traumatized; she hadn't spoken a word since her arrival, and what little sounds she produced imitated a bird—like a phoenix.

"I wish you'd speak," he said softly. She chirped in reply, an almost melancholic tone reverberating against something invisible in his mind. He sighed. "I meant speak in *words*."

She chirped again, and then nothing.

They continued on in silence the rest of the way. When they turned a corner, she started to squirm. Deon lightly squeezed her hand, but it didn't ease her anxiety; she knew what awaited her behind the closed door at the end of the hall.

The closer they got, the more she tried to tug her hand away from him, but he held firm. This happened every time. He'd never personally had his energy drained—that much he could remember—but based on her and Lomos's cries and the way they collapsed afterward, he could only imagine how much it hurt. The fact she continued to survive the ordeal both surprised and impressed him.

"I'm sorry," he said as he pulled her toward more pain.

Her filthy bare feet skidded along the floor, and when she tripped, no longer able to keep up, he spun around and scooped her back into his arms. She wiggled and writhed to get free, but she might as well have been a scruffed kitten; she could do no harm to him as he carried her in.

Deon toed the door open and brought her to the large platform in the center of the room. He set her down, keeping his hold on her bony shoulders to prevent her from escaping. She gripped his hands and looked up at him, tears welling in her pleading golden eyes. His chest tightened.

"Stay here," he instructed before releasing her and taking a step back. Her bottom lip quivered, and she wavered, inching forward. He hastened his backward pace and activated the dome just as an iridescent shimmer coated her hair and her eyes twinkled with fire. "Don't," he warned. "You'll hurt yourself."

But she didn't listen.

Her tiny body lurched back as the dome enclosed around her, ruby feathers sprouting instantaneously all over, expanding in length as she grew in size. But the dome stunted her growth, and the phoenix's anxiety doubled. She shrieked in bird form as she tried to fully spread her wings and failed. She kicked, scratched, and bit at the glass separating them, and each strike pierced his heart like an arrow.

He bit his tongue from retorting that he'd told her so, and he spun around to leave. He couldn't handle this anymore. When he reached the door, he found Shikki standing before him on the other side.

They stared at one another in silence for a moment before Shikki glanced over Deon's shoulder at the phoenix. "Excellent," he said with a wicked grin.

Deon forced himself to surface from the fog, pulling himself out to act. He stepped aside to allow Shikki through. "Master," he acknowledged.

Shikki stepped through the doorway but paused before Deon. His gray eyes darkened, and Deon instantly recognized the look— he'd landed himself in trouble. "What happened?" he asked. "Where is the air elemental, Deon?"

He'd failed. He knew it, Shikki knew it . . . but Shikki wouldn't want to hear that. Deon swallowed hard as he bowed.

"Slight miscalculation," he admitted, as the image of the surprised blonde air user flashed in his mind. "It won't happen again."

"Good."

Shikki said nothing more as he continued on toward the dome, the phoenix's shriek rising with every step he took toward her. Deon straightened from his bow and exited the room, hastening his pace to his private quarters with each high-pitched scream that thrummed through the floor and walls. They vibrated through his bones like a tuning fork until he slammed his door shut in anger.

If only he could remember.

CHAPTER 4
Ferenc

Russia remained just as Ferenc remembered it: majestic, baroque, and interwoven with pragmatism and ambition—even at four o'clock in the morning.

Olivia surprised him by having a decent grasp of Russian, so he'd allowed her to take charge of traveling to a hotel and reserving a room. Bundled up outside in a designated smoking area, he watched Olivia and Dormouse through the lobby doors as he finished his cigarette.

A shudder rattled him as he blew out his smoke, and he momentarily shut his eyes, letting his exhausted mind wander. Nightlife sounds, scents, and even tastes muddled together to become one single muted sense with no distinguishable direction. The sooner he could go to bed, the better.

After one final drag, he extinguished the remainder of the cigarette in the ashtray, then returned inside. The door clicked softly behind him, and the cold dissipated as the warmth of the hotel enveloped him.

Olivia held up the key cards with a bleary-eyed smile before turning and heading for the elevators. Dormouse followed, and Ferenc trailed behind in silence. The fleeting freedom of flying still lingered in his body—no restrictions, no boundaries. A momentary escape from everything that weighed him down.

But the memories of Amy's abduction never trailed far behind, the guilt of *should-haves* and *could-haves* wrapping tighter around him with every flash.

As they rode up to the room, his mind snapped back to the present as he glanced at Dormouse's reflection through the stainless steel of the elevator doors. The anxiety of her first plane ride had left her with dark circles under her eyes. She leaned against the wall, tightly gripping the handrails.

At least he'd protected her from being taken. He couldn't say the same for Amy.

"You good?"

He dragged his attention away from Dormouse to find Olivia watching him, brows raised.

"I'm fine," he muttered. The lingering sensation of flight still buoyed him, like he hadn't quite touched the ground yet. Up there, with the hum of the cabin and the soft drone of the engines, the echo of Amy's scream had been distant. Now it crept back in, but the sky's hold on him remained, keeping him just out of reach of the heaviness waiting to pull him down.

When they entered the room, Dormouse barely made it to the farthest bed before collapsing onto it with a groan. "Ugh. I just want a shower."

"Go ahead and take one," Ferenc replied with a chuckle as he set their suitcases against the wall.

Dormouse zipped into the bathroom, shutting the door behind her.

He turned his attention to Olivia to find her already watching him, her head tilted slightly in silent inquiry.

He nodded. "I'm fine. Really."

She studied him for a moment but didn't press further. She then sat on the edge of the first bed. "So, what's the plan now?"

The urge to act immediately pressed hard, but he knew better. Sheer force wouldn't get them very far, not in this frayed, exhausted state. They all needed to be sharp. If he pushed himself now, he'd be no good for what came next.

"Get some rest." At four o'clock in the morning, most people still slept anyway. "We'll wait to head out until we've recovered from traveling."

"Don't have to tell me twice!" Olivia grabbed her suitcase and unzipped it, reaching for a change of clothes.

Ferenc approached the windows, peeking out at the city lights in the distance between the sheer curtains. He caught sight of Olivia's partial reflection against the window as she carelessly changed, but his focus floated back to the horizon that'd been swallowed up by the night.

The tranquility of the nonjudgmental sky and endless beauty of the landscape when flying struggled against the hostility of everything he couldn't control. Amy's disappearance. Dormouse's safety.

The looming threat of a masked organization. His heart rate lurched back and forth between calm and agitation.

A soft touch to his arm gently drew him out of his thoughts.

"Where did you go?" Dormouse asked quietly.

Ferenc glanced over his shoulder as he forced himself to return to reality to find Olivia fast asleep. His gaze fell to Dormouse, nearly swallowed by the folds of the oversized T-shirt that hung loosely on her tiny frame as she looked up through her mess of long, wet hair.

He turned back to the window, gazing past his reflection. "It's been a long time since I've last been in Russia," he said. "Back then, it was a whole different kind of business trip. One that didn't involve gatekeepers and kings and princes and potentially dangerous stuff. Only flying."

"I'm scared," she whispered.

Ferenc turned back to fully face her as she sat on the edge of the bed. "Scared of what?"

"All of this. Everything Olivia told us. It was one thing when she told me I was an elemental, but it's another thing to be told that not only am I an elemental, but apparently I'm some sort of . . . powerful goddess-like being of an entire realm, and that there are more just like me, and that we're all part of something even bigger. As if being an elemental wasn't big enough. We can't go back to normal. Not now, not ever."

After everything that'd happened on the moon, he'd tried to shield her from this new life, tried to help her live as normally as possible despite his own continued training to keep her safe. But Olivia had relayed more information about the elementals over pizza while they did their research, and as rulers of their respective realms—and the only ones capable of transformation—Dormouse had a point.

Normal no longer existed in their vocabulary. This edged them even further from it, and she had every right to be scared. Hell, even *he* feared what lay ahead.

He pulled the thick curtains closed, then sat next to Dormouse. He gently placed a hand over hers as she fiddled with the hem of her shirt.

"You don't have to be scared. I'll be here for you, no matter what. I won't let anything happen to you."

She nodded. "I know. Because you're my guardian."

"Because I care about you," he corrected.

In the soft, dim light of the bedside lamp, they held each other's gaze for what seemed like an eternity. For someone so guarded, keeping eye contact for as long as Dormouse did without turning away meant something.

"Will you be all right?" she finally asked.

He appreciated her concern more than she'd ever know. "I'll be fine. Nothing a little sleep couldn't fix."

He motioned for her to get to bed with a nod of his chin. Dormouse smiled and whispered goodnight before getting up and making her way to the bed she'd agreed to share with Olivia. She practically disappeared beneath the blankets. Ferenc remained still, watching the subtle rise and fall of her breathing under the covers before finally getting up to freshen up.

And when the room plunged into darkness to match the night after he climbed into his own bed, he rested an arm beneath his head and stared at the ceiling, alone with his thoughts once more.

The regret that built up with each flash of Amy threatened to swallow him whole when his bed shifted. A tiny body crawled atop the covers next to him. She laid her head on his chest, and he reached over to cover her with the blankets before running his fingers through her wet hair, grateful to focus on her instead and keep the suffocating thoughts at bay.

CHAPTER 5
Olivia

Olivia couldn't sleep. It didn't matter how deeply exhaustion rooted in her bones; every time she dozed off, she snapped back awake, her mind buzzing. She kept either replaying the fight against the masked man over and over in her head, searching for something—anything—she could've done differently to save Amy, or her thoughts swirled around every word the lunar princess and the advisers had spoken back on the moon. Her brain refused to quiet.

To top it off, she'd overheard most of what Ferenc and Dormouse had said, both believing she was fast asleep. Ferenc had always been protective of Dormouse, trying to shield her from being forced into this world of elementals and guardians. But as much as guilt pricked at her for pulling them back in, too much had already happened to turn back. Dormouse couldn't escape what she was. They all had a part to play, whether Ferenc liked it or not.

She glanced at the red digits on the clock for the umpteenth time. The dark sky outside stubbornly refused to lighten as the winter months clung to the early morning hours. With a sigh, she turned onto her back, staring at the ceiling.

The masked man must also have been behind the fire elemental and the lunar prince's disappearance. After all, he'd been after Dormouse, even though he'd abducted Amy in the process. Anybody could be next if he succeeded.

Her thoughts shifted to the Keeper of the Realms. The excitement of possibly getting answers about her mission and why the advisers had called her *General* bubbled up, only to fade, replaced instead with a heaviness within. This mission carried weight, each step more complicated than the last.

She snatched her cell phone—a prepaid one Ferenc insisted she get—from the nightstand between both beds and, in the dim light, tried practicing her rusty Russian by reading. Unfortunately, time didn't go by any faster. She tried quietly watching television, and she even paced the room. But time didn't play fair; it continued to crawl.

Olivia glanced toward the bed where Dormouse and Ferenc lay fast asleep, their breathing soft and steady. They needed the rest, especially after the journey they'd had. But Olivia needed to *do* something. If it meant getting a head start while they slept, all the better. She could at least start investigating the leads about Anya on her own and return before they even knew she'd left.

With a long, low sigh, Olivia showered and dressed, then left the room.

Streetlights flickered over the snow-dusted streets as vehicles rumbled by and boots shuffled against pavement in the early hours of the day. Olivia stuck to the sidewalks, glancing down at the directions the hotel clerk had pulled from a map on his phone.

Though slower, traveling by foot to Anya's last-known address kept things safer. Lightning travel carried too much risk in such a populated place; few, if any, would ever consider it a *normal* mode of transportation. The general population always reacted poorly to things they didn't understand or couldn't explain. She couldn't risk attracting unwanted attention.

The Californian in her wanted to immediately escape the frigid temperature and run back to the heat as she shivered inside her thick coat. But the air user—the general, as the people from the moon called her—soldiered through.

Eventually, she arrived at a small community of apartments clustered around a four-way stop. Her eyes traveled up and down the tall complexes, the tacky colors muted from lack of sunlight between the odd mixture of both modern and baroque styles. She found the building in question and tried the front door. It held fast, locked.

A panel of buzzers next to the entrance revealed a slew of name tags: handwritten and typed out, big and small, bold and faded. She inspected them all and could barely make out the name BORDYU-KOVA on the faded tag beneath the tenth button. A faint buzzing occurred when she pressed the button, but nobody replied or allowed her inside.

She pursed her lips and planted her mittened hands on her hips, tapping her foot in thought. If Anya truly didn't live there anymore, how would she get in?

Olivia took a few steps back, her gaze on the various balconies. She tried to calculate which apartment once belonged to Anya, but she couldn't tell—she didn't know the interior layout. She then glanced around, making sure nobody would catch her using her abilities. Even in the darkness, the move risked exposure, but she could probably get a better look by peeking through the hallway windows.

With the coast clear, her heart fluttered, and she flicked her wrists. She'd barely launched off the ground with help from a twister at her feet when one of the tenants stepped out. Panic-stricken, Olivia stumbled instead, tripping over her heavy boots in an effort to stifle her abilities in public.

Despite the cold, her face, neck, and ears burned impossibly hot as she regained her footing and rushed to grab the door before it shut. She muttered, "I locked myself out," in Russian before stepping inside, where she let out a silent breath of relief.

She removed her fur hat and mittens as she made her way up the stairs to apartment ten, running her fingers through her hair to tame the static. The door to apartment ten remained bare in comparison to the others, with their shaggy welcome mats, seasonal wreaths, fake plants, and a single small table with a trio of brightly colored nesting dolls that tried to bring joy in the dim hallway light. She gently knocked on the door.

Nobody answered.

Mindful of the early hour, she waited a bit before knocking again, but still nothing. She knocked a little louder. "Anya?" she tried.

A thin, hushed voice sounded behind her. "She doesn't live there anymore."

A single cloudy-blue eye peeked through the top part of bifocals behind the door facing Anya's. Olivia blinked in confusion. "Pardon me?"

"She doesn't live there anymore," the woman repeated. "Anya Bordyukova, the one you're trying to talk to. She hasn't lived there in years. Are you sure you're looking for the right person?"

"Do you know where she went?" Olivia asked. "I'm an old class-mate of hers. I'm in the area for a job, and I thought I'd surprise her."

The woman shook her head—barely visible through the crack— and Olivia's shoulders sagged in defeat at the impossibility of it all. There had to be a clue of some sort to her whereabouts . . .

"I don't know where she is now," she finally said, "but you might try her parents' house? I'll give you the address. Give me a mo-ment."

The door shut, leaving Olivia alone in the hallway. If this woman really had that address, maybe their mission held some hope after all: they'd be able to find the Gatekeeper, and she'd take them to the Keeper of the Realms, who'd fully awaken them. Finding the fire elemental and the lunar prince and rescuing Amy would be a walk in the park afterward. Or so she hoped.

Olivia wished she had a watch or had brought her cell phone to tell the time because she could've sworn it'd been hours since the elderly woman had told her to wait. She'd left her cell in the hotel room in case she needed to travel via lightning—which would only fry it. Still, the sky remained dark, so it couldn't have been that long. She wanted to knock on her door to inquire but held back as to not seem too impatient, too desperate.

She huffed. "This is ridiculous." Back to square one. She'd just have to return to the hotel and do more research with Ferenc.

The door finally opened, a bit wider than before, just as Olivia took a step to leave. The woman adjusted a curler in her silver hair and flattened her gaudy floral bathrobe before extending her arm, a torn piece of paper in her hand.

Olivia swallowed down her impatience and bowed her head in thanks as she took it and inspected the scribble. She didn't know how or why the woman had Anya's parents' address, but she had to trust the lead would pan out.

"Thank you," she said with a smile. Olivia then glanced at the grimy window at the end of the hall. Still dark. "I'm not from around here," she added, turning her attention back to the woman. "Could you give me directions?"

With any luck, she'd find Anya and make it back before Ferenc and Dormouse woke up.

CHAPTER 6
Olivia

While the directions hadn't been complicated, the address it-self took Olivia halfway across the city. Her winter gear shielded her from the worst of the cold, but it didn't erase the unfamiliarity of the frigid air. The sharp chill still found its way to her cheeks and nose, prickling like a thousand tiny needles. Her body ached, stiff, as if the cold had seeped into her bones. She hunched her neck low, tucking her chin deeper into her coat, nuzzling her nose behind the upturned collar in search of warmth.

Her mind shifted gears, focusing instead on the phantom memory of Californian summers, with heat radiating from sun-baked pavement and the scorching embrace of the afternoon sun on her bare arms. She twitched her fingers and slowly began heating the air, coaxing a tiny bubble of warmth around her. She kept it subtle—just enough to stop her teeth from chattering.

With the directions seared into her brain from repetition, apartment buildings gradually disappeared, replaced instead with large factories and sections of snow-clad trees before lavish houses finally came into view. She whistled, impressed, as she walked down a few side streets. The view reminded her of the first time she walked through Ferenc's fancy neighborhood. Her little one-bedroom apartment in a crowded city could never compare in beauty—or price.

The massive houses sat tall and well kept . . . all except the one corresponding to the address she'd been looking for. Its fence, rotted and cracked with years of exposure to the elements, threatened to crumble beneath one more snowfall. And with each push of the howling wind, she feared the house's rattling foundation would give way at any moment.

The only evidence against complete abandonment came from the shoveled driveway and the car in good enough condition to still be driven. Olivia hoped the Bordyukov family still lived inside.

She made her way up to the weathered wooden steps and porch, which creaked dangerously beneath her light weight. Olivia loudly knocked on the door and waited.

Nobody answered. She pounded once more as loudly as she could before glancing around the frame for a doorbell. Church bells chimed when she pressed the button—resonating, echoing, shaking the very foundation of the house—and Olivia held her breath, almost crossing her fingers inside her mittens that she wouldn't be the one to finally make it collapse.

Eventually, the door opened a crack, and a clouded eye from a wizened older man peeked through. "Can I help you?" he asked, his voice quiet but filled with a calm, steady echo that suggested it once held authority.

"I'm looking for Anya Bordyukova," Olivia said. "Is this her home?"

"This *was* her home." He opened the door a little wider and squinted. "Kseniya? Is that you?"

"No, sir. My name is Olivia Gillies. I'm from the United States."

"An American," he mused out loud. "Ah, forgive me. My eyesight isn't what it used to be. I just—your hair." He raised a trembling finger and pointed at the splay of hair across her shoulders. "Anya had a friend with hair like yours. American, you say? Your Russian is flawless."

She held back a smirk. His ears obviously didn't work as well as they once had either. It'd been so long since she'd spoken Russian that his praise caught her off guard.

"Growing up, I had a Russian friend who taught me," she explained. "Are you Anya's father?"

"I am. Please, come in, don't stand out in the cold . . ."

He opened the door wider, allowing her inside. The hinges squealed and moaned in protest, and old wood and dust assaulted her nostrils, as well as an indeterminable musk that lingered in the corners of the hallway. It took everything she had to not scrunch her nose or cover it up.

Olivia barely had a proper moment to take in the time warp she'd stepped into—the sagging walls with patched holes in the peeling flowery wallpaper, the frayed and faded carpets—when a woman's voice came from upstairs.

"Who is at the door?"

"A friend of Anya's, darling," he replied.

"Show her out."

Olivia blinked at the frigid demand, colder than the winter air outside. The woman approached the staircase, wiping at invisible wrinkles in her black pencil skirt with long, bony fingers before fiddling with the gaudy kerchief around her neck attached to her outdated fuschia blouse—shoulder pads and all.

"Show her out," the woman said again. "No friend of that brat is a friend of ours. She can leave immediately."

"Darling, please." He wrung his hands together, a slight tremble in his voice as he glanced at the top of the stairs. "That's our daughter you're referring to."

"She is no daughter of mine." She huffed and turned around, disappearing back into the upper level.

He lowered his voice. "You will have to excuse my wife. When our daughter was very young, we were expecting company from the greatest and richest socialites in all of Moscow. If dinner was a success, we would join their ranks. But our daughter had a fit, our son ran away, and it ruined us forever."

"And your wife disowned your daughter because of it?" she asked just as quietly, in case his wife hovered around, listening in.

He shifted his weight some, deep in contemplation, before shuffling over to a closet. He donned his coat, grabbed his keys, then opened his arm to show her back out. "Let us speak outside."

They both stepped out, and Olivia immediately shivered, biting down on a lament that threatened to escape with her body heat.

Mister Bordyukov didn't seem to mind—or notice—the state of his decaying porch and stairs as he walked across them without a care in the world. Olivia followed, trying to step only where beams sat beneath, and breathed a sigh of relief once back on terra firma.

He shuffled toward his rusted car and fumbled with his keys. A knot twisted in Olivia's stomach, apprehensive; he couldn't possibly see well enough to drive.

He must've sensed it because he said, "Don't worry; it's only somewhere private and warm."

The car door creaked and groaned as he opened it and slipped into the driver's seat. Olivia got into the passenger side, watching as he struggled to steady his hand enough to put the keys in the ignition. When he succeeded, the blast of cold air from the heating vents caught Olivia off guard. Another shiver coursed through her, and she silently begged the car to warm faster so as to not have to resort to using her abilities next to Mister Bordyukov.

He placed his hands on the steering wheel, his empty focus on his house. "My wife is very upset with our daughter. Anya insisted a fiery monster in a world full of flames devoured her brother when she opened the door. My wife was mortified and devastated. She did not believe Anya and still blames her for our ruin."

"But you believed her?" Olivia's thoughts went a million miles a minute as she tried to make sense of his story compared to the ones the advisers told her. She found it hard to believe the fire elemental, a phoenix, would devour a human, but she'd never actually seen one before, so she had no way of knowing.

He shrugged. "Strange things happen in life. I might have not believed her if it wasn't for the fact that her story never changed over time. She was traumatized—wouldn't open doors for years."

He finally drew his attention to Olivia, tears welling in his pale eyes. "She even fainted. My little kitten!" he added, with a crack in his voice and a quiver of his lips. "A lie could not have frightened a child that badly. But my wife . . ." He dropped his gaze to his hands, clenching the steering wheel as he composed himself. "My wife never believed her. And because my son never returned, she shut my daughter out completely."

"I'm so sorry," Olivia whispered. She couldn't imagine what Anya had gone through—both as a child and as the Gatekeeper. But being part of this *bigger universe* the advisers had introduced her to came with its own set of bigger problems. "Do you know where she is now?"

Mister Bordyukov shook his head. "I haven't heard from her in years. Far too long. I'm sorry I couldn't help you."

Olivia's mouth curved into a polite smile as she nodded, but the disappointment seeped into her bones. Another dead end.

"Tell me," he began. "Will you search for her?"

"Yes," she replied, hoping he wouldn't ask why. She didn't want to lie to him, but she *really* didn't want to tell him the truth.

"Then when you find her, if she is still alive . . ." At that, he took a few deep breaths, which all ended in shaken exhales. When he'd composed himself once more, he turned his attention back to her. "Tell her that her father misses her very much and wants to hear from her."

"I will." A lump formed in her throat. She swallowed it down forcefully before giving him a small smile. "I promise."

Olivia opened the door and slid out while Mister Bordyukov pulled the keys from the ignition and did the same. She thanked him for his time and made sure he got inside the house safely before she walked away.

Her thoughts buzzed like a swarm of insects; she couldn't even focus on how to get back to the hotel. She had no idea what they'd do now. They'd gone out on a limb to find the Gatekeeper, and she'd been *so close* to finding her, only to have Anya slip through her fingers like the wind Olivia controlled.

She rushed down street after street, trying to remember which direction she'd come from and which direction she needed to go in. The sun had finally peeked sleepily over the frozen horizon; Ferenc and Dormouse had to be awake by now. Lightning travel might've been risky, but it gave her the only real shot at getting back to the hotel before Ferenc filed a missing person report. She'd vanished for long stretches before, but never in Russia with her prepaid cell left behind in the hotel room.

Her eyes met the sky, and she pinpointed a cloud. Perfect.

But just as she began quieting her mind to focus on creating a static spark, a hand clamped down on her shoulder.

CHAPTER 7
Olivia

The masked man again—it had to be. He'd somehow found them all the way in Russia. And while she couldn't figure out how, a jolt of relief cut through her—a sharp, fleeting comfort—that he'd stumbled upon *her* again instead of finding Dormouse.

Olivia snapped her arm back, fist curled tight. She spun just enough to give power to the punch, ready to give him the thorough walloping he so deserved. But the person before her had no silver filigree mask, nor a wall-like build.

"Apologies, General. I did not mean to startle you."

"Eeolas!" Olivia instantly dropped out of her defensive stance when she finally recognized the solar king's adviser. The warm smile he gave her chased away the winter chill—until her attention fell on his short-sleeved surcoat. He'd draw too much attention to them both with his arms bare in the harsh, hibernal temperature.

She grasped his wrist and jerked him into the shadows of a nearby alley, only to pause mid-movement as a glint behind him caught her attention.

45

S.W. Raine

Eeolas turned and gestured with his free hand toward the figure in golden armor. "May I introduce King Ariol of the Solar Kingdom."

Her heart rate picked up. "The solar king?" she whispered.

King Ariol nodded in acknowledgment. Olivia, still firmly grasping Eeolas's wrist, marched straight for the king. Ariol's eyes narrowed as he raised his glowing hands, aiming directly for her.

Solar abilities, no doubt. Olivia ignored the subtle warning and snatched him by the arm, yanking them both into the nearest alleyway.

"Are you both *insane*!? People could've seen you! You can't just walk around like you came straight from a Renaissance Festival and flaunt your magic! That's not how it works on Earth!"

King Ariol blinked, muscles tensing in his broad shoulders. Thankfully, the glow in his hands sputtered and dimmed. "I would advise you not to approach a king so . . . aggressively."

Noted. She was probably lucky he hadn't used his magic on her. "Why are you both here?"

"My adviser notified me of your partial awakening and your mission," King Ariol said, "and I wished to meet you, the sylph, and her guardian myself."

An audience with a king was the last thing she'd expected out of this outing—and the last thing she needed when she'd just lost another lead. She didn't currently have said sylph or guardian in her company. "Well, uh, Majesty, I'm afraid they're not with me. They're still recovering from our journey."

46

"We would be happy to accompany you wherever you have taken shelter."

Olivia scrunched her face some. "No offense, but you kind of stand out. *A lot.*" From the fiery hair bristling like porcupine quills beneath a thick golden crown to his sharp-toed armored boots, the solar king couldn't easily be mistaken as belonging here. Even his deeply tanned skin practically glowed like the scatter of early morning sunlight over the horizon.

King Ariol's golden gaze moved to Eeolas, who nodded in Olivia's favor. Ariol dipped his head again. "Very well; I see your point. Let us discuss business here instead." Olivia nodded, and he continued. "My adviser informed me that you agreed to find the Gatekeeper to reawaken the elementals and their guardians."

"I did agree."

"What progress have you to report?"

Olivia sighed. *None.* "The Gatekeeper isn't here," she admitted. "I checked her apartment, I visited with her parents . . . I don't know where else to look. I've hit a dead end."

"Perhaps you need the help of professionals?"

Olivia perked a brow in curiosity. He couldn't possibly mean his own people. From what she'd learned, most of the lunar and solar populations had been sent to Earth, leaving only skeleton crews behind to manage things within the palaces. She doubted they had anyone to spare—and even if they did, she didn't know how helpful they'd be, considering they'd asked *her* to track down the Gatekeeper in the first place. "I'm listening."

"There are certain *soldiers of fortune* in the land you call *Iran*," he said carefully. "One of these people in particular has impressive abilities. They might be able to aid . . . for a price."

Eeolas snapped his attention toward his king, umber hair dancing across his shoulders. "My liege! This isn't prudent, and I advise against—"

"Your advice has no merit, Eeolas; You do not know of which group I speak."

Eeolas clamped his lips shut, though the crease in his brow deepened. Olivia could tell he didn't like the idea, and she could only imagine Ferenc would react much the same way.

Ferenc wouldn't easily agree to working with mercenaries. Olivia didn't like it one bit herself. And even if she did, she couldn't exactly claim to be Miss Moneybags to pay them; she'd lost her job as a personal assistant when she'd followed her gut instincts to find Ferenc and Dormouse, and all her hotel stays had drained her funds. Ferenc had paid for this trip for the three of them—a fact that embarrassed her more than she cared to admit.

"I'm . . . kind of running low on cash with all these wild goose chases . . ." she began.

King Ariol shook his head. "I would never ask another to pay such a steep price. Give the soldiers this instead." He produced a golden envelope from his armor, offering it to her. Olivia studied him before taking it, flipping it recto verso, admiring the gorgeous wax seal with a symbol of the sun. "It is not to be opened by anyone but them. I guarantee you that they shall be satisfied upon seeing this. Once hired, return here with the soldiers and begin your search anew. I promise you will have results."

"Do you have a name to go with this fancy letter?" she asked as she delicately slid it into her pocket, almost afraid to damage it.

Ariol shook his head. "To keep my reputation and that of my kingdom untarnished, I cannot mention any names."

"How are we supposed to know who we're looking for, then?" Olivia asked.

"Fear not. They will find you first."

Olivia bowed her head respectfully in silence, but she furrowed her brows some. She didn't understand why they needed her.

"You appear uncertain." Ariol tipped his head.

"Why me?" She peeked up at him. "If you knew about these people this whole time, then why aren't *you* doing all of this? What makes me so special?"

Ariol smiled just as warmly as Eeolas had. It must've been a Solar Kingdom thing.

"Because you've done it before—you found the sylph and her guardian all on your own. I am confident you can find the others. I believe in you."

"And unlike you," Eeolas added, "our time here is limited to sunlight. I'm afraid we would have to return to the Solar Kingdom each time darkness approached. We would be useless."

"I don't understand." The lunar princess had gifted her a moonstone that allowed her to travel via moonlight back to Earth. If the people from the Lunar Kingdom had the same limits under moonlight that King Ariol's people faced under sunlight, then Richard's

49

presence on Earth didn't make sense. "Richard—er, Alican was able to walk around in the daylight. Isn't he from the Lunar Kingdom?"

"The Solar and Lunar Palaces have an artifact built by the king and the prince," Eeolas offered. "It allows them to open portals anywhere and gives them protection to travel during both day and night."

Ariol's expression darkened. "The relics were stolen right under our noses."

"No doubt by High Priest Alican himself," Eeolas added.

Ariol eyed Eeolas—who sheepishly apologized—before continuing. "Regardless of the thief's identity, I cannot make new ones without my brother."

Things started to make more and more sense. Richard's portals likely existed as a result of those relics.

"You will be compensated for your efforts, of course," King Ariol continued, returning to the matter at hand, "in more ways than one: you'll have your reawakening, and the balance of the universe will be returned to normal. I can also compensate you in gold and riches if that's what you—"

"Ah, well, before we get into that," she cut in with a forced laugh, "how about I find them first? Then we can discuss, uh, compensation."

"As you wish." King Ariol bowed at the waist. "Good luck to you, General."

"Thank you." She forced a smile back at him. The problem of getting back to the hotel still remained.

Eeolas reached into his pristinely white surcoat pocket as if he'd read her mind, producing a stone. "Here," he started, handing it to her.

Olivia couldn't be more thankful for the adviser. She gladly accepted it, inspecting it. Instead of a moonstone, this one gleamed orangish-red in color with gilded detailing.

"Sunstone?" she guessed.

Eeolas nodded. "Just set it in the sun, and it'll take you where you need to go. It's a little more . . . conspicuous than lightning travel," he said with a wink, "but it will do the trick."

Olivia grinned.

Ariol and Eeolas stepped into a beam of sunlight between two buildings and stood tall, their features bathed in the sun's golden embrace. Slowly, their forms faded into glimmering embers until nothing remained. Olivia squinted at the beam of sunlight, shielding her eyes. She'd have to ask Eeolas if sunglasses counted as required fashion in the Solar Kingdom the next time they spoke. She then looked at the stone in her hands—the only proof of their conversation, along with the envelope in her pocket. With an exhausted sigh, she glanced around for potential peepers, then moved the stone toward the sunlight beaming down in the alleyway.

The sunstone's tiny golden flecks glittered, reflecting the light; when Olivia looked back up, she no longer stood in the alley. She spun around, finding herself face-to-face with Ferenc and Dormouse inside their hotel room.

"Whoa," she gasped.

"Olivia!" Dormouse squeaked from behind her fingernails.

Ferenc's eyes held wide in surprise. "How did you—" His brows then furrowed. "Where the *hell* have you been? I was worried sick!"

The frustration in his voice and the sharp edge of worry beneath his anger settled uncomfortably in her chest. "I couldn't sleep," she said quietly, "so I went to see if I could get a lead."

His frown didn't budge. "Without us," he said. It came out as a statement, not a question. "Your phone was on the nightstand with no note, no—no nothing! Christ, they took Amy, so I thought they took you too!" He raked a hand through his disheveled hair as he always did when flustered.

She swallowed down her regret. Ferenc's fear made sense, especially in a foreign country, and specifically after Amy's abduction. "I didn't want to bother you after you finally fell asleep, that's all. But . . . yeah. I should've left a note." Her gaze flicked to Dormouse for a second, who sat cross-legged on the bed in silence, before meeting Ferenc's again. "I'm sorry. I didn't mean to worry you. I just thought—I thought I'd be back before you woke up."

Ferenc didn't respond right away, his lips pressed into a thin line as he processed. Olivia stayed still, letting him work through it.

Finally, he sighed, shaking his head. "Just . . . don't do it again." His voice had lost its sharp edge, though exasperation still clung to it.

The heaviness in her stomach eased, but only a little. "I don't plan to." She then exhaled sharply through her nose, rolling her shoulders as she shifted gears. "But I *did* find something."

Both Ferenc and Dormouse's attentions perked up, and Olivia resisted the urge to just turn around and walk away. She didn't particularly enjoy delivering bad news.

"Unfortunately, nobody's seen the Gatekeeper in years."

That liveliness instantly deflated. "So what do we do now?" asked Dormouse.

"We get help." Olivia reached into her pocket and held up the golden envelope. "King Ariol paid me a visit. He really wanted to meet the both of you, but . . ." She shrugged. "He said to find a band of mercenaries and give them this."

"And where are these mercenaries?" Ferenc crossed his arms over his chest.

"In the very-unspecific location of *Iran*."

"Iran?" Ferenc pulled out his cellphone to start his research. "I mean, it's definitely not as big as Russia. Did he give you a name?"

"No."

Ferenc's head snapped back to her so quick, she half-expected him to give himself whiplash. "What do you mean *no*?"

Olivia tossed the envelope on the desk with a sigh and began removing her winter gear. "This whole needle-in-a-haystack search sure is fun, isn't it?"

She'd require coffee before tackling any kind of research. Things really needed to start being a whole lot simpler than they currently turned out to be.

CHAPTER 8
Ferenc

Ferenc took a drag of his cigarette outside the small Iranian restaurant, trying to make it quick—not just because of the cool winter breeze. He didn't like Dormouse or Olivia being out of his sight for too long. He didn't want to leave them at all, but he had to get his mind under control. Even the scent of grilled meat and saffron couldn't distract him.

His fingers twitched, itching for that weightless feeling, the rush of altitude where the world below no longer mattered. But the ground held firm under his boots. No lift, no escape . . . just a whole foreign country stretching out in every direction, his thoughts as aimless as their search for the Gatekeeper.

At least he'd been able to take on a couple quick freelance flight jobs when they'd been forced to return to Florida and wait on their visas. And every night he'd spent at home, he'd been distracted by training with Olivia at the abandoned furniture store they'd used when he'd first learned to control his abilities. Dormouse joined them, of course, even though she didn't participate. Thankfully,

Olivia didn't push the issue, though she made comments here and there about how Dormouse should be able to protect herself too.

Amy's scream cut through his thoughts, yanking him out of his calm—a sharp, gut-deep pull like a sudden drop.

He couldn't allow those people to lay a finger on Dormouse. But he couldn't ask her to train when it frightened her so much, either.

He scanned the street as he drew in another deep breath of smoke, skimming over every passing face, searching for a glint of silver or gold that didn't belong.

An ember singed his fingertips. He flicked the cigarette filter into the nearest disposal receptacle, watching the last tendril of smoke curl away before he returned inside.

"We ordered two different stews to share," Olivia said as he took his seat. He glanced around, but nothing seemed out of the ordinary on the inside either. "Ferenc? Did you hear me?"

He rubbed his temple, trying to force his mind back to the table. "Yeah, sorry."

"I think it's best we go at night," Olivia then said, cutting straight to the point. "Not so many people to worry about then."

He shook his head. "At night, in the desert? We won't be able to see a thing."

"That's why they invented headlights," Olivia shot back, giving him a look.

"You can't see the horizon with headlights."

"Okay, Mister Analytical, what's your great plan?" she challenged, crossing her arms over her chest.

His jaw tightened. They'd already considered the possibilities: follow old trade routes taken over by smugglers, track where they bought supplies, and stake out the abandoned airstrips and military bases that'd been repurposed over the years. If the mercenaries didn't operate within a city, they had to be using open spaces, somewhere out of reach of government surveillance.

But the desert stretched endlessly. Too many places to hide, too many directions to take. And now Olivia wanted to search in the dark.

He didn't have a better plan because they weren't trying to solve the same problem. In truth, *when* they searched didn't matter half as much as *how* they searched. And every time he got close to a solution, his thoughts looped back on themselves, scattering any focus before he could pin down an answer.

"I'm working on it," he said, turning his attention to Dormouse. She picked at her silk headscarf with one hand, her eyes wandering over the grapevine crawling along the grid-pattern beams on the ceiling. He gently placed his hand over her other one resting on the thick wooden table. When she dropped her gaze to him, he smiled.

"What do you think?" he asked her. "How should we search?"

"I . . ." A soft pinkness spread across her cheeks just as their food arrived, giving her an excuse to look away without answering.

The combination of fresh herbs and spices mingled with a hint of sweetness and a flourish of nuts. Ferenc's stomach loudly growled in response.

"Oh my God, this smells divine!" Olivia moaned, already reaching for a ladle.

A burst of laughter erupted from the door as a boisterous group entered the restaurant. A tight knot formed in the pit of his stomach—not because the group sneered their way as they sat down, but because of the way the rest of the room responded.

The quiet conversational hum died. The modal tunes in the background ended. Chairs scraped against the floor as patrons pushed back from their tables, gathering their things in hurried, almost panicked movements. The server avoided looking up as they shuffled to their table to greet them; an older man left his tea half-finished at the table closest to theirs, setting the cup down with slow precision before slipping out the door without a word.

Ferenc's fingers curled against his thigh before he forced them to relax. He glanced at Olivia; oblivious, she continued explaining to Dormouse why traveling at night made the most sense as she finished serving herself from both bowls of stew.

"We need to leave," he muttered, pushing back his chair.

Olivia frowned. "Why? We just got our food—"

"*Now.*" He helped Dormouse to her feet, herding her toward the door. But when he turned around, a bald man had already cut in front of him, a wicked grin on his crooked face. His eyes glinted, unmistakably unfriendly.

Ferenc instinctively shielded Dormouse and Olivia, throwing his arms in front of both of them as the man spoke. The words meant nothing to him, but the tone mocked. Challenged.

Ferenc pulled his hand away from Olivia, lifting it slowly, palm up, nonthreatening. "We're leaving," he said evenly. Nothing. "We're leaving," he repeated, slower this time, in case the man didn't understand.

The man's threatening grin widened.

"Hey, that one speaks English!" came a voice from the back of the restaurant. "Judging by his accent and mannerisms, he must be a '*Murican*.'"

A few men laughed. Ferenc slowly backed up, making sure he had one hand on both Dormouse and Olivia.

"We don't want any trouble," he said, scanning the room for the English-speaking one.

"Should've thought about that before setting foot in this restaurant." The shaggy redhead at the far table, lighter-skinned than the rest, sneered as he picked up his glass of water. "Or town, for that matter."

The crew sniggered, except for one: a quiet man sitting prim and proper beside the redhead. Instead of joining in the banter, he studied Dormouse with a calculating gaze, entirely still. He exuded no arrogance, no need to prove himself—just silent control. And that terrified Ferenc more than any sneer or threat.

"I'm sorry. We'll be on our way." Ferenc turned to leave in the other direction and found his path blocked again. A woman stood in his way, arms loose at her sides, but unmistakably ready. He cast a quick glance around the room. Figures closed in around them.

"What's the hurry?" the redhead drawled. "Stay a while! The boys could really use some new playmates."

A few cackles escaped some of the crew, along with the unmistakable scrape of metal knives against leather and the sharp clicks of gun safeties being switched off.

Ferenc's stomach dropped. He looked back to the redhead, only to find the quiet man beside him speaking in his ear as if none of this concerned him, his dark, almond-shaped eyes still fixed on Dormouse. The redhead nodded with a smirk, his gaze drifting to Dormouse as well. Ferenc's pulse pounded in his ears. Trouble closed in fast.

"Ferenc?" Olivia's voice held an edge of concern.

He really didn't want to start a fight—not in a foreign country, not with a group that even local patrons avoided like the plague. But when one of them reached for Olivia's arm, she jerked away; when the man grabbed her wrist instead, Ferenc spun around, striking without thinking.

Bone met bone with a sharp crack as he sucker-punched the man square in the jaw, sending him sprawling into a nearby table.

The laughter instantly died, replaced instead by glares and growls. Chairs scraped against the floor as bodies shifted, fingers tightening around weapons.

Ferenc pivoted, stepping between Dormouse and Olivia. He extended one arm to block them and aimed his other palm at the redhead, ready to summon shields of air. Olivia wouldn't have done it— she'd always been cautious about using her abilities in public. But if it gave them a chance to escape, he'd take that risk.

The white swirls forming in his palms drew a chorus of cocking guns. Ferenc swallowed hard, waiting for the barrage.

Then came a voice.

"Stop."

No aggression. Just one word, spoken with simple authority.

The group obeyed instantly. They kept their weapons up, but their bodies went motionless as if held by an invisible force.

Most people would have focused on the loudest man or the most heavily armed or the one standing closest. Instead, Ferenc looked to the real danger in the room: the quiet man. The one everyone listened to without hesitation when he finally did speak.

The real leader.

As the man stood, he clasped his hands behind his back, his posture unaffected by the tension around him. He approached with decorum and purpose, his movements slow and deliberate, as if he never felt the need to rush.

Ferenc forced Dormouse another step back, keeping her shielded behind him. But the man showed no offense at the protective gesture. Instead, he gave a small nod, then held out a hand, palm up.

"May I have that letter in your pocket, miss?"

Ferenc blinked. The man's English came out perfectly—fluent. Precise. His refined manners stood in drastic, unnerving contrast to the rest of the rowdy crew . . . but the fact he knew about the letter in Dormouse's coat pocket unsettled Ferenc the most.

Neither Olivia nor Dormouse moved.

"Please," the man added. His voice remained calm, but firm; Ferenc didn't think he meant it as a request.

Dormouse hesitated, her eyes flicking to Ferenc. He nodded. He didn't care if the letter didn't belong to this crew; he'd do anything to avoid putting her in danger. She slowly reached into her coat pocket, pulled out the folded envelope, and placed it in his hand.

He accepted it with a slight inclination of his head, his fingers gently closing over it. Then, in one swift motion, a blade slipped from his sleeve. With a flick of his wrist, he sliced through the wax seal, barely disturbing the paper beneath. His eyes bounced from one line to the next; though his expression never changed, a huff of amusement escaped him.

"Put your weapons away," he ordered. The Persian crew obeyed at once. He then extended a hand to Ferenc's table. "Please, sit and finish your meal."

Ferenc didn't move. "No offense, but we'd like to leave."

"Surely you have not come all this way to hire me just to leave without discussing the job." The man tipped his head. "And all business is better discussed over good food."

Ferenc studied him, weighing his words carefully. Olivia leaned in, her voice barely above a whisper. "How do we know he's the guy? We never got eyes on the letter."

The man didn't look away from Ferenc as he spoke. "Moses, who am I?"

The redhead smirked, stroking his long, goat-patch beard. "Kamran Rajamir, leader of the Titans."

Kamran handed the letter back to Dormouse and dipped his neatly trimmed chin toward it. She hesitated before taking and unfolding it. At the very top, in crisp ink, the words read exactly that.

To the respected Kamran Rajamir.

CHAPTER 9
Kamran

If one thing terrified Kamran more than anything else in the world—over losing those he cared about, over being unable to live out his childhood dream—nothing struck deeper than being proven wrong. And not just wrong—*fundamentally mistaken.*

A fear he came face-to-face with as he stared at a letter that had shattered years of unquestionable faith in a single moment.

It should've been ordinary. Just ink and paper sealed with wax. But something about it defied that. He'd known before he ever touched it.

The blond man had been the reason he'd activated his ability. Even before the swirling, unnatural power had appeared in the man's palms, Kamran had felt the air shift, had caught the dust in the restaurant briefly moving against the flow.

So, for only a moment, he'd allowed himself to see.

The three of them glowed—not in a way the human eye could perceive, but in the way things revealed themselves to only him.

The small and hesitant woman shined a little brighter than the other two, but the brightest thing of all had been the letter in her coat pocket. It gleamed gold, bright as the sun. Kamran had seen many things in his life, but he'd never seen that specific glow before.

Even before he saw his name written inside, that glow made it unmistakably important. Not only did the letter address him personally, but it bore the signature of a king—from a kingdom on the *sun*, of all places. It didn't mention Mithra, the sun god, but the golden glow reminded him of the old stories Moses used to read to him as children. The tall tales Kamran had long dismissed as just that.

But those stories blended into reality now.

The travelers sat in uneasy silence, all watching warily as his crew returned to their boisterous shenanigans . . . all except Moses. His focus never wavered from the three strangers for the entire duration of the meal.

Beneath the table, the floor trembled in a swift, rhythmic vibration. The restless bounce of Moses's leg sent subtle quakes through the wooden planks, a manifestation of tension with no release.

Kamran set his napkin down after wiping his lips and spoke just loud enough for Moses to hear. "You are making the floor shake."

The movement stopped immediately. Moses gave no response, no apology, no other sign he'd heard Kamran speak.

Kamran exhaled slowly. "Let us set those nerves at ease, shall we? Bring them here."

Without a word, Moses rose from his seat. At the other table, the smallest of the three travelers flinched, her attention snapping toward him before she dropped her head, avoiding all gazes.

An unspoken rule governed the town when it came to Kamran and his mercenaries. People either feared them or treated them like royalty. He accepted either. Fear kept people in line. Respect kept things running smoothly. He had no preference, as long as the outcome remained the same.

Their presence came with benefits—free meals, bowed heads, doors that opened without question. Some gave these things willingly. Others only after they'd learned why refusing never ended well. Foreigners, however, had no way of knowing the rules. They always learned the hard way.

Moses stopped at the travelers' table. Normally, he would've dragged this out, testing their patience, pushing just enough to see how they'd react. He enjoyed playing with his prey, like a cat batting at a wounded bird. But this time, he didn't waste the effort.

He said something—Kamran couldn't hear what—but didn't linger for a reply. He simply turned on his heel and walked back before sitting down again and plucking a toothpick from the table, fiddling it between his teeth as he set his gaze back on the trio.

The three exchanged looks and hushed words. The man rose first, rolling his shoulders back, though the stiffness in his posture betrayed the tension he tried to hide. The green-eyed woman followed, slower, her gaze flicking from Moses to Kamran, measuring, calculating. The third hesitated. Her grip on her headscarf tightened as if she could anchor herself with fabric alone, her knuckles going white as she got to her feet.

Good. They hadn't been foolish enough to ignore the invitation.

Kamran took them in as they approached, noting how they moved not with the aimless uncertainty of tourists, but with the quiet deliberation of people who'd been navigating unknown territory for a while.

He extended a hand toward the empty seats before him. "Please, sit."

The blond man sat first, then the green-eyed woman. Once the timid one sank into her chair, Kamran inclined his head slightly. "Your names, please."

"I'm Ferenc." The man nodded toward his companions. "This is Olivia and Dormouse."

Moses coughed, the sound abrupt, halfway between a laugh and a choke. "I'm sorry, did you say dormouse? Like the rodent?"

Ferenc's expression didn't shift, but something in his gaze hardened. "That's exactly what I said. And that's all you need to know."

Kamran tapped two fingers lightly against the table—a silent command to prevent the inevitable retort. Moses huffed, slumping back in his seat.

"It is a pleasure to meet you, Mister Ferenc, Miss Olivia, and—" Kamran paused only for a second, "Miss Dormouse." Names carried weight. He didn't question the odd ones. "As previously stated, I am Kamran, leader of the Titans. This is Moses, my second-in-command. Now, let us get down to business. How may my mercenaries be of service to you?"

"We need help finding someone. We were told you're the man to do it," Ferenc said.

"You were told correctly." Kamran rested his hands on the table. "What information do you have on the target?"

"'Target' seems a little harsh," Dormouse mumbled from behind her fingertips.

Ferenc reached over, briefly squeezing the hand that fiddled with her headscarf. She exhaled slowly, her eyes closing for a moment before lowering them to the table.

"Her name is Anya Bordyukova," Ferenc finally said. "Her last-known location was just outside Moscow."

Moses huffed again, setting his toothpick down. "That's it? You want us to play a little lost and found?"

Kamran said nothing, only waited to hear the rest. This definitely went beyond a missing persons case. The letter had made that clear.

Ferenc's jaw ticked with restrained irritation. "She doesn't *want* to be found."

Ah. That explained it. Finding someone proved to be simple work. Finding someone who didn't want to be found, that called for a specialist—and Kamran happened to fit that description.

Moses leaned back in his chair. "And what's the price tag on this job?"

"A king's reward," Kamran replied before their guests could open their mouths.

Moses actually choked this time, and the trio stiffened, their eyes widening in genuine surprise. Clearly, they hadn't been filled in on the letter's contents.

Moses cleared his throat and turned to Kamran. "Why didn't you say so in the first place?" he hissed in Farsi.

"Because it did not matter," Kamran replied in English, his focus still on the trio. He had nothing to hide from his clients.

"I still would've liked to know."

"Noted."

Moses exhaled sharply through his nose but didn't argue. He understood the message: they'd talk later.

Kamran studied Ferenc for a moment. Though the man put off an air of calm, the hyperawareness he'd displayed when Kamran's crew had first entered said something different. This trio had been looking over their shoulders for longer than this visit. "Who else is after her?"

Ferenc's fingers curled against the table, but his expression remained unreadable. "We don't know."

That fell short of the answer he wanted. "Do you know why she is running?"

Ferenc hesitated. "She's not running from anyone."

A lie? No. But not the full truth, either. He let the silence stretch, watching Ferenc carefully.

"We only know she doesn't want to be found," Olivia insisted at last. "That's all."

He gave a slow, deliberate nod. The sun god hadn't provided much more than that either. The payment checked out, yet uncertainty hung over every detail.

Still, a contract remained a contract.

"We shall leave first thing in the morning—"

"We're coming with you," Ferenc cut in. "There and back. Safely."

Kamran didn't immediately reply. He kept himself outwardly composed, but his mind ventured elsewhere, puzzling through every possible outcome of having Ferenc and his friends along for the journey. They'd slow them down, possibly get in their way—a minor inconvenience at best. Still, their presence strayed from the ordinary, and that alone made it worth considering.

Unfortunately, Moses saw none of that. He only saw risk. "That's not an option," he said matter-of-factly.

"We need to come with you," Ferenc insisted. "It's . . . complicated."

Kamran raised a hand once more, a simple motion that halted Moses before he could speak. Moses clenched his fists at his sides, but he didn't argue. "We accept your mission and your company, Mister Ferenc," he said. "We leave at dawn."

Ferenc bowed his head. "Thank you." He got to his feet, and both women followed him toward the exit.

The world around him began to warp slightly at the edges as he watched them leave—the telltale sign of a migraine building. Not yet unbearable, but pressing.

The door shut behind the trio. The restaurant carried on with chairs scraping along the floor, loud chatter, and the clatter of dishes, but between him and Moses, the weight of unspoken words thickened the air.

Then— "What the *fuck* was that?"

Kamran inhaled slowly. He'd expected this. Dreaded it. He'd never left Moses in the dark before. Not as a child, not as a teenager, not as an adult. And now, for the first time, he had. And the weight of it coiled tight in his chest.

"I accepted the mission." He offered neither reassurance nor justification.

Moses narrowed his eyes. "You blindsided me. You made the decision without me."

"You are right," he said, meeting his gaze, unwavering. "But the request was in my name."

Moses exhaled sharply in a disbelieving huff. "That's your reason?"

Nothing he said would satisfy Moses—because Moses knew him too well. He knew about Kamran's ability. He'd seen Kamran prove its accuracy time and time again. But he also knew Kamran's faith. He knew no world existed where Kamran should believe in a sun god.

He pushed back his seat, and the other mercenaries did the same, ready to follow his lead. The scrape of chair legs screeched through his skull, sharp and grating, twisting the pressure behind his eyes. But Moses didn't move.

"Which king?" he asked—no, demanded.

No king would offer so much for a search, and they both knew it. But Moses would take the truth even worse than the unknown.

Kamran adjusted his cuffs, smoothing an invisible crease as he walked toward the door, leaving Moses to seethe behind him.

"Why are you ignoring me?"

"I'm not." The lie came easily. *Too* easily.

Moses jumped to his feet, his knee slamming against the table. Dishes rattled and cups tipped, water and tea sloshing over the edges.

"I asked you which king!" he roared.

The restaurant's chatter died. Even the scuff of boots and clatter of dishes halted, as if the entire room recoiled from the outburst. But Kamran barely noticed. The dull throb behind his eyes pressed deeper, like an itch he couldn't scratch.

Moses's hands flexed, knuckles whitening, his face nearly matching his hair color. Around the room, the rest of the crew hesitated before wordlessly filing out, their exit cautious but immediate.

Kamran could only exhale slowly and shut his eyes. The rift between them had already formed. He couldn't keep Moses in the dark, but the truth twisted inside him. He couldn't explain it.

"Kam," Moses said, much more gently.

The name sat in his throat, heavy as stone. "Mithra," he finally replied.

He then opened his eyes and almost regretted it.

71

Moses blinked. Then twitched. "I'm sorry, I'm not sure I heard you right." His voice remained steady, but disbelief bled through every word. "Did you say Mithra? As in the sun god?"

Kamran reached into the inner pocket of his suit's jacket. His fingers brushed the letter, and for a moment, he hesitated. A slight tremble started in his fingertips as he fought the threatening discomfort of the entire situation—ability, lies, and all.

"I did."

"You accepted a mission from someone pretending to be a fucking mythical being?"

"Mo . . ." He held back a sigh. Weight pressed against his skull, dull but persistent. Without another word, he pulled out the letter and handed it over.

Moses practically tore it open. His lips formed a thin line as his gaze flicked across the page.

"*King Ariol of the Solar Kingdom*?" His voice sharpened. "What, are you losing your regular vision? Nowhere on this does it say Mithra."

He barely had time to take a deep breath before Moses looked up again. That stare—flat, unwavering, full of judgment—hit harder than the migraine ever could.

"Who the f—" Moses slowly shook his head, then aimed a different question at him: "What's going on in that head of yours?"

He deserved Moses's anger. Every ounce of it. He'd never kept secrets from him before. Never lied. Never accepted a mission without discussing it with him first. And yet, he'd done it anyway.

But what Moses would never understand—what he *couldn't* understand—lay in the weight of those childhood stories he'd read to him, years ago, before either of them carried guns or titles.

Mithra, the god of the sun. A name spoken like fiction, something told in bedtime tales . . . until now.

The sun should have just been a burning ball of gas, a fact written into every textbook and rational mind. But the letter, signed by the king of the sun, burned with something more. It turned the sun into magic. The same magic Moses had read him stories about.

The words "King" and "Solar" glowed as brightly as that very star, inked into ordinary paper. Ariol and Mithra had to be one and the same. And the Quran spoke of many things, but never that.

The thought alone sent a wave of exhaustion crashing through him. "I have a migraine."

Moses's frustration evaporated. His expression tightened with concern, and the heat in his stance faded as he took a step forward.

"Is that how you knew about the letter? You used your vision?"

Kamran nodded. Just that slight movement almost pushed the pressure behind his eyes crashing through his skull.

Despite never truly understanding the how, when, or why behind his ability to see certain things in color in a superimposed shadowy world, Moses had always understood one part: the toll it took.

The ability had never failed him yet. But the thing that made them rich, made them powerful, made them something *more*—his truth detector, his compass toward reality and deception—came at a price.

"When Mister Ferenc produced *swirls* from his hands, I grew curious." His own voice sounded farther away than it should have. "What I saw . . ." He swallowed hard, his throat tight with exhaustion, but the image had burned into his memory. "All three of them. Their aura, a pale white—Miss Dormouse most of all. But in her pocket, that letter . . ."

The glow had been there before he even thought to look. Normally, color only revealed itself when he focused, when he rewound time to find what lay hidden. But this time, he hadn't even tried. The glow had already been there, pale and steady around them, and blinding in the letter's place in her pocket.

This went beyond magic; it carried power. And not just any power.

"It glowed as bright as the sun," he murmured. "If only you had seen it, Mo."

Moses let out a slow, steady breath. Something between exasperation and reluctant acceptance. "Whatever you say, Highness."

Kamran hated that nickname—one Moses usually used in moments of resignation.

Moses's distrust of the sun king's word needed no explanation. But Kamran had seen the signature; he accepted it as truth, as real as his own breath. More than likely, Moses hated that he couldn't see it himself. But Kamran still hoped he'd see it his way, as he always had. They'd always been unwaveringly loyal to one another. Since the beginning.

He rubbed his temple briefly. A hand touched his arm—Moses's, steady and firm.

"All right, come on," he said, the frustration from before gone, leaving only quiet insistence. "You need to rest."

Kamran pried his eyes open despite his discomfort and exhaustion. He straightened his posture, forcing himself to stand as if nothing weighed on him. His crew couldn't see him like this. Only Moses. Only ever Moses. He remained silent as they walked out, allowing Moses to gently guide him by the elbow.

For now.

CHAPTER 10
Ferenc

When they arrived back in Moscow, Ferenc wasted no time; they only took the time to rent a vehicle large enough for the five of them before beginning their search. And with the scribbled directions fed into the GPS, they set off to the last place anyone had ever seen the Gatekeeper.

Silence enveloped their entire drive to the apartment complex. His grip on the steering wheel never eased after they all packed in, his white knuckles numb. He constantly glanced at the rearview mirror, tracking the mercenaries' every movement, glance, and breath. He remained tense, forever on guard. Contracts meant nothing when lives hung in the balance.

His muscles twitched each time the mercenaries so much as blinked. Olivia's presence in the far back of the SUV served to keep watch over them, not the other way around, but the unease wouldn't leave. Each heartbeat slammed against his ribs, real and undeniable.

Dormouse sat in the front passenger seat, curled into her coat, her hands pulled into her oversized sleeves. She stayed small, as if making herself unseen could shield her from danger.

The apartment complex loomed before them, the gray structure weighed down by thick layers of snow, its windows dark and lifeless. Ferenc parked as close as possible, his fingers twitching against the wheel.

"Well?" he asked.

Kamran didn't answer. His focus darted between empty streets, his head tilting as if following movement that didn't exist. He leaned forward, gaze fixed on something farther down the road, brow furrowing in concentration.

Moses, arms crossed, let out an unimpressed breath. "He's working on it."

He narrowed his eyes. "How?"

Moses merely lifted a single finger, a gesture to *wait*.

Kamran's stare followed something beyond their sight, his body angling ever so slightly, like a man trying to catch a glimpse over an invisible wall. And then, without warning, he turned, dark eyes locking onto Olivia.

Ferenc's heart lurched, and he gripped the wheel so tightly, his wrists and arms protested what his cramped hands couldn't.

Olivia blinked, confusion flickering across her face. Kamran did the same, turning away as if shaking off a stray thought, his attention shifting to Moses.

"She is somewhere far to the east."

Ferenc forced his breathing to steady. "How far?"

"I do not know. I cannot see beyond the horizon."

His grip finally loosened slightly. He pulled his attention away from the rearview mirror and scanned the area. From their position, the horizon hid behind the snow-laden streets, the skeletal trees, and the surrounding buildings. "How did you get all that from here?"

Kamran's expression didn't change. "I have a . . . special ability. I can see things that have happened."

"You're a seer?" Olivia asked.

"Not exactly. I can see things in the past, but as a shadow over-laid atop everything as you see it now. For example, Miss Olivia." Kamran turned in his seat, his movement slow and deliberate. "You were gathering some sort of energy when someone walked out and interrupted you." Olivia stiffened, and Ferenc's jaw ached from the force of his clenched teeth. "You rushed inside," he continued, un-fazed by her reaction, "knocked on an apartment door a few times, then turned around to speak to somebody from the apartment across the hall."

All color from Olivia's face drained. *Careful* never came close to describing how meticulous she'd always been in making sure no-body saw her use her abilities. Yet this mercenary, who'd never even set foot in the building, peeled back the layers of her secret as easily as an onion.

"When my vision is activated, I cannot see exactly what you wear or whom you speak with. I simply see hazy, pale forms up against a darker background. But when I focus, I can see certain things in color. And over there . . ." He shifted his attention back toward the side of the building and pointed. Ferenc followed his finger but saw nothing. "Right there, before you get interrupted, I see color. Pale yellow beneath your feet. Like a cloud, or . . ." Kamran trailed off, shaking his head.

Ferenc's stomach tightened as his eyes darted back to the rearview mirror. Olivia sat rigid, her eyes wide and lips slightly parted.

"That's impossible," he said, forcing himself to sound certain. Anything to pull the attention away from her and keep her abilities secret a little longer.

"It's not," Moses said flatly.

"I see it happening," Kamran insisted.

Ferenc inhaled deeply, forcing himself to stay calm. "Okay, let's say you can. How do you know it's *her* form and not someone else's?"

Kamran's eyes flicked toward him, sharp with quiet certainty. "I can focus on one figure in particular—or a select few, depending on my concentration—and the form will become clearer than the rest. However, in this particular instance, Miss Olivia's form gives off a soft white signature—all three of you do."

Ferenc forced another steady breath, keeping his expression neutral, but his mind reeled with the weight of that statement.

He didn't doubt Kamran. Too much had happened for him to brush off something like that as a lie. But the logical part of his mind—the part that'd spent years relying on hard facts and tangible evidence—wanted to pick it apart. He wanted to pull out his phone and research how this mercenary's ability worked, its limits, anything. But he wouldn't find any answers. He never did.

But damn, if that didn't make for one hell of an ability. If Kamran could really track people this way, then maybe finding the Gatekeeper bordered on possible again.

Kamran turned back to Olivia. "Where did you go after leaving here?"

"I—I went to investigate her parents' house," she stuttered. "But I wasn't doing anything special before—"

"Miss Olivia," Kamran interrupted smoothly, his tone firm but not unkind. "I have been open with you, and I would appreciate the same openness in return."

Ferenc exhaled sharply. Ridiculous didn't even begin to cover it. Kamran refused to back down, and if they kept dodging, they'd simply be wasting time. If the solar king trusted these mercenaries enough to hire them, then, for the sake of the mission—for the sake of Dormouse's safety—Ferenc had to trust them too.

"She can manipulate air," he admitted, crossing his arms over his chest.

"Ferenc!" Dormouse squeaked, horrified.

"Look, he's right. As much as I hate to admit it, he needs to know if he's going to help us. Because receiving a letter addressed to him personally from the solar king about a mission to retrieve the Gatekeeper isn't weird enough on its own." He found Kamran's eyes through the rearview mirror once more. "That yellow cloud you saw. That was her manipulating air."

Kamran inclined his head slightly. "I thank you for your honesty." He then peered out the window, back toward the apartment complex.

"I can as well," Ferenc added, ignoring how Dormouse shrank deeper into her coat. Her hand flew to her lips, and her teeth nibbled at her fingernails—an old habit she'd never fully shaken. "I'm a guardian, and Olivia's one of my warriors."

Kamran's attention returned to Ferenc. He studied him, his expression unreadable, but the intensity in his gaze sharpened. "A guardian and warrior of what?"

"Me." Dormouse spoke so quietly, the word nearly disappeared under the hum of the vehicle's heater. She slouched into her massive winter coat as everyone's attention focused on her, avoiding their eyes, her cheeks flushing pink. Ferenc placed his hand atop of hers and squeezed lightly, letting her know he'd protect her.

"She's an elemental," Ferenc clarified. He didn't want to go into any more detail than he had to.

Kamran's lips curled slightly in understanding. "So she is," he said simply. Dormouse's stare remained fixed on her lap. "I saw this as well."

Ferenc inhaled deeply, letting the moment settle before pressing on and removing the focus from Dormouse. "So what now?"

"We follow the trail," Kamran answered, leaning back into his seat.

Ferenc and Olivia traded looks in the rearview mirror, his thought reflected on her face: that following the trail would prove easier said than done when Kamran alone could see it.

As if reading their thoughts, Kamran added, "I will tell you the way." He glanced back at the apartment complex, eyes distant, unreadable. "But first," he said, his voice quieter now, "I would like to stop by her old home."

CHAPTER 11
Kamran

Tracking a ghost through time took patience. Thankfully, Kamran had an infinite supply. Patience mattered when no clear leads existed, and he had nothing more than a name and a house to work with. No direction, no tangible clues, and no certainty that rewinding time here would reveal anything useful. But if something waited to be found, he'd find it.

The vehicle slowed, tires crunching over ice and packed snow. He remained still as he took in the quiet neighborhood: its stately townhouses stood tall, stretched in elegance, their ornate facades softened by winter's hush.

"This is it," Olivia said.

He believed her. But this house . . . it didn't belong.

Even without knowing its history, he could see it'd once stood on equal footing with the others. But something had stripped it of its status. Whatever event had ruined the home had not been kind enough to finish the job. Instead, it'd left behind a reminder that lingered, silent and heavy.

Ferenc leaned forward slightly. "Does anybody even still live there?"

"Believe it or not . . ." Olivia replied.

The temperature greeted Kamran brusquely as he stepped out of the car, seeping through whatever opening of his thick coat it could find. He nestled his nose and cheeks deep into his scarf as the cold nipped unpleasantly at his skin, bringing back unwanted flashes of splattered crimson atop fresh blankets of crystalline white. With a shuddered exhale, he shoved his childhood memories back into the depths of his mind by focusing on the crumbling house.

At first, he rewound time slowly. The present softened at the edges, flaking away in increments. Figures emerged in the muted grayscale overlay. They moved fluidly, their actions like a film playing in reverse. Some entered the house, others left, their interactions silent but unbroken. Kamran continued rewinding the events when a familiar pale-white aura entered the picture.

He adjusted his focus, watching as Olivia's figure spoke with someone inside a car. Their postures suggested conversation, but no sound accompanied the exchange, their words locked in the past.

"What do you see?" Though Moses had exited the vehicle and stood next to him on the sidewalk, his voice barely broke through the thick haze of Kamran's ability, distant and muted as if struggling to carry through deep water.

Kamran squinted, trying to extract more details. He focused on the second figure as time continued to rewind, placing them inside the house. A third figure lingered on the second floor for a moment, but nothing out of the ordinary stood out.

He forced his tongue to move, but his body resisted, trapped in the weight of the past. "What . . . did . . . her . . . parents . . . say?" he asked instead.

Each movement cost him extra effort to accomplish, his muscles nearly unresponsive. Even talking felt like his tongue fought its way through a spoonful of peanut butter. Every syllable sluggishly resisted, his voice dragging behind the rest of him.

"They don't know where she is," Olivia replied from inside the vehicle, her voice carrying through the open door. "And her mother doesn't care. She disowned her as a child."

"Why?" Ferenc asked.

"She claims Anya threw a fit, but her father says something spooked her pretty bad."

This new information sharpened Kamran's focus, giving him permission to delve deeper into the past. He forced time to rewind faster, pushing beyond his usual careful pace. He turned the clock back so far, pain coiled around his skull, the pressure growing with each passing second until he could no longer hide the wince that rippled uncomfortably through his muscles.

Body and mind fought for control. Instinct urged him to pull out, but he refused. Hesitation had no place here. His job depended on it. And a king's bounty hung in the balance—Mithra's fortune.

"Hey. You're pushing too far."

Moses's voice drifted further away, distance warping the sound. The warning lingered, offering a tether back to reality, but Kamran

85

ignored it. He couldn't afford to heed. His persistence earned him a flash of red splitting through the past before it vanished just as quickly as it appeared.

He steadied his breath, forcing himself to stay present despite the discomfort. "There," he said, trying to point with his chin. Whether he succeeded or not remained to be seen.

With controlled precision, he slowed time to a natural flow, allowing the past to unfold at its own pace so he could study the upcoming event.

The house's past played out before him in layered shadows, each movement ghostlike and detached. A family of four resided inside the house—one adult and two children in one bedroom, and a slender figure in a dress in another bedroom. Nothing out of the ordinary.

A vehicle diverted his attention as it pulled into the driveway. Two adults and a single child emerged and approached the door. Through the transparent house, the children rushed down the stairs and reached for the handle.

Then the entire world around him shifted from blacks and grays to bright red. Fire blazed everywhere.

He'd braced himself for the flash he'd seen earlier, but it still startled him. His muscles tensed, and he might've even jumped—a feat, considering the disconnect between his mind and body.

The overlay of the red world jammed into reality like a square peg forced through a circular hole. It distorted and twisted in ways the mind refused to accept. Jahannam—hell itself—had appeared into the past.

A monstrous, demonic creature unlike any he'd seen before swiped its enormous clawed hand through the flames, its massive maw stretched wide. Kamran's throat constricted as it swallowed one of the children whole.

Then, as instantly as it had appeared, hell vanished.

The world about him turned shadowy once more, the demonic being vanishing with it. Only a faint red glow clung to the remaining child, flickering before fading entirely as their small body crumpled.

Darkness pressed in around him. Kamran's mind reeled as he tried to return to the present, but his body refused to follow.

Move. Return. Escape, he commanded, but nothing obeyed.

His brain jackhammered against his skull at the same speed and intensity as his heart against his ribcage. The past still clung to him, refusing to let go, locking him in a place that no longer existed. In all the times he'd ever used his ability, he'd never witnessed anything like what he just saw.

Kamran tried to reach for something—anything—to help him distinguish the past from the present, but his limbs remained paralyzed, trapped beneath the weight of the past. He'd pushed too far. The darkness deepened, nothingness stretching in every direction.

Time had lost all meaning. It'd been seconds since he rewound time. Minutes. Hours. Or maybe none of it at all.

A sound drifted through the void, faint and shapeless. A voice, maybe, but the words blurred together, too faint, too distant, too *warped* to grasp. Or maybe he'd imagined it. But the sound came again and again.

His world jolted violently, the tremor buzzing through every nerve. A voice—urgent, calling—reached him through the darkness. "Come on, Kamran. Come back!"

The name—*his* name—cut through everything. A spark, a flicker of light then rekindled inside the suffocating black. *Moses.*

Another violent shake. The sensation crawled over his skin, pressure beckoning him forward, but the past resisted, clinging to him like quicksand, threatening to drag him under. Kamran latched onto the familiarity of Moses's voice, clawing his way toward it, tearing through the paralysis by sheer force of will. He used Moses's voice as an anchor, and reality slammed back into him, finally breaking him free of his bond with the past.

Every nerve inside his body roared back to life in sharp, electric agony. His vision blurred. His senses overloaded all at once in a disorienting mess as light blazed too bright, cold stabbed too deep, and sound crashed too loud. The air reeked of sulfur, the acrid burn stinging his nostrils. And a sour taste curdled at the back of his throat, threatening to make him choke. The nausea hit immediately, his stomach lurching with violent protest.

Moses's grip tightened on his shoulders. "Come back!" he urged through gritted teeth, his voice rough with something dangerously close to panic. Then he gave a sharp exhale. "Oh, *alhamdulillah.*" His forehead pressed against Kamran's, the relief in the gesture more telling than words.

"You do not even believe in Allah." His voice barely scraped out, hoarse and paper-thin, but he forced his lips into the faintest of smiles. The words should've come with a teasing edge, something to lighten the crushing weight of the moment, but they didn't. Because, after receiving that letter from Ariol—from Mithra—he didn't know if he believed in Allah anymore either.

Moses huffed, a breath almost like a laugh but carried too much leftover tension to be anything close to amusement.

Kamran wanted to say more, to tell Moses he'd never been so relieved to see him. But the pain crashed in again, tearing through his skull with ruthless force. His stomach clenched and his limbs trembled.

"Come on," Ferenc said from next to them, his tone steady but urging. "Before we get any unwanted attention."

Hands gripped Kamran's arms, and only then did he register the hard-packed snow beneath him. He hadn't even realized he'd gone down. His stomach coiled tight from the sudden movement as they lifted him, and his balance wavered as the cold air bit against his overheated cheeks.

Then it struck.

His stomach twisted violently, the migraine too much to handle. He barely managed to turn before he doubled over, violently retching.

Footsteps shifted nearby, controlled but weighted, before something cool pressed into his palm—not harsh or hurried, just firm and steady. Snow.

"Here." Moses's voice remained quiet and gentle, only ever reserved for him. "Clean yourself up."

Kamran tightened his grip on the snow, pressing it against his lips. His limbs trembled, his muscles weak from the strain, but the sharp chill grounded him enough to breathe through the worst of it.

Ferenc exhaled sharply. "Is he all right?"

Moses positioned himself between him and Ferenc, creating a barrier. Though Kamran didn't lift his head, he recognized the unwavering stillness. "He's fine."

The words rang false, but their purpose mattered more than the truth. Kamran closed his eyes for a moment, centering himself before straightening his spine. His scarf had loosened during the ordeal, the thick wool uneven against his coat. Before Moses could adjust it for him, he lifted a shaky hand and fixed it himself, tugging the fabric back into place. Moses remained still, watching but not interfering.

Kamran tightened his jaw, drawing in a slow breath through his nose. The trembling hadn't yet subsided, and the ache behind his eyes throbbed nonstop. Without wasting another second, Moses helped him into the SUV. He sank into the seat, barely holding back a sigh of relief. The cold from the snow still clung to his fingers, but heat started creeping under his skin once more. As the vehicle pulled away, every tiny bump in the road sent another sharp pulse through his skull. He shut his eyes and exhaled through his nose before tearing off his scarf and cracking the window. The air brushed against his face, cool and grounding. He focused on it, hoping to keep the nausea from getting worse.

"What did you see?" Moses asked.

Kamran wanted to answer, to tell him about the impossible and terrifying scene he'd witnessed, but he only managed a low groan. Between his pounding skull and the nausea still twisting in his stomach, the words remained lodged in his throat. He shut his eyes tighter, pressing his fingers against the bridge of his nose. The pressure did nothing to dull the sharp pain from behind his eyes. Every small jolt from the road sent another ripple through his gut, the nausea churning like an aftershock.

"Don't throw up in the rental," Ferenc warned from the driver's seat.

Kamran barely acknowledged the comment.

Once back at the hotel, the trio stepped out, their boots crunching over the snow. But Kamran remained in his seat, unmoving. The moment he'd try to stand, he'd risk passing out, throwing up, or something worse. None of the options appealed to him much.

Moses shifted beside him. Of course he'd stayed. That should've reassured him, but it only confirmed what he already suspected—a lecture loomed.

It didn't loom long.

"You pushed too hard." Moses's scolding carried no bite, but the low rasp to it stirred up shame anyway. He'd frightened him.

Kamran exhaled slowly, his eyes still shut. "I needed to see it."

"You could've been lost forever."

"But I wasn't." His voice barely held any strength, each syllable requiring more effort than it should've. "You were there to save me."

Moses hissed out a breath, irritation crackling just beneath the surface. "Kam, I'm serious. That was reckless—even for a king's bounty, let alone for some fucking fictional character."

He peeked through one eye. His vision swam from the effort, but he caught enough—Moses's rust-colored eyebrows furrowed deeper than he'd ever seen before. He shut his eye again. "Enough."

Moses sighed in his tone of surrender. "Yes, Highness."

Kamran would've bristled at the name if his head hadn't been pounding. Instead, he let it slide, unwilling to waste the effort.

Moses shifted again, no doubt getting comfortable to stay as long as needed. "I'm glad you're back," he said quietly.

The tension in his body eased as he sank into the quiet steadiness of Moses's presence. They sat in silence—not awkward, not heavy, just there. It stretched on for ages, or maybe only a few minutes. Time had lost meaning beneath the pounding in his skull.

Finally, Moses spoke again. "What do we do now?"

He didn't answer right away. The thought of using his ability again twisted his stomach, the sickening knot coiling tighter. But their mission hadn't finished. Not even close. "We rest. We buy warmer clothing. Then we follow the horizon to the Gatekeeper."

"Are you up for it?"

If every use of his ability took this much out of him for this contract, he doubted he'd be able to physically handle it. But this job promised a king's reward. A god's reward.

"I will be after I rest."

A quick knock rattled the window, sending a fresh spike of pain through Kamran's skull and his stomach twisting in protest. His eyes shot open long enough to see Ferenc before the searing pain forced them shut once more.

"We have rooms," Ferenc said.

CHAPTER 12
Shikki

Revenge had a flavor, and Shikki savored every rich and intoxicating bite. The slow-burning satisfaction curled in his chest like a well-fed flame.

He lightly squeezed the silver filigree mask in his hands, the cool metal pressing into his skin as he descended the platform to the center of the chamber. The room's stillness swallowed the dull thump of his boots as they struck against the smooth lunar stone with each step.

At the chamber's center, the lunar prince dangled from blackened iron chains, his arms stretched taut above his head, wrists enclosed in heavy shackles. His body sagged under its own weight, but the chains held him fast, refusing to allow even the small mercy of collapse. His long silver hair clung to his sweat-dampened skin, strands falling in a tangled curtain over his face. The moonstone beads threaded within—once gleaming with ethereal light—had dulled to a lifeless gray, their luster stolen by time and suffering.

Shadows pooled beneath him, stretching outward as if the darkness itself sought to claim him.

Shikki loathed royalty who couldn't be bothered to learn the names of their own staff. It didn't matter if they had thousands under their rule—any kingdom ruler worth their weight in gold should know them all. Alican had taught him that.

And high priest or not, Alican would've made a far better ruler than Prince Lomos.

A sharp slap echoed through the room as Shikki's palm struck Lomos's cheek. The blow twisted the prince's head to the side, and Shikki savored the sting radiating through his fingers. A weak groan slipped from Lomos's lips, and a wince flickered across his features, but he barely stirred.

"Wake up, Highness," he said, his voice lilting with false sweetness.

Lomos's breath hitched, but his eyes only fluttered before rolling back again. Shikki sighed and struck him again, the force reverberating through his palm.

"Not so fast," he warned. "I want you awake for this."

Damp metal and stale incense lingered in the chamber, mixing with the underlying musk of stone and the prince's sweat. The air itself pressed down, thick with the residual energy that had been siphoned from Lomos and the phoenix over time.

Shikki had been patient. He'd drained the lunar prince's energy a few times now, and each session unraveled something new.

Lomos differed from the phoenix. The fire elemental only physically weakened with every wisp of her essence drained. But

Lomos's energy drain decayed the entire moon along with him. His lunar glow had shifted, first dimming, then darkening into a rusty orange, like an eclipsed moon. And with it, the Lunar Kingdom suffered. Structures crumbled. The palace eroded. Even the sacred temple . . .

Shikki's jaw tightened. He loathed that temple.

Lomos's head lolled forward, his breath shallow, barely conscious but awake enough. Shikki leaned in, studying the prince's gaunt features. Malnutrition and mistreatment had carved away at him, thinning his face into something ghostlike.

"Do you remember a priest by the name of Kaydo, Highness?" he asked softly. He lifted the filigree mask, pressing the cool metal against his skin before settling it over his face. He let it rest there, let it mold to his features, revealing his previous position within the kingdom. "Hmm?" he prompted. Maybe, just maybe, the prince would recognize him now.

Lomos's brow barely twitched. His gaze remained unfocused, hollow.

Something inside Shikki snapped. He ripped the mask away and hurled it against the stone floor, the sharp clang echoing through the chamber. His hands curled into fists as rage flooded his veins, the weight of years of insignificance pressing against his ribs. Again. Forgotten. His teeth clenched so tight, his jaw ached. Before he could stop himself, he reeled back and slammed his fist into Lomos's face.

The prince's head snapped to the side, and chains rattled as his body jerked, but no sound escaped his lips. Not even a gasp.

The lack of reaction only made it worse.

His nostrils flared. His breath came sharp and uneven, every inhale stoking the fire roaring in his chest. He pulled back his fist again, fingers tightening until his knuckles burned, seconds from repeating the blow—

Shikki exhaled. The breath dragged through his teeth, long and slow, the effort to release it almost painful. His fingers uncurled, shoulders rolling back as he smoothed the fabric of his priestly robe with deliberate precision.

When he spoke again, his voice curled with venom. "Of course you don't." A sharp click of his tongue followed, unimpressed. Then, louder, "Well, it doesn't matter." He took a step back, tilting his head as if studying an insect beneath his boot. "Kaydo is dead. My name is Shikki now. And you best remember that name, because *I'm* very much alive. And so is Alican—thanks to your energy."

Lomos's eyes snapped wide.

Shikki almost laughed. Of course he remembered *that* name. Alican carried a title that demanded recognition, a name that held weight.

That's where Lomos and Alican differed. Lomos only knew the names that mattered to his court, the ones with influence. But Alican knew them all—elder and newborn alike.

As Kaydo, he'd always been an afterthought. Not just to royalty, but to all lunar beings. He came second to everything. Another voice spoke over him, another hand reached past him, another decision made without his opinion. Always overlooked. Always forgotten.

He loathed it.

97

But Alican had been different. Alican saw him, spoke to him, and even remembered his name, unprompted and unforced. Kaydo had clung to that. And when Alican took him in and made him his apprentice, teaching him everything he knew, Kaydo had followed without question.

And then Alican asked for his help as he sought revenge on the Lunar Kingdom, asking only for one small thing: to let Kaydo die— let them all forget him completely. And from the ashes, a new name would rise. One they would never forget.

Shikki, the *Death* Elemental.

With a final glance at the chained prince, Shikki spun around and strode out of the chamber. He pressed a large button, and the mechanism whirred to life, the dome sealing Lomos inside.

He climbed the steps to the platform and pressed the controls, his fingers gliding over the cold metal. With a pull of a lever, he activated the siphon. Lomos's body jerked as his energy drained from him, siphoning into the canister along the panel. A sharp cry of pain tore through the chamber, but Shikki didn't flinch. The moment the prince had forgotten his name, he'd lost the right to sympathy.

The door groaned open, and the heavy thud of approaching footsteps rattled through the platform beneath Shikki's boots. He didn't need to turn to know who neared—Deon moved like a man carved from stone, solid and unshakable, with a deliberate, weighted pace.

The footsteps stopped just behind him before Deon dropped to one knee, the soft scrape of fabric against metal. "You beckoned, Master?"

Shikki finally turned from the control panel, the hum of the siphon thrumming pleasantly in his ears. His lips curled into a slow, satisfied smile. Deon had been his greatest experiment: a walking weapon, stripped of hesitation and reforged into something greater. "I have a mission for you."

Deon lifted his head slightly, one hazel eye locking onto him, the other hidden behind a thick curtain of long, wavy blond hair.

"The solar king made contact with the air elemental and her guardian," he continued, his tone clipped with irritation. "Which puts a rather large damper on my plans."

The king's interference didn't just slow their progress—it threatened everything. Alican needed the elementals' power to prove his worth to the Keeper of the Realms. He needed her to respect him as ruler over the realms. He wanted to reshape them, to carve his name into history with an iron grip.

None of that would happen if the elementals slipped through their grasp. The solar king's interference tipped the scales, giving the air guardian and his little crew a lead they couldn't afford . . . unless Shikki stripped that advantage away.

Deon straightened with a fist at his chest, his jaw set. "Then I'll handle it—"

"Hold on," he cut in, a slow smirk curling his lips. "I have something better in mind."

He'd let them scramble to find the Gatekeeper, let them believe they'd edged ahead. Shikki only had to pluck a few from the fray, twist the narrative, and turn them against their so-called allies. No one fought harder than those who believed they'd been betrayed.

"I want to find as many of the elementals and guardians as possible," he continued, "and pit them against the royal little lapdogs. Convince them the air guardian and his group are the enemy, so to speak."

Deon nodded once. "Of course."

The solar king's interference posed not just a problem but a challenge. And Shikki had never backed down from a challenge. He'd rewrite the rules before the guardian's crew ever realized they'd lost.

"I have their general locations, but that won't be enough. What I need from you is to pluck their wild card. You see, the king sent them to fetch a mercenary with an extraordinary ability, which puts us at a severe disadvantage. Bring him here."

Deon bowed his head once more. "As you wish, Master."

Lomos's broken cries died out, and the chamber fell silent, save for the constant hum of the siphon. Shikki barely spared a glance toward the prince hanging limp in the chains, unconscious, as he flicked his attention to the swirling silver mist gathering inside the canister. Satisfied, he shifted his gaze back to Deon in silent expectation with a tilt of his head.

Deon didn't hesitate. He smoothly rose to his feet and strode toward the exit.

Shikki turned back to the control panel and shut the siphon down. The steady hum quieted, replaced by the distant echoes of the palace's endless corridors. With a practiced motion, he detached the canister from its slot, cradling it in his hands. Lunar energy swirled inside, a shimmering silver mist tinged with something dimmer, weaker than before. He tilted the container slightly, watching the mist shift and dance within.

A kingdom's lifeblood, stolen pulse by pulse.

His lips curled in satisfaction as he exited the chamber, leaving Lomos behind. The heavy door slid back into place, sealing the unconscious prince inside with a deep, resonant thud.

With each step down the hall, recessed sconces embedded in the dark stone flared to life, casting pale violet light. The glow stretched over the polished surfaces, warping in long reflections that wavered like ghosts. Shadows clung to the edges, untouched, settling deep in the corners.

At the end of the corridor, a pair of heavy doors loomed. Shikki pressed his palm against the eclipse carved at the center—a full moon swallowing a thin crescent. At his touch, the sigil pulsed with pale violet light, flickering through the cracks like veins drawing breath for the first time. The surrounding stone trembled, vibrations rippling through the floor beneath his boots. With a deep, echoing groan, the doors parted, revealing the chamber beyond.

Inside, Alican sat hunched in his black throne, his form swallowed by the thick folds of his dark hooded cloak. Shadows clung to him like a second skin, his figure little more than a silhouette against the dim violet glow of the recessed sconces along the walls. Long skeletal fingers rested lightly on the surface of a large labradorite scrying sphere atop a pedestal in front of the throne.

Beside him, Amy stood with the uneasy stiffness of someone caught between her own will and another's.

Shikki stepped forward, his voice soft. "Master, I brought you more energy."

Alican coughed into his sleeve, a dry, rasping sound. "Excellent."

Alican's voice no longer carried the steady, soothing tone it once had. It'd decayed into a wicked, gritty grumble that scraped against the air like sandpaper. His skin had burned, nothing left but charred flesh and exposed bone.

No decent being would've ever harmed the high priest of the Lunar Kingdom. Only monsters would do that. So Shikki had deemed the Realm of Air and all its inhabitants his mortal enemies. And they would all pay.

He handed Amy the canister, and she pressed the release valve. A thin mist of stolen lunar energy hissed free, swirling upward before Alican greedily inhaled it, his breath shuddering.

His gaze flicked to Amy as they waited. She served as their wild card, the piece of the puzzle still unsettled. Alican had a natural pull on her, but not enough. The air guardian could still manipulate her emotions, using her lingering doubts against them. And Shikki refused to take that risk. A true soldier couldn't waver.

He'd suggested sealing her memories, placing them behind a barrier the same way they had with Deon. Forge her into something unshakable. To his surprise, Alican had agreed.

The last tendrils of mist dissipated as the canister emptied. Alican raised his hand, the motion slow but deliberate. The sleeve of his cloak slipped back, and he flexed his restored, fleshy fingers. With a controlled exhale, he reached for the edge of his hood and slowly pulled it back, rolling his shoulders as though shedding the weight of weakness.

Relief flooded through Shikki's chest as he took in the familiar face. The decay had been reversed, if only for now. His master looked like himself again.

Alican's gaze met his own, sharp and knowing. "Thank you, Shikki."

His relief didn't last. It never did. The decay would creep back—it always did—undoing everything they fought to keep together. He'd witnessed the cycle repeat too many times since dragging Alican back from the brink of death, no thanks to the air guardian.

He exhaled sharply and snatched the empty canister from Amy, irritation flowing through him. "This won't work, Master. You keep reverting back."

Alican's gaze remained steady, unreadable. "No, it's working as it should." He adjusted the sleeve of his cloak, flexing his fingers as if testing how much time they had before the decay started again. "The prince's energy is tied to the moon, and the moon to him. The more energy I take, the harder it becomes for him to replenish it." A soft smile curled his lips. "Don't worry. Everything is still going to plan."

Shikki wanted to believe that. He needed to. But doubt stalked at the edges of his mind, pacing like a restless predator. He forced it down, choosing instead to trust Alican implicitly.

"You alerted Deon to our plan, yes?" Alican asked, his voice soft but firm.

Shikki smirked at the mention of his greatest success. After Alican's defeat, they'd needed a new strategy to rebuild their army, one that didn't rely on sheer numbers alone.

Pure dumb luck had led them to the guardian of the Realm of Earth, but controlling him had taken far more effort. The man stood as sturdy as a fortress—broad-shouldered and unyielding—but raw strength meant little when the mind could be reshaped. The process had been experimental, but they'd succeeded in burying his memories behind an impenetrable wall, turning him into something obedient.

"I have, Master," he said, a flicker of satisfaction curling through him. "He's on his way now. We shall have the mercenary on our side in no time."

Alican hummed in approval. "Perfect." He then raised a hand, and Amy moved instantly, stepping forward to help him to his feet. She took his arm with careful precision, guiding him as he rose.

Shikki grabbed the walking cane from its place nearby, handing it over with a small bow. His jaw tensed as he watched Alican straighten. Each slow, deliberate step served as a reminder of how far they still had to go, how much more energy they needed to take.

Alican needed the Keeper of the Realms for the plan to work. She held the key to restoring him, whether she wanted to or not. And if she slipped beyond their reach . . .

Then Shikki would raze the Solar Kingdom to nothing but cinders.

CHAPTER 13
Ferenc

Ferenc couldn't decide what unsettled him more: how quickly Moses had secured their passage north, how effortlessly he'd acquired the best equipment along the way, or the fact the easiest and most direct route led them across a river.

Their journey had taken them from paved roads and a rented SUV to an old all-terrain cargo truck—built to withstand brutal temperatures that would kill most vehicles—to finally, snowmobiles and sleds trailing behind like tethered lifelines. The farther they traveled, the more civilization faded into a distant memory.

To make good time before dark, they'd avoided the shelter of snow-capped forests and instead streaked across the open ice, where an unforgiving wind howled against them. Ferenc brought up the rear, his nerves stretched thin over the constant risk of flips, falls, or worse—the ice betraying them and plunging them into a watery grave. But they reached a tiny, secluded village without incident as the temperature plummeted along with the sun.

The locals, shy but warm, welcomed them with steaming bowls of food that thawed the cold from Ferenc's bones. Their host, Moses's contact, had arranged a tiny room for the night, and by sunrise—mid-morning, this far north—they continued their journey.

Majestic mountains loomed ahead, their jagged peaks piercing the overcast sky as they rode single file, trusting a mercenary who could see a beacon-like signature no one else could. With every mile, Ferenc's stomach tightened. They followed two men armed with automatic weapons, men trained to handle the most extreme situations—including, presumably, killing people. And now, those same men led them to a place where nobody would ever find their bodies.

"Are you sure it's not *this* mountain range?" Ferenc asked over the helmet intercom system.

Moses, who'd been casually exchanging words in Farsi with Kamran over his shoulder, switched to English without missing a beat. "I swear, if you ask that question one more time—" He cut himself off when Kamran tapped his arm.

"I am certain," Kamran replied smoothly. "Her signature is farther still."

"Why would anyone want to live out here?" Olivia mused, uncertainty laced through her voice.

"If you had seen what I did, you would understand."

Kamran had explained the fiery world and the demon after their visit to Anya's parents' house, though he'd needed the night to recover first. The strain of using his ability to peer that far in the past had left him physically spent and ill. But even after hearing the details, Ferenc struggled to make sense of it.

Only Kamran could see Anya's so-called *beacon*, and everyone else had to blindly take his word for it. Ferenc's gaze drifted to Moses's helmet at the head of the line. The mercenary followed Kamran's lead without hesitation, as if second nature. But whatever history existed between the two, he didn't share it.

Moses switched back to speaking Farsi, and Ferenc tuned him out, focusing instead on Dormouse—the only one without a headset.

While he wished she could be kept in the loop, their intercom system only allowed for four speakers. Her silence came naturally, but it became deafening during the long stretch of their journey as she sat behind Olivia on their snowmobile. His heart ached for just a single word or two from her instead of Moses and Kamran's sporadic back and forth.

He exhaled and turned his attention back to the journey ahead. No physical proof supported Kamran's claims—no visible landmark, no measurable trail. Discomfort twisted deep in his gut. The only thing keeping them from freezing to death in the middle of nowhere came down to the word of a mercenary handpicked by a solar king.

"Not much farther now," Kamran announced. "The aura is getting brighter."

That hit somewhere between worrisome and encouraging. They'd finally escape the blistering cold, but isolation carried its own risks. Anything could be waiting for them out there, and with mercenaries leading the way, one wrong move might set off a trigger-happy response.

The river faded behind them as the forest swallowed them up, thick trees closing in on either side. Smooth riding turned into a dangerous game of precision as they weaved through obstacles buried beneath the snow.

Then, the trees broke away, leaving them fully exposed to the elements. Wind tore through the expansive wilderness, no longer softened by the cover of the forest. It cut through Ferenc's layers, straight to his core. His skin instantly prickled with goose bumps, a shiver rolling through him.

Ahead, Moses veered toward a large rock outcrop jutting from the base of the steep incline. Olivia followed, and Ferenc pulled in behind them, keeping close. He eyed the rock wall, hoping for some hidden tunnel entrance that would get them the hell off the mountain.

Moses swung off his snowmobile and pulled off his helmet. "This is where we walk. It's too steep to keep riding through."

Olivia groaned, shoulders slumping. Ferenc couldn't blame her. The heaviness settling over his own body had nothing to do with the gear he wore. He wanted the Gatekeeper found, Amy rescued, and to be back home playing fetch with Max in his backyard.

But for now, he'd settle for a cigarette.

He climbed off his snowmobile, helmet tucked under his arm as he reached into his coat pocket. Despite the outcrop, the wind whipped from every angle, killing every flick of his lighter before the flame could take.

After the fifth failed attempt, when he'd growled in irritation, a mittened hand lifted in front of his face. The air stilled. He exhaled, flicking a glance at Olivia. She didn't say anything, just kept her focus where it mattered. He gave her a quick nod and finally lit his cigarette, dragging in a long pull of nicotine. He should've been able to think of that on his own—he could've blamed the frozen tundra, but he knew better. His mind had tangled itself while running over every possible way things could go wrong, every risk of trusting Kamran and Moses as they led them further into nowhere. No wonder he'd fumbled over something as simple as blocking the damn wind.

"Save your energy," Moses called, steadying Kamran against the rock. "We're close, but far enough for you to pass out if you don't pace yourself."

Ferenc took another slow drag, watching Kamran massage his temples through his ski mask, head bowed and eyes shut. His ability had left him sick before, and Ferenc doubted this time would be any different. He tipped his chin toward Kamran. "What about him?"

"He's my concern, not yours."

"Sympathy's no reason to be an ass," Olivia shot back with a frown.

With his eyes still shut, Kamran raised a hand before anyone could keep going. "I appreciate the concern," he said, his voice steady despite the strain, "but I assure you I am also being conservative with my energy."

Ferenc studied Kamran. He spoke with certainty and carried himself like someone who understood his limits, but certainty didn't guarantee he wouldn't drop at any moment. The last time he'd used his ability, it had wiped him out completely. Out in the middle of nowhere, that kind of miscalculation could get them all killed.

Ferenc finished his cigarette just as Moses returned from gathering supplies from the sleds. The redhead handed Ferenc a rucksack. "Let's go."

Kamran pushed off the outcrop, tightening his hood as he started up the incline, Moses close behind. Ferenc adjusted his ski mask higher over his nose, slung the heavy rucksack over his shoulders, and turned to Olivia and Dormouse.

"One last push," he said. "Stay close."

They both nodded in unison, then followed Kamran and Moses through the relentless climb, each step a battle against the biting wind and uneven terrain, a grueling test of endurance. Ferenc gripped Dormouse's hand, anchoring them both as hearty gusts tried to knock them off balance. At first, he thought she'd started shivering—faint tremors vibrated through his thick gloves—but then he felt it in his boots. A faint, rhythmic pulse rippled through the ground beneath them, subtle but distinct. He froze mid-step.

Up ahead, Kamran had stopped as well. He turned sharply, his posture rigid with awareness. His gaze swept behind them, searching for something. But when Ferenc followed his line of sight, the Siberian tundra remained vast and desolate, white swallowing the horizon. No movement. No obvious threat.

He turned back to Kamran. "You felt that too?"

Moses flicked his attention between them. "What?"

Kamran shook his head in silent dismissal. He turned forward and pressed on, moving with the kind of deliberate focus that kept people from asking questions.

Ferenc peered down at Dormouse, her lashes rimmed in frost, thick brows drawn in confusion. He squeezed her hand reassuringly before continuing on.

"What happened?" Olivia asked when he fell back into step beside her.

"I'm not sure."

He'd always understood air, long before discovering his role as the air elemental's guardian. His instincts as a pilot recognized the subtle language of the wind before his mind ever caught up—every gust, every shifting current. But whatever had passed through the ground felt foreign, beyond his natural awareness; avalanches and earthquakes sat too far outside his element.

The tremors had come and gone so fast, he couldn't tell if they meant anything. If it'd been an avalanche, Kamran would've turned toward the peak, not away from it. Maybe Ferenc had imagined it and Kamran had stopped for an entirely different reason. He didn't know, and the bitter cold did nothing to help him figure it out.

They trudged through the incline in suffocating silence. Kamran's pace gradually slowed, and Ferenc tensed when Moses leaned in close, speaking in hushed tones as Kamran rubbed his eyes.

The way Moses hovered over Kamran mirrored how Ferenc had been protective of Dormouse when they first met. He hadn't recognized it as the guardian instinct back then; he just assumed decency drove him. But concern lingered at the back of his mind, always tugging at him, wondering where she went, what she did, and if she needed anything. Even now, that protectiveness remained.

Kamran finally stopped, nowhere near a cave entrance or shelter. Ferenc's stomach churned when Kamran dropped to his knees. Moses crouched beside him instantly.

"What's wrong?" Ferenc asked, trying to keep his voice even.

Moses rubbed Kamran's arms, trying to warm him. "He's cold. And something's in his eyes."

Ferenc clenched his jaw. He hoped whatever irritated Kamran's vision wouldn't interfere with his ability. Without it, they blindly marched into nothing.

Olivia kneeled behind Kamran. "Here. Let me—"

Moses knocked her hands away before she could touch him. "What do you think you're doing?"

She shot him a glare and reached again. "I'm going to warm him up."

"She won't hurt him," Ferenc cut in, pulling Dormouse close for warmth.

Moses didn't budge. "Save your energy." His scowl matched Olivia's, the tension between them thick enough to slice.

She exhaled sharply. "Look, I don't have time for your holier-than-thou leadership complex, and neither does your friend, here. Either huddle in with a little bit of gratitude and let me help, or go elsewhere and freeze in self-righteous silence." She then pressed her hands on Kamran's back, irritation still etched into her face. Moses didn't budge.

She focused, and the air around her shimmered, bending to the heat she generated. Friction built in the molecules, forcing warmth into the space around her. The harsh, turbulent winds distorted the effect, warping Ferenc's view with rippling waves, like a mirage in the middle of a tundra, as she worked her magic.

Kamran paused mid-motion as he rubbed at his eyes, cracking one eye open and peering past his gloves. He nodded once at Moses, who instantly dropped his defensiveness and shifted back into protective concern.

Ferenc exhaled, tension easing—but only slightly. Olivia had never been one to back down from confrontation. Her assertiveness, stubbornness, and confidence naturally clashed with Moses's more aggressive approach, and their bickering spiraling into an all-out argument served no one. Not while they remained out in the open, vulnerable to the elements.

He gently tugged Dormouse's hand, guiding her to sit beside Kamran. Olivia arched a brow at him, but he said nothing as he imitated her actions, kneeling behind Dormouse and warming the air around them. When he placed a gloved hand over Olivia's, she gave a small nod before refocusing on Kamran's back. He then placed his other hand on Moses's shoulder.

Moses stiffened, his gaze snapping to Ferenc in a glare that faded almost as fast as it appeared. He nodded—maybe in understanding, maybe in thanks. Either way, he didn't protest, his focus returning to Kamran.

"Is this the farthest north you've been?" Dormouse asked Kamran. Between the howling wind, the thick scarf muffling her words, and her usual quiet tone, Ferenc barely heard her.

The corners of Kamran's eyes crinkled slightly, a telltale sign of a smile hidden behind his ski mask. "It is not," he admitted, "but it has been far too long."

Ferenc and Olivia continued their efforts, and soon enough, the shivering eased. Color returned to Dormouse's wind-chilled face, and Kamran no longer hunched in on himself for warmth.

Olivia tilted her head back to the sky, exhaling sharply through her nose. She shut her eyes, her chest rising and falling heavily. "Sorry, that's all I have in me."

"It's fine." He squeezed her shoulder lightly. "You did good."

Moses helped Kamran back to his feet. "Let's keep moving."

Olivia's brows furrowed, irritation flickering across her features, but Kamran turned, offering a slight bow. "Thank you," he said, sincerity woven into his words.

"Anytime," Olivia replied, her tone less assertive than usual.

Ferenc simply nodded before falling back into step.

They pressed on, the wind clawing at their backs while the snow-covered ground shifted unpredictably beneath their boots. When they finally reached a break in the jagged rock face, Dormouse squeaked, elated, and pulled ahead of Ferenc, slipping inside the cave.

Sheltered from the blistering wind, the sudden stillness hit like stepping into another world. The cave's cool air settled over them, still crisp but nothing compared to the brutal sting from outside.

114

Ferenc rubbed at his face, grimacing as blood flow returned, his cheeks prickling with uncomfortable warmth.

Kamran dropped to his knees, freeing his hands from his gloves before clawing at the layers covering his face. Moses reacted instantly, kneeling beside him. "What's wrong?"

"I can't—I can't breathe!"

Kamran yanked his ski mask free, then tore at the scarf tangled around his neck before unzipping his heavy coat. His breaths came fast and uneven, shoulders rising and falling with each desperate gulp of air. A sheen of sweat clung to Kamran's forehead as his body slowly unwound. After a few moments, he pulled his coat back around himself. Whether from overheating or from exhaustion, the worst of whatever had hit him seemed to have passed.

Dormouse hesitated near the entrance. "What now?" she asked quietly.

Ferenc pulled the flashlight from his rucksack, clicking it on. The beam cut through the darkness, revealing the cavern ahead. "Looks like there are a few different paths."

Dormouse dropped her gaze to the uneven ground in defeat. "She could be anywhere."

"We will split up," Kamran said, tone firm. "We can cover more ground." He left no room for argument, but his hardened gaze lingered on the entrance.

Curious, Ferenc followed Kamran's line of sight, searching for whatever held his attention. Nothing but the same wind-blown snow covered the horizon.

Kamran exhaled, finally shifting his focus to Ferenc. "You and Miss Dormouse. And Moses with Miss Olivia."

Ferenc caught the cold glare Olivia shot Moses. He would've offered to switch—he implicitly trusted Olivia when it came to Dormouse's safety—but something told him Kamran had deliberately chosen the pairs. It made sense to pair the elemental with her guardian. A more unsettling possibility lingered, however—Moses picking them off one by one.

Moses narrowed his eyes. "And leave you on your own?"

"Yes."

Moses said something in Farsi, his tone edged with suspicion.

Kamran exhaled, his breath curling into the cold. "I cannot see— I am too cold—so I am in the dark just as much as you are." He'd switched back to English again. Whatever Moses had accused him of, Kamran clearly had no interest in hiding anything from the rest of them.

"Then come with us," Moses said.

Kamran shook his head. "Go. Time is of the essence."

Ferenc stepped in before Moses could argue, handing him a flashlight. "All right, there are four paths. Dormouse and I will take the far left. Kamran can take the next one, and you and Olivia can take the one after that." His voice stayed even, authoritative, but his gut twisted at the plan. Splitting up always made things more dangerous. "If anybody reaches a dead end, come back here and take the path to the far right. Leave an item so we know you've returned. The next group out will take the path of whoever hasn't returned yet to check on them." Everyone nodded. "If anyone comes across the Gatekeeper—"

"Do not engage," Kamran interrupted.

Ferenc adjusted his grip on his flashlight, the weight grounding him. "Try talking to her first. We need her help."

Moses straightened to his full height, eyes still locked onto Kamran on the ground. "And if she attacks?"

"Do not engage," Kamran repeated. "She is not to be harmed."

Moses exhaled sharply, then removed a few layers of clothing, practically making a show of how easily he could reach his weapons. "Let's just hope she doesn't view us as the enemy, then."

Ferenc gritted his teeth. "We'll make this quick. Get in, get out." He met Olivia's gaze and bumped fists with her. "Be careful."

"Always," she whispered, following Moses down their designated path.

He turned to Kamran, finding his head bowed, eyes shut. "How's your head?"

Kamran masked his condition well, but Ferenc had seen how the mercenary staggered, how the cold clung to him more than the rest of them. The last time he'd pushed himself, he'd nearly collapsed.

Kamran kept his head bowed, his voice steady despite the strain. "I assure you, my condition is manageable. But I appreciate the concern."

Ferenc hesitated. "You sure you'll be fine?"

Kamran exhaled, slow and controlled. "Yes."

That answer left too much unsaid. The tremors. The way Kamran had turned, scanning the horizon as if pinpointing something just beyond their sight. Later, his attention locked onto the entrance, unwavering.

Kamran's ability allowed him to see what the rest of them couldn't. Either he still worked to piece things together, or he actively kept them in the dark on purpose. Assessing the situation before raising an alarm made sense—but so did leading them straight into an ambush.

Ferenc's shoulders tensed before he forced them to loosen. He could keep dissecting Kamran's motives, or he could focus on the task ahead—the only thing that might keep them from getting killed. Anya held the key to all of this. If they found her first, they controlled the field.

He gave a short nod—though Kamran wouldn't see it—before turning to Dormouse. "Let's move."

Together, they stepped toward their designated path, leaving Kamran alone. Ferenc forced away the negative thoughts clawing at the back of his mind. He had no time to hesitate. Finding the Gatekeeper had to come first. The sooner they found her, the sooner they could get out of this frozen abyss.

CHAPTER 14
Kamran

Kamran forced himself to ignore the unpleasant tingling in his fingers and the sluggish numbness creeping into his thoughts. He leaned back against the cave wall and focused on his breathing instead, slow and steady, hoping to clear his head. Or at least distract himself from the cold air assaulting his face now that he'd removed his mask and scarf.

Beyond the entrance, the wind screamed through the desolate tundra; inside, only his own breathing broke the silence. The others had already left.

He needed to think.

At first, he'd assumed the cold interfered with his ability. He'd been careful not to overuse his sight—both because migraines typically followed and because the more he strained, the weaker the signature appeared. But he'd endured bitter temperatures before. He'd been sent into far worse for the sake of a mission. This felt different. *Something* interfered with his sight.

He rubbed at his eyes again but froze mid-motion. The grittiness grinding against his eyelids came from more than exhaustion or dryness.

Sand.

That shouldn't be possible.

Tremors pulsed through the ground—a faint, rhythmic vibration beneath him, almost like a second heartbeat. His fingers inched toward the handgun holstered at his ribs, instincts bristling.

The moment the tremors stopped, a shuffle echoed just beyond the entrance. A deep voice followed, in English, the words measured and deliberate: "I'm unarmed."

Kamran activated his sight past his blurred, tear-filled vision. His ability registered a faint forest-green aura before the sting forced his eyes shut again.

"If you call manipulating sand being *unarmed*," he countered smoothly.

A brief pause. Then, "I apologize. It was meant to mask my presence."

Kamran's thoughts raced. Sand bowed to no one. And tremors didn't follow a mortal man's steps. He adjusted his grip on the gun, keeping it low but ready as he cautiously got to his feet. "What can I do for you?"

"My master's impressed with your skills. He requests your help."

Kamran had dealt with unusual offers before, but being tracked through the Siberian wilderness for a job request reached a new level of absurdity.

"It must be urgent," he said evenly, "to have followed me all the way here. Unfortunately, it will have to wait, as I am currently engaged in another job."

The stranger stepped inside, his long, wavy blond hair splayed about his shoulders like a lion's mane beneath his ski mask. "My master's aware. But this *is* urgent, so he's not offering you a choice."

Kamran's stomach twisted. He recognized a threat when he heard one. And after taking in the imposing size of the man, he didn't like his odds in a struggle.

The man moved his hand, and the earth split beneath Kamran's feet. He barely threw himself aside, weighed down by his winter gear, before the hole beneath him erupted. A jagged pillar of stone speared upward.

The ground *obeyed* this stranger.

He'd met only two other people who could control an element— Ferenc and Olivia. Between them and the letter from Mithra, his faith and understanding of reality had already been shaken. And now this.

His thoughts flicked to the legends of the *daevas*—ancient demons of destruction, creatures of earth and chaos that twisted the world beneath them.

Fiction. Myth. And yet . . .

A rock the size of a human skull hurtled toward his head. Kamran ducked, the projectile smashing against the cave wall behind him. Before he could regain his footing, another one shot toward his ribs.

He twisted, firing twice in rapid succession. The bullets struck solid stone—a wall that hadn't been there a second ago.

The daeva redirected the terrain itself. Kamran ground his teeth, throwing himself into a roll as another slab of rock slammed into where he'd stood only moments ago. He landed low, bracing himself against the shifting floor, trying to predict the daeva's next move.

The ground lurched under his boots, the stone shifting like a wave. Kamran's balance gave out as the terrain betrayed him, sending him into a skid. A pillar of stone shot up behind him, forcing him forward—right into the daeva's range.

Kamran fired again, aiming for center mass. But the bullet never made it. A wall of earth rose between them, swallowing the shot. The impact splintered the stone but left the stranger untouched.

Kamran growled, pivoting to fire again, but the hard ground beneath him softened. Sand dragged him down, swallowing him to his knees in seconds. His heart skipped a beat, but he shot again, only for the bullet to ricochet off another sudden protective barrier of stone.

The stranger flicked his wrist, and the stones under his command shot toward Kamran, pinning his weapon arm against the ground.

The stranger loomed over him, a shadow against the dim cave light. "You're lucky my master needs you alive."

The man had only taken one step forward when a piercing cry rang out from the cave entrance. Kamran's gaze snapped toward the sound.

A figure stood silhouetted against the snow-brightened light filtering in from outside. It lunged forward with a flash of bone in hand and drove a knife into the daeva's back.

A strangled grunt left the stranger's lips, his visible eye going wide in surprise. He twisted to face his aggressor, the blade dislodging slightly from his thick coat. Kamran caught the gasp from the new figure—a woman—her terror breaking through as the stranger turned to face her.

A gunshot cracked through the cave; Kamran barely made the connection before the stranger lurched forward from the impact. The gunfire had come from the opposite direction—Moses had returned.

The daeva reached for his shoulder, his gloved fingers brushing the wound. Slowly, he turned back toward the tunnels, glare smoldering beneath his ski mask.

"Step away," Moses warned, weapon still aimed, his stance unyielding.

Olivia skidded to a halt beside Moses, gasping sharply as her eyes locked onto the daeva. Her reaction shifted from alarm to immediate, calculated action. With another quick breath, she shoved both hands forward.

The air roared. A massive gust slammed into the stranger's chest, lifting him clear off his feet. The force ripped him from the cave, sending him hurtling backward into the snow beyond the entrance.

Moses blinked, brows lifting as his gun remained locked on the empty space where the stranger had been. His grip didn't waver. "Huh."

Kamran exhaled slowly, tension bleeding from his limbs as the stones pinning his arm collapsed into dust. He flexed his fingers, testing the muscles before shifting his attention to the trembling figure near the wall.

The second stranger—the woman near the entrance—had pressed herself against the wall, her rapid breaths breaking through the cavern's sudden stillness. Wide, dark eyes darted between them, her posture stiff with uncertainty.

Moses didn't lower his gun. His boots crunched against loose grit as he closed the distance to Kamran in seconds, his free hand extending as he turned his weapon on the woman.

Her scream ripped through the cavern, bouncing off the stone walls. Olivia immediately rattled something off in a foreign language, her hands held open in a calming gesture.

Kamran reached for Moses's offered hand, pulling himself free from the sand that had swallowed him moments before. His legs ached from the strain, but he ignored the discomfort.

Moses barely spared him a glance. "What the hell did you get us into?"

Kamran straightened, brushing dust from his sleeves with slow, deliberate movements—a distraction from the unease tightening in his chest. His mind fought to reconcile what he'd witnessed with what he knew, what he believed. He schooled his expression into something unreadable, but the weight of doubt settled deep.

Boots pounded against stone as Ferenc barreled in from his tunnel. A harsh beam of light slashed through the dim cavern mouth as he swung his flashlight ahead, scanning for a threat. He barely made it two steps into the mouth before Kamran swiftly lifted a hand—a gesture to *stand down*.

Ferenc skidded to a halt, his gaze darting from Kamran to Olivia, then falling on the new woman. His flashlight steadied, the beam lingering on the woman for a fraction longer before he lowered it slightly. But his other arm remained extended, keeping Dormouse tucked behind him, blocking her from stepping into view.

The woman shook her head, muttering something back to Olivia. Her mittened hands curled into fists, her stance shifting like she might bolt. Kamran recognized the instinct. She'd fought, but she hadn't been prepared for what followed.

Olivia switched to English, desperation in her voice. "Please, Anya, wait! I need your help."

Suspicion hardened Anya's features. "How do you know my name?" she demanded, accent thick.

"We've been searching for you," Olivia explained, keeping her hands visible. "We mean no harm. My name is Olivia, and these are my friends."

Friends. Kamran resisted the urge to correct her. They'd hired him, not befriended him. But for the moment, he held his tongue, allowing Olivia to lead. She spoke the woman's language, and they needed Anya to listen. He flicked two fingers at Moses—a silent order. Moses hesitated, but after a beat, he lowered his weapon. Not holstered, but no longer a direct threat.

Anya slowly removed her yarn mittens and fur hat, fingers raking through her dark, pixie-cut hair. Her gaze swept over them, lingering briefly on Moses and his gun before flicking back to Olivia. "What do you want?"

"I need you to open a portal to the Keeper of the Realms."

Kamran's interest perked up. The Keeper of the Realms. The name meant nothing to him—nowhere in Mithra's letter had it been mentioned—yet Olivia spoke as if Anya should understand.

Anya's fingers twitched at her sides as she continued to sweep her gaze over them. Her lips parted just for a second before she pressed them into a thin line. "I don't open portals." Without another word, she strode toward the path Ferenc and Dormouse had taken earlier, unzipping her coat and reaching into the interior pocket. A small flashlight clicked to life in her hand, its narrow beam cutting through the dark ahead.

Moses muttered something under his breath and moved to the cave opening, gun still in hand, to check for the stranger with earth manipulation. Kamran retrieved his own weapon from the ground and holstered it as he returned his attention to Anya.

"Please," Olivia tried again, stepping forward to block her path. "The fire elemental and the lunar prince—"

Anya stiffened, tension rolling off her in waves. "I don't know any elementals or princes. I don't know any keepers of realms, either. And I sure as hell don't know you." She gestured toward the entrance, where the daeva had vanished. "Or the man you blew out. Who the hell was that, and how did you do it?"

126

Olivia froze. Not a full stop, just a moment too long between breath and movement, a blink that lingered, her fingers tightening subtly around the fabric of her coat.

"What?" Her voice came steady, but her weight shifted ever so slightly, as if preparing for something worse than the question itself.

Ferenc frowned, attention snapping toward Olivia. "Wait, what happened?"

"That thing you did." Anya motioned with her hands, mimicking a push. "I saw it. Wind doesn't just do that."

Olivia hesitated, glancing at Ferenc. "I—"

"Liv . . ." His expression softened.

"Answer the question." Anya's focus remained on her.

Olivia exhaled, shoulders tensing. "I manipulated the wind."

Anya's expression barely shifted, but her fingers slightly twitched again, as if considering something. "That's not possible," she said, but the certainty in her voice faltered.

"'Fraid so, cupcake," Moses drawled as he returned.

Kamran stepped in. "Manipulating earth is not possible either. And yet, you saw it happen." Anya's jaw tightened, her gaze darting back toward the entrance. "You do not have to trust us," he added. "But you saw what that man could do. You saw what Miss Olivia *can* do . . ." He paused, then delivered the final blow. "And I saw what you did when you opened that door so many years ago. The day your mother disowned you."

Anya's guarded expression cracked. A flicker of something raw passed through her dark eyes, her fingers flexing at her sides as if bracing against an unseen force. Then her walls snapped back into

127

place. Her lips curled with skepticism before she turned on her heel, stalking deeper inside the tunnel. "Nice try," she said, voice edged with forced detachment. "I don't open portals. No portals, no gates, no doors. You made the trip for nothing."

Kamran didn't buy that for a second. "I can see past events. Shadows." His next words landed heavy between them. "I saw you, as a child, open the door into a world of fire." Her fingers curled into fists, her pace quickening, as if distance alone could silence him. But he stayed close. "I saw the demon," he pressed, each word deliberate. "And I saw it devour your brother."

She spun, her face inches away from his, her dark eyes wild. "*Stop!*"

Moses aimed his gun, but Kamran lifted a hand, halting him before he could interfere. His attention never wavered from Anya. "It was not your fault."

Silence clamped down like a vice. Then Olivia spoke, her voice softer. "Your father believes you."

Anya's gaze snapped over his shoulder toward her, suspicion darkening her features. Kamran seized the moment. "You unknowingly opened a portal and have feared yourself ever since." He tapped just beneath his right eye. "I know that fear. I felt the same when I first used my sight."

The first time it had happened as a child, the vision came without warning—disjointed echoes of things that had already happened or would one day.

The ability hadn't arrived gently. It had grabbed hold of him, splintered his understanding of time, and left him isolated in a world that no longer moved in a straight line. Like her, he'd tried to shut it down, to pretend it didn't exist. But it had never stopped. And in time, he'd learned to carry it with discipline. He recognized that fear in Anya.

She swallowed hard. The mist in her eyes caught the flashlight beams, but she turned away before they could betray her further.

Moses let out a low whistle. "So your mother was right, then. You made all that fire fuckery up for kicks, huh?"

Anya stiffened, glaring over her shoulder. "If you think trying to make me prove myself is going to work, you're mistaken."

"Wasn't trying to make you do anything. My job was to find you." He gestured vaguely at the cave tunnel. "I've done that. Now I can claim my reward. Don't care what lies you told to get away with whatever you did to your brother."

Anya's temper flared like the fire he'd seen in her past. "I told no *lie*!"

Kamran raised a hand to stop Moses. "I believe you. So tell me the truth. You *will* not open portals . . . or you *cannot*?"

"I won't." Anya snapped around on her heel and marched deeper through the winding tunnel. "Nothing will ever be so important to make me open anything ever again."

Olivia groaned and hurried after her. "Please—this is important!"

"You do not have to be alone," Kamran insisted, following them both.

"Alone is what I chose."

"But you do not have to suffer in solitude," he corrected. "Extreme isolation warps the mind. It—"

The moment the words left his mouth, a pressure built behind his eyes, his skull tightening as if something clawed at the back of his thoughts. He parted his lips to finish his sentence, but nothing came out as childhood memories flooded through—*Shackles. Spikes. Darkness.* His mind braced against the oncoming tide as the past threatened to drown him.

Moses's voice cut through the deluge in his mind. "He would know."

Kamran inhaled sharply. He clung to Moses's voice and allowed it to pull him from the abyss, to ground him. The tension in his muscles barely eased, but the storm in his head abated.

"No one deserves to be alone, no matter what," Moses added. Then, quieter, he spoke to Kamran in Farsi. "Are you all right?"

Kamran forced a nod as he returned to the present. A lie, but a necessary one. Anya had stopped in her tracks and had been watching him. A flicker of something unreadable passed over her face before she lowered her gaze.

"Miss Bordyukova," he said softly, "we are no different from you."

"Exactly." Olivia stepped in. "You can open portals to different dimensions, Kamran can see things no one else can, and I can control air. So can Ferenc—and Dormouse too."

At the mention of her name, Dormouse shrank further behind Ferenc, disappearing from view.

Anya's keen gaze flicked between them before landing on Moses. "And you?"

Moses shrugged. "I can say the alphabet backward. That's about where my special skills stop."

"You can shoot a gun," Ferenc offered helpfully, at the same time Olivia said, "Which alphabet?"

Anya ignored them all, meeting Kamran's gaze again. She didn't look away this time. Her eyes gleamed, but she didn't let the tears fall. "I won't open a portal. I'm sorry."

The finality in her tone left no room for argument.

Kamran nodded. He wanted to change her mind, but unfortunately, he'd told the truth—he did understand. More than anyone, he knew what it meant to be trapped by something beyond control—an ability that refused to release him, threatening to pull him into the past and keep him there forever.

A heavy silence followed, then Moses turned to leave. "All right. Let's go, Kamran."

Olivia blinked at him. "Wait, what? Why?"

"The mission was to find the Gatekeeper," Moses said flatly. "We found her. She said no. Job done. So we're leaving before that guy comes back."

"We can't just leave her," Olivia argued. "He could come back at any moment. He's after Dormouse, he's holding someone hostage—what's stopping him from taking Anya too?"

"He wanted me." Kamran measured his words carefully. "He followed us. He . . ." Kamran exhaled slowly, waving a hand briefly in front of his eyes to illustrate the grit that had clouded his vision.

"You can't leave," Anya stated firmly. "It's too late. You'll never make it back before the sun sets. You'll end up freezing to death."

A heavy silence settled over the group. Olivia's brows furrowed, lips slightly parted, as if caught between questions and realization. Moses stood rigid, his stance shifting ever so slightly, assessing. And Ferenc crossed his arms over his chest, deep in thought.

Dormouse's quiet voice finally broke through. "What do we do?"

Kamran parted his lips, but Ferenc beat him to it, sighing as his arms dropped.

"We'll stay the night, at least. We can all take turns keeping watch and figure the rest out tomorrow."

Kamran gave a curt nod, his focus shifting between Ferenc and Olivia. "Agreed. But in the meantime, Mister Ferenc and Miss Olivia, I believe you owe me more information."

Olivia raised a brow. "Information about what?"

"The truth." His voice cut through the cavern's chill, cool and measured. "The Keeper of the Realms. The fire elemental. The lunar prince. And most importantly, the daeva who just came for me. I want to know what other threats await us."

Moses sighed. "*Daeva*," he muttered while shaking his head, the motion slow and skeptical.

Olivia shot Ferenc a quick, hesitant look—subtle, but laced with concern. Ferenc studied Kamran for a long moment, his gaze un-readable, before he gave a small, conceding nod.

Anya shifted, breaking the tension. She continued on down the tunnel. "Come. Best get comfy for the night."

CHAPTER 15
Olivia

Olivia had to admit, Anya had her act together. Not only had she transformed the cave's open center into a fully functional living space—complete with fur rugs, a fire stove, and shelves packed with dried goods and supplies—but she handled everything herself. Hunting, foraging, and repairing gear all fell under Anya's capable hands. She even knit—as proven by the blankets, mittens, hats, socks, and other various items neatly stacked or draped across the space like a walking Pinterest board for survivalists.

Despite the main cave's openness, the wood-burning stove steadily radiated heat, loosening the chill that had burrowed in deep through Olivia's bones during the long journey. Anya's thick and hearty stew had helped too, and the tea that followed chased away the last bits of numbness clinging to her fingers.

A wide battery-powered clock displayed large red digits across the room as the time crept toward midnight. The hours stretched thin in the hush of the cave, softened by the whisper of firelight.

"You have a curious bunch of friends," Anya mused, handing her another mug of tea.

Olivia accepted it with a quiet thanks, glancing toward Ferenc and Dormouse curled against the wall closest to the warmth of the stove. Both slept soundly, their breathing slow and even, tucked beneath thick knitted blankets. She didn't know how she'd convinced them to come this far on the off chance she might discover who—or *what*—she used to be. They hadn't needed to say yes, but they had. And she'd never forget that.

Even if it had all been for nothing, since Anya refused to help.

Her gaze then shifted to the corner, where Kamran slept atop a nest of pillows and wool. Earlier that evening, she and Ferenc had given him as much information as they could—everything they'd learned about the Keeper of the Realms, the elementals, and the lunar court. Kamran had listened without interruption, his posture rigid, his questions sparse but precise. He hadn't challenged a single word, and his silence afterward had stretched long. Not dismissive or skeptical, just . . . measured. Like he needed to carry the weight of the truth before deciding what to do with it. Then, without fanfare, he'd thanked them and turned in for the night.

Moses lay nearby, sprawled on his back, finally quiet. He'd stood guard most of the night like a hypervigilant watchdog, and he hadn't left Kamran's side—like a loyal little puppy. Olivia had even watched him help with Kamran's prayers, steadying him like he'd done it a hundred times before. Unfortunately, that quiet, caring nature began and ended with Kamran. The rest of them had to endure his sarcastic commentary and general superiority complex—neither of which Olivia had the patience for. She'd lost count of how many times she'd fantasized about chucking something at his head just to shut him up.

Still, irritating or not, they'd pulled their weight earlier. Kamran especially.

She'd been terrified of him when they first met. Among his rowdy crew, his composure had bordered on inhuman. That kind of calm meant one of two things: psychopathic tendencies or extreme discipline. Luckily, Kamran landed on the better side of that spectrum—at least for now.

Moses, on the other hand, grated on her nerves like sandpaper on a sunburn. She couldn't tell if his default setting involved picking fights or if he just didn't know how to be positive. Either way, he pushed her buttons. But he'd shot the blond man before she'd used her ability, and that alone might've kept them safe this long.

She took a sip of her weak, flavorless tea. She missed the heat of her Mexican mochas from back home.

"Got any spices?" she asked, trying to keep the grimace off her face. Anya crossed to a wooden cabinet, shifting around glass containers until she pulled one out. She returned and poured a splash of something dark into Olivia's mug.

"Whiskey?" Her eyebrows lifted. "Thought you Russians only drank vodka."

"Cognac," Anya corrected, then tipped the bottle back for a swig. "And we drink everything. Vodka, whiskey, beer, wine. Wine's shit unless you spend a fortune, though." She settled onto the fur rug, dropping the bottle beside her with a soft thump. "So. Tell your story. How did you first control the wind?"

Olivia tensed, her insides knotting. People feared what they didn't understand. And fear turned violent faster than most cared to admit. If the situation hadn't been dire, she never would've revealed her abilities like that. Not in front of strangers. But she'd already fought that dangerous man once, before he'd kidnapped Amy.

She took a sip of her tea and swallowed hard. The cognac cut through the brew with a surprising bite—a strange pairing of warm spice layered with faint notes of fruit and caramel, but not unpleasant.

So much had happened since leaving California in search of Ferenc and Dormouse, Olivia didn't know where to start. She took another slow sip. "Well, this is going to sound weird, but I had a dream one night. It told me to find elementals and guardians. I thought it meant nothing—just a dream—until I realized I could . . ." She paused, uncertain if speaking it aloud counted as brave or reckless. Admitting it to a stranger felt like a gamble. "You know . . ."

"Do magic?" Anya raised an eyebrow, lifting the bottle back to her lips.

"Kind of. I guess. I don't know. I can—" She swallowed hard, shifting in the armchair. "I can control the element of air, but not much else."

"Show me."

Olivia's insides froze as frigid as the Siberian weather outside the cave. "Um."

136

Ferenc hadn't remembered his life as a guardian, even after she'd created snowflakes in the Florida heat. But he'd chosen to protect Dormouse anyway and allowed her to train him to control air. As the Gatekeeper, Anya might've held a role just as important, but she didn't seem to remember anything either—no Keeper, no elementals, no flicker of recognition when she looked at any of them. That made this harder. Olivia didn't just fear Anya turning violent; she feared another dead end, another person who couldn't help her understand who and what she might truly be.

"Show me," Anya repeated, her tone firm. "I want to see this magic—this *air power* properly."

A frown tugged at Olivia's brows. "You show me yours, I'll show you mine," she shot back.

Anya held her gaze for a moment, then took a big swig before wiping her mouth with the back of her knitted sleeve. "I can't do what I do on command. You can."

The tension in Olivia's shoulders eased slightly. If any hope remained of Anya opening a portal to the Keeper of the Realms, the woman needed to harness her abilities—just as Ferenc had. Maybe seeing Olivia do it would trigger something.

Olivia inhaled slowly, grounding herself in the warmth of the cave, then exhaled with intention. She focused on the tea in her hands, letting her control settle around the air around the mug. Frost curled past her fingers, creeping up the ceramic in delicate white veins. When Anya's eyes widened, every nerve in Olivia's system screamed to shut it down. But then Anya nodded, visibly impressed.

"All right," Anya said slowly. "But I thought you said you could only control air, not water."

"Oh, I didn't control the water," Olivia replied. "I cooled the air around the mug."

Anya tilted her head some, then nodded her chin toward the others. "And what about them? Did they have the same dream as you?"

The memory of Ferenc crashing into her with his jet blinked across her mind, fast and vivid. That moment would stay with her forever. Olivia shook her head. "No. I . . . I was the only one tasked with finding Ferenc and Dormouse. The other two—well, that's complicated."

"Not an easy task." Anya took another sip and extended the bottle.

Olivia declined with a shake of her head. "No, definitely not. Especially since I came from California and found him in Florida. That's all the way across the States."

Anya's frown returned, her eyes narrowing slightly as if trying to map the geography. Olivia prepared to explain, but before she could, Anya asked a simple question: "How?"

Olivia had expected skepticism—like with Ferenc—not genuine curiosity. She licked her lips, sorting her thoughts. Part of her almost preferred explaining the physical distance instead. At least *that* made sense. "I had this—this feeling. Deep inside. Like a pull. And I followed it across the country. The closer I got to Ferenc, the stronger it became. Like a—a magnet. Y'know?"

Anya made a quiet, noncommittal sound in the back of her throat.

"I don't know why I was specifically chosen to find Ferenc and Dormouse. But I was told the Keeper of the Realms can answer that, and more. That's why we had to find you; you're the only one who can open a—"

"No," Anya cut her off, her voice flat and hard. Her entire expression dimmed like someone had flipped a switch.

"But—"

Anya rose to her feet, taking another swig. "If you were me, and you opened the door to find the world on fire and this large . . . *thing*—" Anya's eyes closed, her mouth tightening as if to hold back the memory. But the trembled words escaped anyway. "It *ate* my brother." She swallowed whatever sorrow still clung to her voice with a sniffle and a shallow breath. Then she lifted her chin. "I don't know how to open portals on command, and I won't try. I can't even bring myself to open doors. I'm sorry you came for nothing."

Olivia sat frozen, fists curled tight against her knees. If she'd seen what Anya had—lived through that horror—maybe she would've refused too. Frustration bubbled dangerously, and the familiar sting of tears pressed at the corners of her eyes, demanding release.

Another dead end.

She swallowed hard and straightened her spine. The fate of the world hinged on this. That had to count for something. She wouldn't take no for an answer. She couldn't.

"It's not all about me," she said carefully. "Sure, I'd love to get answers about who I am and why I can control the air. But the real reason we need to find the Keeper of the Realms is because something dangerous is happening. The fire elemental and the lunar prince have been taken. And that blond guy? He's after Dormouse. He tried to take her back at Ferenc's house. We stopped him."

A deep snore, like an angry tiger's snarl, interrupted her thoughts. The sound grated on every nerve like nails down a chalkboard. Olivia twisted around with a glare just as Moses shifted in his sleep, completely oblivious. Her eyelid twitched. Just one pillow. One well-placed fluff. But the thought vanished, and she turned back to Anya.

"We need to stop this before it snowballs. We need the Keeper's help. And you're the only one who can take us to her."

Anya sucked in a breath, jaw tight. She poked the inside of her cheek with her tongue before answering. "I don't know of any Keeper. And even if I did, I wouldn't open a—a *portal* to get to them! What part of 'world on fire' makes you think I'd *ever* want to do that again?"

The snoring cut off sharply, followed by a groggy grumble from Moses: "Keep it down over there. Some of us are trying to sleep."

Olivia ground her teeth as tears stung her eyes once more. She had nowhere to go and nowhere to vent. The cave offered no escape, no open air, and no distractions.

She shut her eyes, forcing herself to think of something—anything—else. A movie she hadn't seen. Popcorn. The sound of previews. But the moment she let go, her mind yanked the conversation back. A shaky breath escaped her.

"I won't open a portal." Anya's voice came quieter this time. More controlled. "But this seems important to you. All of you. So I'll still try to help."

Olivia opened her eyes. "How?"

"Maybe the same way you found him." Anya nodded toward Ferenc.

It didn't add up. According to the lunar princess, Olivia had been tasked with finding her own elemental and guardian. She couldn't sense the others; she'd never been meant to. That part had always been clear. She nearly shook her head, dismissing the thought, until something sparked.

Anya didn't have an element. She didn't need one as the Gatekeeper. But she *could* open a portal to the Keeper of the Realms. Maybe a connection existed.

Olivia leaned forward, her heart thudding as the thought took root. "If I teach you what to feel for . . . do you think you'd be able to find the Keeper?"

Anya gave a slow shrug, her eyes narrowing in consideration. "It's worth a shot."

The warmth that bloomed in Olivia's chest had nothing to do with the fire or the cognac. Hope flickered, small and stubborn. And for now, it would be enough.

CHAPTER 16
Ferenc

The frigid temperature gnawed through Ferenc's gloves, numbing his fingertips. Smoking in the middle of a Siberian winter ranked high on his list of terrible ideas, but the nicotine helped curb the tight knot of stress in his stomach.

They'd found the mercenaries. They'd found the Gatekeeper. But the Gatekeeper refused to open a gate. And to top it off, the blond man who'd taken Amy had come back—this time for Kamran.

He rubbed his hands together to generate heat as he approached the small shack nestled at the edge of the secluded village. They'd left Anya's cave at sunrise, hiked down to where they'd parked the snowmobiles, then rode the rest of the way through biting wind and ice-glazed slopes until they finally reached the safety of the settlement by nightfall. The one-room structure they'd been granted creaked with every movement and barely fit them all, but it beat freezing to death outside.

Ferenc fumbled with the knob before knocking. Olivia answered.

"I can't feel my fingers," he said.

She stepped aside, careful not to trip on the sleeping bags, rucksacks, or the sprawl of limbs along the floor. "You can control air, silly. Heat it up."

"I'm trying! It's not working fast enough!"

She clasped her hands around his. Warmth slowly seeped into his fingers, the tingling ache returning. He groaned in relief.

Olivia smirked. "Maybe that's a sign to quit smoking."

"You can keep that Californian opinion to yourself," he shot back. She cackled.

"But you've been here before. You're telling me you haven't learned your lesson?"

Ferenc shot her a look. "First of all, I traveled to Moscow, not middle-of-nowhere Siberia. Second, it happened in the summer."

She pulled away with a mischievous grin. "Uh huh . . ."

"You want some of this?" He wiggled his fingers, then playfully snatched at her wrist, aiming a cold touch toward her back.

She yelped, pulling away with a half-laugh. "Don't you dare!"

He parted his lips to retort, but Moses pointedly cleared his throat from the back wall. And just like that, the lightness Ferenc had shared with Olivia for a fleeting moment vanished.

"Are you two done?" he drawled.

"Jealous?" Olivia quipped without missing a beat.

Moses muttered something under his breath.

Ferenc ignored him as he sidestepped a crumpled jacket and a half-zipped rucksack to sit beside Dormouse on the narrow bed. The frame creaked beneath him, its joints stiff from disuse.

Anya stirred in the beat-up armchair at the foot of the bed. Her eyes opened slowly, frustration already brewing beneath her otherwise calm demeanor. She'd been trying to hone her sense of the pull—just as Olivia had trained her to—but still showed no sign of progress.

"I don't feel anything," she said.

Dormouse's shoulders drooped. Ferenc shifted closer and rubbed her back, trying to offer silent reassurance while his gaze found Olivia.

She stood over Kamran's sleeping bag, arms folded, thoughtful. How she'd tracked him across the country from California based only on instinct remained a mystery. But she had.

"What did you feel?" she asked. "What was the sensation?"

"I don't feel anything," Anya repeated. "There's no . . . pull. There's nothing."

Olivia's mouth pulled into a tight line, her disappointment loud and clear.

"What did you do with the sunstone?" Ferenc asked.

Olivia raised a brow. "It's in my bag. Why?"

"Even if Anya could sense something, where would it lead us? If the only way to find the Keeper is through a portal, then they're probably not on Earth. And if they're not on Earth, then we need the solar king's help."

Olivia stepped over to her rucksack and unzipped the bottom pouch. She pulled out the sunstone—given to her by the solar king's adviser, Eeolas—and a moonstone on a fine silver chain that once belonged to Marisol, the lunar princess. "Well, we can't use the sunstone at night. And the lunar prince has been kidnapped, so I don't know how much help the moonstone would be. I don't even know if we can use these to reach out to them."

He held back a sigh. Another plan slipping through their fingers. At this rate, he'd need a cigarette just to keep his thoughts from spiraling.

"Why can't you just have her feel for the other elementals and guardians?" Moses asked. "Someone's gotta know how to reach your Keeper."

"Because unlike me, she's not attached to any realm in particular," Olivia replied.

"Yeah? You know that for a fact?" he challenged. "Did your *sun king* tell you that?"

She turned toward him, gaze sharp, tone colder. "If you know better, then by all means—enlighten us."

Ferenc waited for Kamran to rein Moses in, but he remained silent, eyes closed, head slightly tilted back against the wall. The faintest crease edged into his forehead—barely perceptible, but enough to betray the growing strain from the endless bickering.

Finally, Kamran opened his eyes and glanced at his watch. With a quiet breath, he sat forward and reached for his coat. His movements remained smooth and deliberate, every action wrapped in that usual calm control.

"Mo," he called out, barely above the hum of the argument. Moses still responded immediately, striding away like he and Olivia hadn't been arguing at all.

"Where are you going?" Ferenc asked. No one casually wandered out into subzero Siberian wilderness at night without a valid reason—even smoking had been a bad idea.

"Salah," he replied, sliding his arms into the sleeves. "It is too loud and crowded to pray in here. So I will borrow another room."

"Why can't your seeing friend find the others?" Anya asked, gesturing toward Kamran. "He found me . . ."

"Because it's not part of the contract, and we can't afford to tack it on," Olivia replied, hands landing on her hips.

Moses finished lacing up his boots. "We don't even have a lead," he added, not missing a beat. "And in case you missed it, the more he uses his sight, the worse off he gets. We don't just take jobs without thinking it through, you know." He grabbed his coat and shrugged it on with ease. His eyes tracked Kamran as he reached for the door.

"Be careful," Ferenc quietly offered to Kamran.

Since their travels began, Moses had always stayed close during Kamran's prayers. It made sense he'd continue, especially with the earth controller still out there.

Kamran nodded once and stepped outside.

"The only thing you think through is your paycheck," Olivia shot back at Moses, apparently still focused on getting the last word.

He snarled something harsh and guttural—definitely Farsi, and probably an insult—before heading out and slamming the door behind him.

Olivia growled, fingers splayed, reaching as though to throttle the air. "He drives me up the damn wall!"

Ferenc blinked slowly, willing the mental weariness to recede. Moses and Olivia had spent most of their Siberian journey sniping at each other. He and Kamran had become the unofficial referees, not that it ever helped for long.

It didn't matter. They'd needed Kamran—and that meant putting up with Moses, attitude and all. The two came as a package deal.

"You didn't know your pull was to air, specifically," Dormouse said quietly, still cross-legged on the bed. She pulled her fingers away from her mouth, her nails chewed to uneven edges. "Can't you just train her to feel for something unusual?"

"There's nothing about this that *isn't* unusual," Anya pointed out.

Olivia dropped her hands with a sigh. "It's not that simple."

"We'll figure it out," Ferenc said. He stood and stepped toward the door, reaching into his coat for another cigarette. On his way past Olivia, he paused, placing a reassuring hand on her shoulder. "Give it time. We—"

Before he could say more, a voice outside caught his attention. A shout.

His stomach dropped. For a split second, everything in him braced for the blond man's return. But the noise outside didn't match the chaos of a fight—no clash of movement, no weapons . . . just muffled bursts of sound. A single syllable. Then two. The tone climbed, sharp and uneven, more urgent with each call.

Olivia folded her arms and rolled her eyes. "*Now* what's his problem?"

The door burst open. Wind slashed through the room, dragging a flurry of snowflakes in its wake. Moses stood in the frame, his gaze bouncing across the faces inside—searching.

Ferenc's heart skipped a beat. "What's wrong?"

Moses didn't answer. He slammed the door shut behind him, sealing in the silence but not the cold.

Anya leaned forward in her chair, eyes narrowing. "Where's his friend?"

Ferenc crossed the room in two strides and threw the door back open. The cold instantly bit at his cheeks. "Stay here," he said over his shoulder, then slipped into the night after Moses.

They couldn't afford to lose their most expensive mercenary. Not now.

CHAPTER 17
Ferenc

Ferenc stepped into the bitter night air, eyes scanning the dark—but Moses had already disappeared. A sharp knot cinched tight in the pit of his stomach. If Moses had vanished too, then it didn't bode well for the rest of them.

The rapid crunch of boots over snow dragged his attention to his left. He spun around, only to be blinded by a flashlight beam.

"*Kam!*" Moses's scream rang out into the darkness as he surged past, his light bobbing ahead.

Ferenc blinked away the strobing impression of the flashlight beam and fell into stride behind him. "Did you find him? What happened?"

Moses shook his head, feet crunching hard as he veered toward the back of the shack. His shouts drew attention; nearby doors opened, and villagers spilled out with flashlights and oil lanterns. Confusion rippled through the settlement. Moses returned from around the bend and instantly beelined for his contact.

While they exchanged words he couldn't understand, Ferenc swept his flashlight beam low to examine the snow. Outlines of footprints scattered across the area, but none told a clear story—no signs of a struggle, no drag marks. Just cold, crusted snow and the aimless tread of daily activity.

The wind gnawed at his skin. He hadn't grabbed his ski mask or gloves when he ran after Moses. Minutes stretched into something colder, heavier. The longer they stayed out, the less likely they'd find Kamran without freezing to death first.

He finally returned to the shack, staggering with the stiffness of half-frozen limbs. As he stood by the wood stove, he fed extra heat into the air, thawing himself out while concerned faces watched him.

"What happened?" Olivia asked, stepping closer to help warm him up. "Where's Kamran?"

"No idea. We couldn't find him."

Anya lifted an eyebrow. "How does someone disappear into thin air?"

"Oh, we've got a pretty good idea," Olivia muttered.

He caught the flash in her eyes and recognized the same dread that clung to his own thoughts: the blond man had come back for Kamran.

The door flew open. Moses stormed in, searching every face in the room again before landing on Ferenc. "He's not here."

"You were literally *seconds* behind him," Anya said. "How did you lose him so fast?"

150

"I don't *know*," Moses ground out, frustration tightening his voice. "When I stepped out, he was gone."

He crossed the room and dropped to one knee beside Kamran's sleeping area, yanking open his bag and rummaging through it until he pulled out the satellite phone with a hissed curse.

Kamran wouldn't have needed the phone for prayer—especially with Moses by his side.

Amy had time to scream when she'd been taken. But that time, the blond man had wanted something in return—Dormouse.

This time, the man hadn't needed to bargain. Kamran would've had no time to scream, to struggle. They would have simply . . . disappeared.

Moses turned for the door with a furious, fearful scowl, but Ferenc stepped into his path, both palms raised.

"Wait."

"Get out of my way," Moses ordered, pushing forward.

Ferenc didn't budge. "Look, we'll help find him, but we need a plan to make sure we do it safely and effectively."

Anya left her chair and planted herself beside him. "I already told you—it's dangerous out there at night unless you know your way around." Her voice rose slightly. "You'll freeze before you find anything. Then we'll be down two people and no closer to finding your friend."

"With how fast he vanished," Ferenc added, "I doubt he's wandering the woods. These masked figures use portals."

Moses's eyes narrowed. "Get out of my way," he repeated with a dangerous growl.

151

He shoved again, but neither Anya nor Ferenc gave way.

Ferenc's muscles clenched so tightly in irritation, it bordered on pain. A part of him almost wished he'd been the one lost instead. The pull of solitude called out to him like a siren's song, but he resisted. "You're a mercenary, for crying out loud! You're trained for situations like these—"

Moses stepped back, arm drawing in close—then came the click of metal. In half a second, Ferenc found himself staring down the barrel of a gun.

"Yes," Moses replied through clenched teeth, "and unless you want to see that training up close and personal, you'll get out of my fucking way."

Ferenc froze, hands lifting instinctively. Anya mirrored the gesture. Across the room, Dormouse froze in place.

He understood Moses's concern for Kamran more than anyone else in the room—he lived it every day with Dormouse. But that didn't change the fact that Moses needed to keep a clear head if they wanted to find Kamran.

Ferenc wanted to shove Moses back with a gust of air, but he couldn't risk it in such a tiny room. One misstep and someone else could get hurt. But before he could act, Olivia stormed forward.

She drove her fingers through Moses's shaggy red hair, gripping him by the base of his skull. His eyes rolled back. Ferenc caught him as he dropped, guiding him to the floor atop the mess of sleeping bags.

Olivia wiped her palms on her yarn sweater with a hiss. "I can't stand him!"

Ferenc glanced back at Anya. "You okay?"

She gave a slow nod, though her wide eyes stayed locked on Moses.

He then turned his attention to Dormouse, lifting a brow in silent question. She gave a shaky nod but wrapped her arms around herself anyway. He wanted to pull her close and comfort her, but Moses stirred, already coming to. Thankfully, Olivia hadn't used too much electrical stimulation.

Moses groaned as he sat up, rubbing the back of his neck. "What the hell was that?"

"You were a little out of control, so I zapped you before you hurt someone." Ferenc crouched beside him, voice even, tone steady. He took the fall without blinking, heading off an argument before it could ignite. "Now listen carefully. We'll find Kamran. But we need your head clear. We'll miss important things if we're not one hundred percent." Olivia had often reminded him of that. "Understood?"

Moses still glared, but the heat behind it faded. He nodded once.

Olivia crossed her arms. "So what do we know?"

"There's nothing," Moses said, running a hand through his hair. "No trail. No sign of him. The villagers started a quick sweep—only a few of them. They say the terrain's too dangerous at night for anything extensive. They'll give it thirty minutes tops before calling it and trying again at first light."

Ferenc nodded. "Makes sense. They know the terrain better than we do. If Kamran left a trail, they'll spot it faster than we could."

"They say it's unlikely he could have made it that far that quickly," Moses added. "He's just . . . gone."

"Unlikely, but not impossible," Ferenc said, rising to his full height. "Not if someone pulled him through a portal. They're instantaneous. Given what we've seen, it's the most logical explanation."

Olivia dropped onto the bed beside Dormouse. "You said there wasn't a struggle?"

"Not that I could tell," Ferenc said. The next words hurt more than he'd expected. "But I'm no expert."

"What's the deal between you two?" Anya asked.

Moses shifted, eyes narrowing at her. Ferenc braced for something dismissive and snide, but Moses just let out a long sigh, scooting until his back hit the wall.

"He's . . . we grew up together," he said. "Child soldiers."

Olivia slapped a hand over her mouth, her gasp muffled by her fingers. Ferenc's breath caught. The words landed like a blow—*child soldiers.*

"Believe it or not, the ringleader of that whole clown operation was my father," Moses went on. "Total bastard. Beat me, beat my mom, and however many wives came before her."

Ferenc's pity surged, tangled with something heavier he couldn't yet name. From a mercenary, that admission carried weight. His hands curled into fists, not from anger, but from the pressure of questions piling up, none of which he dared ask.

"We moved to Iran when I was five. Didn't see him much after that. But when we did? He always had a crowd with him—war buddies, minions, whatever. I didn't know who the hell they were. I just knew to stay in bed. Not that it stopped me from sneaking out now and then."

He paused, fingers dragging absently through the scruff of his goat-patch beard, eyes unfocused, like the memory pulled him sideways for a second.

"There were sounds," he said, quieter now. "Haunting stuff. Crying. Screaming. Chains. All coming from the basement. I was scared shitless. But after a while . . . I got curious."

His eyes shut, and silence followed. Ferenc eyed him warily; he didn't want to poke the bear by asking questions, but the mention of haunting sounds still didn't track. So the silence held—until Anya gave voice to the confusion that had started to creep in.

"You had ghosts in your basement?"

Moses's brow furrowed, eyes snapping open. "No! Kamran was in the basement!" He shook his head, a scoff slipping out. "Weren't you following along?" He exhaled through his nose, the fire dimming behind his eyes. His arms crossed tight over his chest as he looked down at the floor, quiet for a beat. When he spoke again, his voice came low. "Kid wasn't much older than me. Scrawny as hell. First time I saw him, he was locked in this hanging iron maiden—"

"Oh my God," Olivia gasped from behind her hand.

He glanced up at her, expression flat. "Yeah. The medieval-torture kind."

Dormouse shifted her focus to a knot in the wooden floor. Anya crossed her arms, mouth pressing into a line. Her expression didn't shift much, but her posture spoke volumes.

Moses's gaze dropped again. "But he was so small, the spikes didn't even touch him. I read to him that night. Went back whenever I could, when my old man wasn't around. Taught him English. He taught me Farsi. We kind of became friends." He let out a humorless breath and shook his head. "One day, my father came home early. Caught me down there. Boy, did I ever get a whoopin'. After that, I didn't go back. I should've, but I didn't."

No one moved. The weight of what Moses had said anchored the room in silence. Ferenc braced himself. As much as he didn't want to hear the rest, he needed to understand.

"What happened to him?" he asked.

"I don't know. It broke my heart every time I heard him cry in the middle of the night. But one day, it just . . . stopped."

Ferenc's stomach twisted. That kind of silence usually meant the worst. But Kamran had made it out. Somehow.

Moses leaned his head back. "I didn't see him again until I was eight, when my father shoved an automatic weapon in my hands and threw me into a room full of other kids. Kamran was one of them. He looked different. Tougher. But I recognized him. Still had the same eyes."

Ferenc gave a small nod. He understood that kind of bond.

"He recognized me too," Moses said. "After that, we stuck to-gether. No mission could separate us. We used to talk about what we'd do when we got out—run away, start over. Live like kings, y'know?"

Anya leaned forward slightly. "So how'd you get out?"

Moses looked up at her. "We forcefully ended my father's tyranny."

Ferenc swallowed hard. If they could take down someone like Moses's father, they could take down anyone. "You both—"

"No," Moses cut in, flat and sharp. "*I* killed him. You think I'd let Kamran get his hands dirty like that?"

"But you were child soldiers," Olivia said, finally dropping her hand from her mouth. "Surely, he's killed before."

Moses shut his eyes once more. "There's a difference between being forced to kill and choosing to do it. Kamran's never killed willingly."

Ferenc raised a brow in confusion. "But he's a mercenary."

"*I'm* a mercenary," Moses said, cracking one eye open. "Kamran's the group leader." His eyelid closed again. "I get my hands dirty to keep his clean."

That changed everything. Moses's attitude still grated, but after what he'd just revealed, Ferenc recognized it for what it was: self-preservation. A hard-edged coping mechanism, not unlike Dormouse's. Just shaped differently.

A knock at the door cut through the heaviness. Everyone turned. A man stepped inside—Moses's contact. Moses jumped to his feet and approached. They spoke in low, clipped tones. The language slipped past Ferenc's understanding, but he didn't need a translation. The way Moses's shoulders sagged told him everything he needed to know.

No Kamran.

He shifted aside to let them finish talking when a pair of arms wrapped around his waist. He blinked and glanced down. Dormouse. He smiled softly and pulled her in for a hug. After everything Moses had said, he needed a little sunshine to cut through the shadow, and Dormouse had always been exactly that for him.

"Thank you," he murmured into her hair.

The contact left. Moses stayed by the door, eyes fixed on the sky through the narrow window set into the frame. Moonlight touched his face as he stared, fingers absently stroking his goat-patch beard, before he turned back to the room. His gaze landed on Ferenc.

"So. What's the plan?"

"I take it they haven't found Kamran." Dormouse angled her head up, watching Ferenc as if the question belonged to him alone.

"No," Moses replied, even though the question hadn't been meant for him. "And I don't think they will. You said it yourself—he was probably taken." His gaze slid back to Ferenc. "So I ask again: what's the plan?"

All eyes turned to him, and he suddenly found himself suffocating under the pressure for an answer.

He needed air. Solitude. And lots of nicotine.

Ferenc released Dormouse and stepped back abruptly; maybe putting distance between them might help him breathe again. But the air only thinned further, offering no relief.

His mind ran in loops he didn't have time to finish. He had no way to research, no time to investigate leads. He could only work with the information they already had.

He hadn't been able to stop them from taking Amy. Moses hadn't been able to stop them from taking Kamran. They'd probably keep disappearing, one after the other, until the masked organization finally got what they wanted: Dormouse.

Ferenc forced himself to breathe deeply. He couldn't freeze up. Moses needed closure, to know Kamran hadn't just wandered off to die in the cold. Olivia needed answers about why she'd been chosen to find the elementals and guardians. They had to come up with something.

His attention settled on Anya. If she had even the slightest chance of leading them to the Keeper, they needed to follow it.

"Olivia will keep working with Anya to see if she can sense the Keeper," he said. "That's our only lead now. We'll look for Kamran again in the morning, see if we can find a trail in the light. If there's still no trace, we'll regroup and come up with a new plan."

Moses didn't reply at first. He kept his eyes on the floor, stroking the long tuft hanging from his chin. Then, without warning, he dropped to the floor and started unlacing his boots.

"Best get to it, then," he muttered, removing his boots and coat, climbing into his sleeping bag, and turning his back on the rest of them.

Ferenc watched him settle, the heaviness refusing to lift. Sleep wouldn't come easily—not with this much hanging over them. But they had to try.

CHAPTER 18
Deon

Deon stepped out of the swirling portal and shoved the merce-nary down the cold, dark corridor. Shikki had ordered the re-trieval, and Deon had followed the group from a distance—far enough that he should've remained unseen. He didn't know how the mercenary had spotted him. An unfortunate fluke.

He'd taken a knife and a bullet from certain members of the group, which only fueled his irritation. He could've buried them all beneath the mountain, but Shikki had been clear: bring the merce-nary back alive.

The man recovered quickly from his stumble, twisting around with his gun already drawn and ready. Deon didn't flinch. With a flick of his hand, the weapon disintegrated—the metal reduced to dust, the polymer frame clattering harmlessly to the floor.

Surprise flickered for only a second—an expert recovery. Then the mercenary lunged, dagger drawn from his boot, blade catching the dim corridor light.

The narrow hallway, combined with the bulk of his winter gear, left little room to maneuver. Deon braced, raising his hands defensively as he backstepped, the thick fabric tugging at his range of motion while he narrowly evaded each slash. The man pressed forward, relentless. With the next strike, he caught Deon by the back of the neck as he readied to pierce his midsection.

Even with the size advantage, that grip stole his range of motion. He needed to end this fast. Thanks to Shikki's healing, his earlier wounds no longer slowed him.

He trapped the man's wrist against his hip, locking the knife in place. Then, with a swift, precise chop to the side of the neck, the mercenary dropped hard—unconscious.

Deon stood over him, pulse still pounding. His body had reacted like instinct, every movement fluid and effective. Like his control over earth and metal, he couldn't explain *how* he knew what to do— only that he did. The thought barely surfaced before another shoved it aside: Shikki wouldn't approve.

He'd never known anyone whose moods fluctuated as intensely as Shikki's. Usually soft-spoken and respectful, the moment his plans shifted or his orders went unfulfilled to even the slightest degree, his temper erupted like a raging volcano. He became violent and extremely dangerous.

He hoisted the mercenary's dead weight over his shoulder, then pulled off his ski mask and shoved it into his pocket. His hair slipped free—staticky, tangled, clinging to his face—but he ignored it, heading to the throne room just as Shikki had instructed.

"Deon?" Shikki's soft voice came from behind him, sending a chill down his spine. "What happened?"

He paused in his steps and slowly turned around. "He's not dead. Just unconscious. It was him or me." He spoke the truth, but that didn't make it the right answer.

Shikki said nothing. His grip on the canister didn't tighten. His expression didn't change. No eye twitch, no scowl. Nothing Deon could read.

Shikki hadn't mentioned how much damage counted as acceptable—just that Kamran needed to be brought back alive. Maybe knocking him out *had* been too much. Maybe Deon had taken too long. Maybe Shikki had expected no resistance at all.

With Shikki, the rules shifted without warning. And for the briefest moment, he wondered—again—why he still worked for such a violent man. But the thought proved unreachable. He couldn't remember ever *not* serving him. He couldn't remember a time he hadn't lived in the shadowed halls of this palace.

"Follow me," Shikki said. The coolness in his tone offered no comfort, but Deon didn't dare disobey.

"Yes, Master."

He followed Shikki until they entered the grand, shadow-cloaked room where High Priest Alican sat slumped upon the throne, hidden beneath a dark hooded cloak. Deon paused at the center, lowering the mercenary to the icy floor as Shikki approached the throne and settled the canister in Alican's lap.

A hiss escaped as Shikki released the seal. Deon bowed low, eyes locked to the floor, shoulders tense while Alican inhaled the mist.

The mercenary groaned and lifted a hand to rub the side of his neck.

"Ah. He awakens," Shikki said.

The man's body stiffened in sudden awareness, and his eyes snapped open. In one swift motion, he pushed to his feet—but Deon caught his forearm and pivoted behind him, locking an arm beneath the man's chin. The pressure forced a surprised cry from his throat.

"Easy," Shikki warned. "He's our guest, not our enemy."

Deon held firm, the mercenary's breath passing harshly through gritted teeth. No trust passed between them—only tension and stillness. Then the man gave a small, tight nod. Deon loosened his grip with reluctance and stepped back, still on guard.

Shikki moved forward, stopping a few paces away, studying him. "I've heard a great deal about you and your feats."

"You flatter me," Kamran rasped, clearing his throat as he rubbed at his neck. His focus remained on Shikki, but a passing glare flicked toward Deon.

"No flattery. Just fact. That's why we need your help."

"I do not work with kidnappers."

Shikki clicked his tongue. "That's unfortunate."

From the throne, Alican rose with effort as Amy stepped in to retrieve the empty canister. He slid the hooded cloak from his shoulders and let it drop onto the seat behind him, revealing skin worn and weathered. He accepted his cane from Amy and descended the platform, each step deliberate.

"Mister Kamran Rajamir, I presume?"

Kamran stayed silent, tension still coiled through his stance. Beside him, Shikki gave a single, deliberate nod to Deon. He understood the command without question.

Alican paused a safe distance from Kamran and leaned forward, supported by his cane. "I want to extend my apologies for the conduct of my subordinates," he said slowly. "The aggression you faced didn't reflect my intention, nor the standards I hold myself to. This isn't how I do business, and it certainly isn't how I intended this encounter to begin. But as a leader, I accept responsibility." He kept his clear, earnest gaze locked with Kamran's. "I respect men like you—men who value integrity, restraint, and control. That's why I believe we could have approached this differently, had we both been given the chance." He exhaled softly, a breath that hovered on the edge of a sigh. "I've already instructed Deon to return you safely to your team. You're free to walk away. But I'd ask, before you do— consider whether this has to end in distance. Frankly, I don't think either of us wants this encounter to define us."

As Alican spoke, Deon swept his hair away from his face. He gathered the strands and twisted them into a loose knot at the base of his neck—just enough to uncover the eye he usually kept hidden. Static clung to the ends, and a few stray pieces drifted free, but his view remained unobstructed.

He'd done this once before—to Amy.

He couldn't recall ever learning how to hypnotize anyone. No technique surfaced, no memory he could reach. Every time he delved into the recesses of his mind for an answer, he hit that fog. Then the wall. Maybe he'd gone through this same process himself.

He didn't know—and didn't dare ask. Shikki had no patience for questions.

Kamran narrowed his eyes at Alican, posture rigid and skeptical. "Save your apologies. I have dealt with your kind before—smooth talkers, manipulators. Words do not erase the fact that your people dragged me here against my will. And now you expect me to believe you are offering an olive branch? Why should I trust anything you say?"

Alican maintained his composed demeanor, meeting Kamran's gaze without flinching. Every movement marked him as an expert at this kind of interaction. "I understand your skepticism, Kamran. Your trust is hard-earned, and I respect that. I want to make this right. Your skills are valuable, and I believe we can find common ground—without resorting to force. There is a better way forward for both of us."

"Better for you, maybe," Kamran said, his stance shifting slightly. "You want something from me, and I have already said I am not interested. Your fancy words will not change that."

Alican sighed. "I can't force you to believe me. All I can do is show you through action. You're free to leave with Deon."

Kamran's distrust lingered a moment longer before he turned his head toward Deon. In an instant, his posture eased, and his gaze turned vacant—lost in a trance.

Shikki lifted a hand, and dark mist spilled from his palm. It curled through the air and coiled around Kamran, dissolving into his skin before fading completely.

When Kamran's eyes closed, Deon released the knot in his hair. The curtain returned, veiling his eye once more.

"Kamran," Shikki said, his voice laced with confidence. Kamran's eyes snapped open, glowing red for a single breath before fading back to normal. "We need the elementals and their guardians before it's too late. You're our best tracker. Find them."

Like a puppet under command, Kamran dropped to one knee in a bow. "Yes, Master."

Shikki watched him for a moment, a smug smile tugging at the corner of his mouth. He then handed Deon a folded note.

"These are the general locations High Priest Alican remembers the elementals traveling to. Take Kamran."

Deon accepted the paper with a bow. "Yes, Master."

He turned and started down the hall, Kamran falling into step behind him. They had only just reached the archway when Shikki's voice rang out again.

"Save the fire guardian for last. I have special plans for her."

Deon spun on his heel and gave a swift bow before continuing forward, boots echoing against the stone.

Orders demanded obedience. And with Kamran on their side, the search would be faster. Cleaner. But something gnawed at the edge of his thoughts.

Shikki had made the mind control look effortless, the trance smooth and unbreakable. Deon dove into the fog within his own mind again, searching for any memory from before he'd served under Shikki's rule. He pressed far, determined to find even a glimpse. But, as always, the fog thickened—and the wall stood in his way.

166

Frustration stirred inside him, low and hot. But he couldn't afford to indulge it. Not now. He had a job to do. So he pushed the questions down, buried the itch, and kept walking.

CHAPTER 19
Ferenc

Ferenc hadn't gotten much sleep. He'd stayed half-awake through the night, eyes flicking toward Moses whenever he stirred. If Moses decided to slip off into the dark alone, he intended to catch him before he got far. Between that and the endless loop of *should-haves* and *could-haves* playing in his head—about Amy, about Kamran—sleep had come in short, fractured pieces.

And what little sleep he managed brought no comfort. The dreams came hard—intense enough to leave him breathless and on edge, but the details vanished the moment he woke, dissolving like smoke in the air.

By morning, he'd shoved aside the doubts, dreams, and distractions and joined Moses and the villagers in combing the area for any sign of Kamran. But they'd found nothing. The usual tracks pressed into the snow—some old, some fresh—but nothing pointed to a struggle or a path diverging from the rest. Just the hush of snow and evergreens, untouched and unchanged.

Ferenc returned to the shack stiff and cold, his cheeks wind-burned and his thoughts restless. Flakes and frost still clung to his winter gear when he stepped inside.

Anya sat cross-legged in the armchair, her eyes closed, deep in meditation. Olivia stood beside her, hand planted on her hip. She glanced over her shoulder when he entered, offering a small nod before turning back to Anya.

"Good morning," he offered, his voice low, not to disturb them. Then, to Dormouse, softer: "Hey. Did you grab some breakfast?"

She nodded. "It was good."

Olivia nudged her chin toward the wood stove. A dented silver thermos sat waiting.

"I brought you back some coffee," she said.

"Please tell me it's not that instant stuff from earlier." He shrugged off his winter gear with a wince.

"Okay, I won't tell you."

He groaned, and Olivia snickered. Then her focus shifted back to Anya, whose breathing remained steady.

Ferenc turned to the stove and unscrewed the thermos lid. Steam rose, carrying that same bitter, earthy scent that had failed to impress him earlier. He lifted it toward his face, careful not to burn himself, and his nose wrinkled. The smell alone triggered a vivid reminder of the thin, disappointing taste. For once, he actually wished he had sugar or milk to add.

He brought the rim to his lips, bracing for the first sip, when a single gunshot cracked through the morning air.

He froze, listening. Maybe the villagers had fired at a wild animal.

When three more shots followed in quick succession, his stomach dropped. He slammed the thermos back onto the stove, metal clattering, then yanked open the door and rushed outside.

The cold hit him hard, slicing across his exposed skin. He sprinted forward a few steps, scanning the field.

A supply sled lay tipped in the snow, gear spilled across the ground. Two reindeer still tangled in their harness bucked and kicked, the sled lurching against a buried stump with a splintering crack. The search party had formed a tight circle facing outward, all braced with weapons ready, but hesitation flickered through the circle. No one attacked the gangly creature that leaped toward them—limbs twisted, claws sharp.

A lunanite. He hadn't seen one since he'd defeated Richard.

Moses fired again, the shots cracking through the cold air. The lunanite jerked as the bullet struck, but it shook off the blow, driving forward with claws outstretched.

Two more beasts took shape from the snow on either side, dark mist coiling into twisted flesh. Moses pivoted, tracking the sudden new threats.

Ferenc spun halfway back toward the shack. "Stay here!" he ordered, locking eyes with Olivia. "Protect them."

He turned and surged forward, a twister gathering at his feet. With a sweep of his arm, he pushed the wind into a low, punishing blast. The gust battered the nearest lunanites, forcing them back just long enough for Moses and the villagers to react.

Shots cracked through the cold air. A spear sailed across the churned snow. The search party had found their courage. The first lunanite stumbled under the assault—hit once, twice—before collapsing and disintegrating like ash in the wind.

The second twisted low, claws carving through the snow as the blast of wind caught it broadside. A villager lunged with a spear, driving it deep into the creature's ribs. The lunanite hissed once, then dissolved like the first one.

Only one remained. As it staggered upright, its injury knitting itself back together, the snow around the circle rippled, and four more lunanites erupted from the ground, terrors of gnarled skin and snarling teeth spun from smoke. The search party tightened their circle, weapons raised. Moses fired again, sharp and fast, but the creatures kept coming.

"What the fuck are these things?" Moses barked between shots, backing closer to the others.

"Those would be the lunanites we told you about back in the cave," Ferenc said, still tracking the field.

Two of the lunanites peeled from the group and lunged straight for him. He thrust out a hand, shaping the wind into razor-sharp blades. The currents spun into slicing arcs, hissing through the air.

He moved to strike—but his fingers moved too slowly, numb from the cold. The first lunanite veered, almost slipping past his guard. Ferenc gritted his teeth and adjusted, driving the blades harder. They slashed through both creatures mid-lunge, tearing them apart in twin bursts like ash and smoke.

Moses pulled the trigger on the lunanite rushing toward him, but his weapon clicked dry. He gritted his teeth with a furious roar and ripped a dagger from a sheath on his thigh, ready to meet the charge head-on.

Ferenc lunged forward, thrusting his arm in a sharp arc. The wind curled tightly around his wrist, forming into a coiled whip. He snapped his hand outward. The strike cracked against the frozen air, slamming into the gangly creature's torso, tearing through flesh in one brutal sweep. Pain flared along his knuckles, the freezing air biting harder where the motion pulled skin tight over bone—but he didn't slow.

The lunanite let out a broken hiss before collapsing, its form vanishing into the air.

Ferenc lowered his arms, wind settling at his feet. A quick scan of the field confirmed the last lunanite lay crumbling into ash, and the search party stood braced, weapons raised, shoulders tight with readiness.

Across the churned snow, Moses caught his gaze. He gave a single nod of thanks—then flicked a glance past Ferenc's shoulder toward the shack.

"Hey, thanks for the help!" he called out, sarcasm dripping from every word.

"You had it handled just fine!" Olivia shot back, voice cutting across the cold.

Ferenc turned, finding Olivia standing firm in the doorframe, fists balled tight at her sides.

Dormouse and Anya hovered behind her, still tucked safely inside.

A glint at the edge of his vision caught Ferenc's attention. He turned toward it, heart still pounding, just in time to catch a figure in a familiar silver filigree mask slipping out of sight behind a nearby shack.

His hands clenched into fists, and he charged toward them—but when he rounded the corner, the figure had vanished, leaving only a set of fresh tracks pressed into the windblown snow, leading nowhere.

Moses jogged up behind him, boots crunching hard in the frost. "Our blond friend?" he asked, breath misting the air.

"No," Ferenc said, scanning the nearby structures. The figure he'd glimpsed stood much smaller than the man who'd taken Amy. "It's weird," he added, voice low. "Hiding isn't their style."

"They toying with us?" Moses asked, narrowing his eyes.

"Who knows." His gaze landed on the search party who'd gathered cautiously nearby. He couldn't tell whether they hesitated because of the lunanites . . . or because of him. He jerked his chin toward them. "I think your contact's waiting."

Moses stalked off without a word.

Ferenc returned to the sleep shack, the cutting cold gnawing along his exposed skin now more than ever.

"Everything okay?" Olivia asked, brow arched. She moved aside as he reached the door, allowing him to step through.

He glanced back toward Moses and the villagers before shutting the door against the cold and parking himself in front of the wood stove. "No," he said flatly. The hesitation written across the search party's faces flickered through his mind, but he filed that away for later.

Ferenc shook out his stiff hands, then rubbed them together briskly, willing heat into his frozen skin. He stirred the air molecules faster alongside the warmth from the stove.

Anya's voice broke his thoughts. "Olivia said those were the lunanites you spoke about."

The words hung in the air, and Ferenc could only manage a slow nod.

"We haven't seen those since . . ." Olivia trailed off, and Ferenc finished the sentence.

"Since the moon." The words scraped in his throat. "Since we fought Richard."

"Does that mean he's definitely still alive?" Dormouse whispered, barely louder than the flickering fire.

The question snagged in the back of his mind, refusing to let go. His mind flashed back to the blond man at his house, the silver mask identical to the ones Richard's old law firm used. His thoughts shifted to Amy and her shifting moods—the way hatred kept rising and falling inside her like a tide, long after Richard should've lost his grip.

Amy had fought it, but Ferenc had always found it curious she still struggled months later. Now, after seeing the lunanites again, the pieces slid into place with a grim kind of logic. Maybe Richard's hold had never broken at all—only weakened.

"Ferenc?" Dormouse's voice tugged him back.

He turned to find all three girls watching him—concern painted on their faces, questions hanging in the tight space between them.

His gaze landed on Olivia. She'd remained behind on the moon after their battle, searching for the fire elemental, and she'd been the last to speak to Amy face-to-face.

"Did you bring Amy back to Earth after our battle with Richard?" he asked.

Olivia shook her head, brow furrowing. "No, why? What's on your mind?"

"What if Amy knew Richard wasn't dead?" After all, she'd refused his offer to accompany her home after the battle.

Olivia pressed her lips together for a beat. "It doesn't matter. We can't ask her now."

The door creaked open, dragging a blast of cold air into the room. Moses sauntered in, face blank, not even sparing them a glance. He parked himself near the stove beside Ferenc, rubbing his hands together against the heat.

"Is that coffee?" Moses asked, nudging his chin toward the thermos. Of all the things he could've opened with—like the lunanites or the villagers' involvement—small talk hadn't been on Ferenc's list of guesses.

"Instant," Ferenc replied.

Moses shrugged. "I've had worse." He took a sip, grimaced, swallowed with effort—then immediately went back for another mouthful, as if sheer stubbornness could fix the taste.

Ferenc silently suspected he preferred cream and sugar.

175

He waited a moment longer, hoping for Moses to explain whatever the villagers had told him, but Moses stayed silent. If it had been Kamran, Moses wouldn't have needed an invitation, so he cut straight to the point.

"What did the villagers say?"

Moses set the thermos down and finally turned toward them. "Well, they're spooked. Moon monsters don't exactly show up every day, and neither do people throwing wind around like it's a weapon. Hard to blame them."

Ferenc barely nodded.

"They asked if you're dangerous," he added. "Told 'em to figure it out for themselves. You helped save their asses. They know what they saw."

"Gee, thanks," Ferenc muttered. A little backup wouldn't have killed the guy.

Moses shifted. "So, those ugly things were lunanites, huh?"

Ferenc nodded. "We thought they vanished when I beat Richard, but . . ."

"First his masked henchmen, now his lunanites," Olivia mused. "This can't be a coincidence."

Ferenc's attention landed on Dormouse. The blond man had come after her in Florida, taken Amy hostage instead, cornered Kamran, and likely captured him too. The pattern pointed back to her—Richard wanted her again, and he wouldn't stop until he had her in his grasp. He'd stolen her elemental energy once before. He might be planning to take more.

"We need to leave," Ferenc said.

Olivia blinked. "Like, right now?"

"They know we're here, and we know he's coming back for Alexis next. The longer we stay, the bigger the target on our backs—and the more danger we put the villagers in."

Anya's brow ticked up at the name, confusion flickering across her face, but her question remained unspoken.

"Yeah, have fun with that," Moses said, turning back to the thermos.

Anya looked at him. "Wait, you're not coming?"

"Not without Kamran."

"There's no way he's out there," Ferenc said. "Richard more than likely has him."

Moses bristled, narrowing his eyes. "You don't know that for a fact. If he comes back—"

"Then he or your contact can call you," Olivia interrupted. "Why are you still stuck on this?"

"Because I trust my instincts more than your airy theories."

Olivia rolled her eyes. "Instincts? You mean the ones that make you sit, stay, and roll over when Kamran's around? You're like a lost puppy right now."

"At least I'm not the third wheel without a clue . . . must be the hair color."

"Okay, knock it off!" Ferenc threw out a hand to stop Olivia from pummeling Moses. Even Anya grabbed her shoulder. "They only sent seven lunanites this time, but next time, we might not be so lucky. People will get hurt. Hell, the whole village might burn in their search for her."

Anya stiffened at the word *burn*. Dormouse shrank back to the bed, avoiding eye contact. She curled in on herself, shoulders small, spine pressed to the wall as far from the conversation as she could get.

Regret tugged at his heart, sharper than he expected. She hadn't asked for any of this—not the attention, not the power, not the target painted on her back. And now they wanted her again.

She deserved peace; she needed space, safety, distance from it all. That much, at least, he could still give her.

He glanced back at Moses and straightened. "You're still under contract until we get back to Iran, but no one's forcing you to come with us. If you want to stay here and wait, that's your call. I promise you, we want Kamran back just as much as you do. And we'll get him back—whether you join us or not. But we sure could use your resources and expertise to make it easier."

Anya stepped in, somehow the calmest presence in the room. "You said he was the leader of your group, yes? Trust that he'll know what to do. He's your leader—and your friend." Anya didn't blink. "Don't let him down."

Moses stared at her, jaw tight, as silence pulsed through the room. After a beat, he sighed, bent down, and started rolling up his sleeping bag.

"What are you doing?" Ferenc asked, though Moses's answer had already unfolded in the quiet way he moved.

"Thought we were leaving."

"So you're coming after all?" Olivia asked with a hint of disappointment in her voice.

"Haven't seen a dime from the job yet," he muttered. "Guess you're stuck with me a little longer, doll."

His reply came in typical Moses fashion. Still, Ferenc had no doubt Anya had struck a nerve.

Olivia huffed and whirled through her packing with jerky efficiency while Dormouse crouched to fish her bag out from beneath the bed. Anya moved in serene contrast, quietly gathering what little she'd brought with her.

He wished Olivia and Moses would quit fighting and take advantage of their similarities instead. She and Moses clashed constantly, but at their core, they both ran hot. Quick tempers, sharp tongues, no brakes. And like Moses's dogged devotion to Kamran, Olivia's loyalty always came through when it counted.

Ferenc stepped closer to Olivia. "Hey," he said, keeping his voice low, private despite the cramped quarters. "Don't let him get under your skin. You're not a third wheel. Honestly, you're not just along for the ride—you're the one driving most of the time."

Olivia turned, a smile tugging at her lips—playful, but not quite soft. "Does that mean I get VIP treatment now?"

He smirked. "Sure. But VIP treatment includes being the first to dodge flying objects when things go south."

Olivia chuckled and turned back to her gear. "I should've negotiated terms."

Her humor returned, and with it, some of the weight lifted from his chest.

But it didn't last.

Reality pressed back in like quicksand, dread swallowing him up. Things had started shifting in ways they couldn't plan for. And Ferenc hated it.

CHAPTER 20
Ferenc

Ferenc steered the rented SUV along the highway as distant city lights flickered on the horizon—a beacon of civilization breaking through the desolate, wind-carved plains. At least they'd made it out of the mountains and onto paved roads again. No more white-knuckling it across a frozen river. No more direct exposure to the elements.

Every so often, a freight truck or snow-dusted sedan passed in the opposite direction, headlights sweeping across the windshield. Inside the SUV, things stayed just as quiet. What little conversation surfaced as day shifted to night came from Olivia and Anya, continuing their training in short bursts between meditative stretches.

He yawned as fatigue settled over him like a blanket. A rest stop loomed ahead, and the thought of acquiring coffee to chase the heaviness from his body tempted him. But the city sat just ahead, with the promise of a real bed and a real shower.

From the back seat, Anya gasped. Her eyes flew open from her meditative state, and she shot forward, gripping the seat in front of her. "Pull over!"

Ferenc's heart skipped a beat; instinct slammed his foot down on the brake, harder than he intended. Gravel and slush crunched under the tires as the SUV slowed to a stop.

Moses jolted awake beside her. "What the—?"

Anya had already unbuckled. She pressed her hand urgently against Olivia's arm, her voice thin but forceful. "Open the door."

Olivia didn't hesitate. The handle clicked. Anya shoved the door wide and darted out, boots vanishing into knee-deep snow. In the rearview mirror, Ferenc caught Olivia's blink and brief pause before she unbuckled and stepped out after her.

He turned to Dormouse in the passenger seat. Her hands gripped the seatbelt, knuckles pale, breath shallow. "Stay here," he said, voice low. She nodded quickly, unmoving.

The cold knifed through the space between coat and collar the second he stepped out of the vehicle, stinging his skin and shocking the last of the weariness out of his bones. He zipped up fast and trudged through the drift.

"She feels something," Olivia said, almost breathless with anticipation.

Anya didn't turn. Her arm stretched forward, index finger steady. "That way."

"What's 'that way?'" Olivia asked.

Ferenc pulled out his phone, the screen flickering to life with a GPS signal. Finally. The mountains had choked reception for days.

He studied the map. "Finland," he started. "Could be Sweden. Maybe Norway or Greenland. Take your pick."

Olivia peered at the screen, then turned back to Anya. "Can you be more specific?"

Anya's arm dropped. She spun to face them, posture rigid, exasperated.

"Right. Sorry," Olivia said, backing off with a sigh. "We'll work on fine-tuning it as we go . . . 'that way.'" Her hand gestured vaguely toward the horizon, then fell limp. She turned and walked back to the SUV without looking at anyone.

Ferenc recognized the signs. He'd seen this boil-over before—most notably on the beach months ago, in the quiet, frustrated tilt of her shoulders when a plan slipped out of reach. Olivia didn't panic when things got hard; she bristled when control fell through her hands.

Anya's eyes fluttered closed, chin dipping. "I'm sorry."

Ferenc suppressed a groan. So much for a shower and a real bed. He ran a hand through his hair, the weight of the moment pressing down harder than the miles behind them.

She hadn't needed to come. Hadn't needed to stay. And she sure as hell hadn't needed to help. Yet she'd still tried and caught on to her training a hell of a lot faster than he ever had. Now, she probably regretted it.

"Don't apologize," he said gently, offering her an empathetic smile. "You're doing great."

She didn't answer. She just stepped past him in silence and headed back toward the vehicle, defeated.

His head throbbed, sharp and low behind the eyes. He fished a cigarette from his coat pocket, then the lighter. Something to dull the noise, just for a second.

After a few fast puffs at the hood of the SUV, Ferenc exhaled a final stream of smoke. The cold bit into his lungs on the inhale, but the burn helped chase off the creeping fatigue. He flicked the cigarette and slid back into the driver's seat—then froze. Dormouse sat stiffly beside him, wide-eyed, staring straight ahead. His stomach clenched.

"What's wrong?" he asked.

Moses answered instead by cocking his handgun.

Ferenc's pulse jumped, and the knot in his stomach twisted tighter. He went to confront Moses, but something glinted out of the corner of his eye. His attention snapped to the windshield.

A masked figure stood in the headlights. Probably the same one from the village. But one detail stopped him cold: familiar brown curls spilling from the hood's fur trim.

Ferenc's skin tingled uncomfortably, like his body couldn't decide how to feel. "Stay here," he said—then, catching Moses's gaze in the mirror, he added, "*Everyone.*"

"Not happening," Moses replied, raising his gun. "So far, these masked freaks have come with ambushes, abductions, and nightmare fuel. So I'll pass on sticking to the sidelines, thanks."

"It's Amy."

Ferenc stepped back out, boots crunching through snow.

The door had barely closed when the window whirred down, Moses calling after him: "Wait—Amy, like your ex?"

He marched forward and stopped at a safe distance. Who knew what Richard had done to her, what hold he still had. Amy stood still, her freckled face hidden behind the silver filigree mask. Hundreds of questions clawed their way up his throat, but only one word made it out.

"Why?"

She didn't hesitate. "I told you I'd never forgive you."

The words hit like a slap. She'd said those very words on the moon when he'd tried to help her home—and she'd meant it then. He'd hoped she'd come to her senses.

When Olivia returned later, she'd said Amy hated him *a little less*. And Ferenc had believed it.

Richard's influence had never been a spell. He hadn't enchanted her or twisted her mind. He'd just let the moon do what it did best: pull. In Richard's presence, her emotions—her anger—surged and intensified like the tide.

When she'd returned to Earth, Richard's hold had loosened. Sure, she still had bad days—snippy words, colder silences—but she hadn't looked at him like she wanted him dead. Not like she did at high tide. He thought she'd finally broken free.

"So Richard's alive," he said flatly.

"Yes. Barely. No thanks to you."

Her tone sliced into him, the venom stinging. After everything—being turned into a lunanite, used to guard Richard while he drained Dormouse, being kidnapped by the same masked organization—she still blamed him.

"This isn't you talking."

185

"Of course it is. Who else would it be?"

"He's controlling you again. He's—"

She stepped forward. "I'm not doing anything against my will. Never have been."

Richard had always claimed as much. And with his title as lunar high priest, it made sense—just being near gave him the power to warp her emotions.

"How can you still be with him after everything he's done?"

Her hands balled into fists. "Don't you dare judge him, Ferenc Janos! *You're* the one who nearly killed *him*."

"He was hurting Alexis." Ferenc saw a flash of Dormouse in his mind—wisps of cloud and sparks in the dome, writhing and screaming as bright fronds stole her energy. And then Amy: the way she lurched away from him, just before her bones snapped and twisted into a lunanite's frame. "Christ, he turned you into a monster, Amy! Why can't you see I'm not the bad guy here?"

"I'm done talking."

Amy opened her hands, and black swirls coiled in the snow at her sides. Ferenc stepped back defensively, the cold biting into his ankles. He recognized that magic: lunanites.

Two of them formed, gnarled and gangly, their red eyes glowing in the dark as they bared jagged fangs from their maws.

"I don't want to hurt you," Ferenc said, hands raised, "but I'll do what I have to if you come for those I care about."

She tossed her head back, amusement breaking free—big, warm, and achingly familiar. He'd seen that tilt and heard that burst of laughter a hundred times when they'd dated. They hit like a blow to the chest. His heart clenched, memories stirring with a bitterness he didn't have time for. Nothing about this counted as a laughing matter—he meant every word.

"You're so clueless," she said, amusement draining from her voice.

Behind him, car doors opened and shut. He should've known they wouldn't stay put. Snow crunched under boots, but he didn't dare turn away from Amy.

"You good?" Olivia stopped at his right, hands charged with energy, eyes locked on the threat.

Moses took position on his left, gun trained on Amy. "I suggest you take your pets and crawl back to wherever you came from."

"Don't hurt her," Ferenc said, more plea than command.

"I'll do what I damn well need to," Moses shot back.

Amy's bitterness twisted her smirk into a scowl. "It's too late to pretend like you care." She raised her hand, palm out. "Get 'em, boys!"

The lunanites lunged. And a low rumble rose in the distance.

Ferenc shot out his arm, wind lashing forward in a slicing gale. The first beast took the hit square in the chest and went flying, limbs flailing before it disintegrated. But the second moved faster.

It sidestepped Moses's first shot, then leaped straight toward the SUV. Olivia reacted instantly—one hand braced, the other driving a wall of compressed air along the vehicle's side, protecting Dormouse inside. The creature slammed into the barrier with a hiss, claws skittering across the surface.

"Someone's coming!" Olivia shouted, eyes snapping toward the road.

A pair of headlights cut through the darkness ahead, and the deep rumble of an engine grew closer.

Moses cursed and fired again—twice—one bullet piercing the lunanite's shoulder, the other missing as it stumbled and rolled. It then sprang for him, limbs stretching unnaturally wide.

Ferenc didn't hesitate. He dropped low, shoved both hands toward the ground, and flung a surge of wind beneath the creature. The blast flipped it midair, its gangly limbs flailing just long enough for Moses to step forward and fire point-blank. The lunanite shrieked, body shuddering, then disintegrating.

The semitruck bore down on them, horn blaring in one long, urgent blast. Ferenc swept his arm wide, dispersing the last ash-like flakes of dark magic into the wind, clearing the highway by the time the truck roared past. The driver shouted something in Russian, none the wiser.

When the wind settled and the headlights faded, Amy had vanished.

Ferenc scanned the area. Only a shallow impression marked where she'd stood. No movement. Just cold wind and silence.

Moses holstered his weapon. "Why even bother attacking? She's toying with us."

Ferenc's mind raced, retracing every moment. She hadn't stayed to fight—she didn't need to. She wanted them on edge. Distracted. Unsteady.

"What is it?" Olivia asked.

He didn't answer right away. Through the windows, the SUV's interior lit up as Moses opened the door and slipped inside—just enough for Ferenc to catch a glimpse of Dormouse, hunched low in her seat, watching. Then the door shut, and darkness swallowed her again.

Ferenc stared at her outline a beat longer before finally facing Olivia.

"I just—I can't figure out what she's up to," he said. "And I really hate how they keep finding us."

"Was she behind the village attack?"

He nodded. The hair. He saw it again tonight—the same curls as before. He dug into his coat pocket and pulled out his phone, holding it for a second before powering it down. Even without a signal in the mountains, it might've pinged something, somewhere. He refused to take any more risks.

"Let's move," he said, already striding toward the SUV. "The faster we reach whatever Anya's sensing, the better."

Determination lit the coals in his core, stoking his purpose as Dormouse's guardian. He wouldn't let them hurt her or have her. He'd protect her to his last breath—no matter what game Richard set in motion.

CHAPTER 21
Olivia

Olivia didn't know how the others tolerated him—especially Kamran—but Moses dragged at her patience like nails on a chalkboard.

Sure, he'd worked his mercenary magic and secured forged documents that sped them through border crossings, but his smug, aloof attitude left much to be desired. Any sentence from anyone seemed like an open invitation for him to chime in with sarcasm, arrogance, or negativity. And every time, it scraped against her raw nerves.

The monotonous hum of the engine filled the SUV as Ferenc spoke with the border agent. Fatigue wrapped around Olivia like a weighted fog, pulling at her focus while she listened carefully to the exchange just in case the agent requested anything from her. They'd stopped for food, fuel, and rest more times than she could count, but the long drive had still taken its toll.

The border agent directed most of his questions toward Moses and Anya after speaking with Ferenc. Moses answered with respectful professionalism—a complete one-eighty from the insufferable routine he defaulted to—and somehow, it aggravated her even more.

Her stomach writhed with more than just nerves. Sure, the anxiety from the forged documents passing inspection sat high on the list, but so did the weight of uncertainty pressing from within the vehicle. Anya's emerging ability had become their one lead, and Olivia couldn't afford for it to be a false one. They'd followed her northwest for days, but the strain of holding that connection quickly drained her. Olivia just wanted answers. And she desperately hoped Anya's trail didn't lead to another dead end.

She'd trained Anya to follow the pull, but she couldn't feel it herself. And that accentuated the internal churning. Back on the moon, Eeolas had explained that she'd only found the air elemental and her guardian because she belonged to the realm too. And as far as Olivia knew, as the Gatekeeper, Anya held no attachment to any specific realm. Part of Olivia's inner turmoil stemmed from the hope that Anya truly felt the pull rather than pretending to please her. Ferenc eased them away from the customs booth. They'd successfully made it through the border without anyone questioning the documents. Olivia exhaled, tension slipping from her shoulders—until a voice shattered the peace.

"Doubt my liaison's abilities, doll?"

The thing that irritated her most about Moses had to be his condescending pet names. Every "doll," "cupcake," and "sweetheart" made her want to knock out his teeth with the nearest steel-toed boot.

"I really find your name-calling offensive," she said through clenched teeth.

"Don't worry," Anya piped in. "I'm keeping track of all the times *cupcake* over here does it. He has it coming." She patted Moses on the head. He swatted her hand away with a glare.

Olivia smirked despite herself. Anya had been the first target of Moses's names, and the fact she hated it too only made the satisfaction burn hotter. But when Moses turned around, her satisfaction instantly vanished, replaced by a different kind of fire behind her eyes.

"Lighten up, would ya?" he said, irritation edging into his voice.

She hadn't come along to entertain him or make the ride more pleasant. "What we're doing is bigger than your Rolodex. It's even bigger than finding Kamran."

"My *Rolodex* got us across the border without a hitch," he said. "I'd think you'd be a little more grateful. And for the record, Kamran matters more to me than any of this nonsense."

She rolled her eyes. "Yeah, yeah. You're loyal. I heard the story."

"You wouldn't understand loyalty if it slapped you in the face."

Olivia huffed, her patience thinning. "Loyalty doesn't excuse your disrespectful behavior. I'm tired of your chauvinistic garbage. Cut it out."

He laughed—a derisive sound that made Olivia bristle. "Sweetheart, respect goes both ways. You act like you're above it all, but you're just as lost in all this as the rest of us. Maybe a little humility would do you some good."

Ferenc sighed loudly from the driver's seat. *"Children,* don't make me pull over."

Olivia's pulse thudded in her ears, irritation prickling at the edge of her composure. Ferenc could pull over if he wanted—she couldn't let this go unanswered.

"I'm not above it all," she said tightly. "Can we go back to the part where I said this whole thing is bigger than anything—*including* me?"

"Yeah, well, some of us have more pressing priorities."

Her voice hitched. "Kamran isn't our only priority!"

Moses's eyes narrowed, his tone clipped. "I'm dealing with the *reality* of Kamran being in danger. Your mystical detour won't change that."

"You've got a pretty narrow one-track mind, you know that?" she shot back.

"So do you. Let's not pretend your noble quest is the only thing that matters."

She threw her hands up in exasperation, breath catching on the way out. "It's *not* the only thing that matters! Why can't you get that through your thick skull!"

"Enough!"

Ferenc's voice sliced through the argument as he hit the brakes and pulled the SUV off the road. The sudden stop jolted everyone in their seats. Even Dormouse ducked lower in the front passenger seat, her eyes wide.

Olivia found Ferenc's stern gaze in the rearview mirror, and for a second, her thoughts scattered like leaves. When he'd intervened in their arguments before, he'd never been that assertive. She didn't know if she liked it.

"You're *both* in the wrong."

Her heart skipped a beat. For a second, she swore she'd misheard him. He stood as her friend—usually in her corner. But not this time. And it stung.

"You've been on his case since Siberia, Liv. All you've done is criticize him. His childhood friend's been taken. Are you saying you wouldn't act the same way if it was Alexis or me? I think you're being a little harsh, and it's not fair to him."

His words landed hard, grinding against the simmer of her frustration. She didn't like hearing it, but she couldn't retort. Instead, she dropped her gaze to her lap and stayed quiet. No denying it— she'd do the same in a heartbeat if their positions reversed.

Ferenc then shifted his attention to Moses. "And Moses. I don't have the same ability to stop you in your tracks as Kamran does, but the name-calling really needs to stop. You think it's harmless, but you're clearly pushing her buttons, and it's not helping. I know Kamran's your priority—believe me, I'd be the same way in your shoes—but you need to see that our situation isn't all that different. We need to find these new elementals and guardians. Preferably before Richard's goons do, or all this gets a lot worse. This 'mystical detour,' as you call it, might be what leads us to Kamran. So show some patience. And a little trust."

She lifted her eyes and found Ferenc's gaze waiting in the mirror—still hardened, still annoyed. Olivia held it, throat tight. Then his attention shifted to Moses, whose clenched jaw and fixed stare out the window said everything.

"This pissing contest needs to end *now*," he continued. "You're both loyal—to the people you care about and to your missions—but this constant bickering? It's not helping. It won't help us get Amy or Kamran back, nor will it help protect Alexis. It's going to get someone hurt or worse. So let's be a team, not a battleground." His voice softened, but the edge remained. "Olivia, give Moses the understanding you expect from him. Moses, recognize that Olivia's quest might be the very thing that saves Kamran. We're up against a dark force, and Richard sure as hell won't care about personal grudges. He'll take advantage of them."

Olivia drew in a long breath and let it out slow, her shoulders easing slightly as she gave a small nod in acknowledgment. Moses turned to her again, and she braced herself, jaw tight, for whatever nonsense might slip past his teeth—because clearly, he'd chosen to ignore Ferenc's warning.

"I'm not sorry about my priorities," he began.

A growl nearly broke loose. Typical.

"But I *am* sorry about the names," he finished, glancing toward Anya. "Truly."

Anya blinked, caught off guard, then narrowed her eyes with a skeptical frown. The tension inside the SUV lingered until she finally gave a small nod. When Moses turned to Olivia, waiting, she crossed her arms.

"I'll forgive, but I won't forget."

195

"Don't worry," Anya said, stretching as far as the cramped space allowed. She discreetly flashed four fingers at Olivia—proof she still kept count. "He has it coming."

A reluctant smirk tugged at Olivia's lips, and Moses grumbled under his breath. The situation left much to be desired, but Ferenc had been right to call them out.

She glanced at the rearview mirror and found him still watching her. The temper in his gaze had faded, replaced by something gentler. When she gave him a silent nod, his attention returned to the road, and the SUV rolled forward once more.

Olivia leaned her head back and closed her eyes, exhaling her tension away. She didn't have to like Moses. She didn't have to agree with him. But they had a lot in common, including a shared purpose: they both wanted to protect the people they cared about. And when it came time to confront Richard's looming threats, none of them could afford to be anything less than their best.

That fight would demand everything.

CHAPTER 22
Ferenc

Despite the seasonal darkness, the drive through snow-covered Finland and Norway offered a panorama of pristine forests, rolling hills, icy lakes, and jagged mountain peaks. But none of it compared to the green ribbons dancing in the sky.

Ferenc had seen the northern lights a few times before in his travels. They still managed to awe him, every time. And at that moment, they served as a welcome distraction from the thoughts clawing at the edge of his mind—Amy, her mask, her monsters. The beauty of the Scandinavian night sky stretched above them, vast and dreamlike, clashing hard against the cramped press of the SUV around him.

The seat pressed against his back, more obstacle than support, and the ceiling seemed to lower with every mile. He'd spent years in jet cockpits—tight spaces didn't bother him—but he itched for open air, for freedom under a wide sky. Or maybe his lack of nicotine had more to do with it than the SUV itself.

He stole a glance at Dormouse. Childlike wonder lit her face, her eyes wide with awe as she watched the ethereal dance in the sky. The heaviness of his previous thoughts and discomfort vanished, and a soft smile broke through.

Just weeks ago, she hadn't even left Florida. Now she'd crossed Russia, passed through Finland, and the road ahead carried them through Norway. He couldn't imagine what all of this looked like through her eyes.

Ferenc returned his focus to the road and slid a hand over, resting it atop the one in her lap. He hadn't had a real chance to tell her how he felt—Olivia had crashed his one opportunity, and every other moment since hadn't felt right. When Dormouse shifted her hand and laced her fingers through his, warmth flooded through him. His heart raced, and so did his thoughts, but he forced both to settle. Another chance would come. This quiet, tentative connection would have to hold him over for now.

A fireball exploded in the distance just as they passed through a village, a sharp blaze tearing across the night. Ferenc narrowed his eyes just as Olivia echoed his thoughts.

"What was that?"

He shook his head. "Not sure—"

"*Ferenc!*"

Dormouse's screech shot through him like a live wire, and the guardian inside roared to life. His instincts kicked hard, every nerve on alert. For one harrowing beat, he feared she'd been hurt—but then a molten boulder the size of a van crashed into the road ahead.

He slammed on the brakes. The SUV fishtailed on the slick road, frozen snow scattering in a wild arc. The memory of his jet spiraling after Olivia dropped onto the nose flashed hard and fast. Jaw clenched, his grip tightened around the wheel, and he maneuvered past the obstacle, letting the car slide into the snow-packed shoulder. The tires groaned, the vehicle shuddered, and then everything stopped.

A flurry of sharp words flew from the backseat—none of them in English. At least one of them probably cursed, judging by the tone.

Ferenc's heart jackhammered against his ribcage. He turned immediately, eyes locking on Dormouse. "Are you okay?"

She nodded, though her eyes stayed wide. She twisted around to look at the steaming chunk of rock behind them.

"What the hell was that?!" Moses barked, squinting out the window. "Where the hell did it come from? A volcano?"

Ferenc didn't have an answer. He'd done zero research on Norway's geology, and right now, it didn't matter. Olivia's voice cut through the shock.

"Anya? What's wrong?"

In the back seat, Anya squirmed in place, one hand clutching her chest as she gasped for breath. "I feel something!" Her voice shook, laced with panic. "It hurts!" Her trembling hand shot out, pointing somewhere into the dark.

"You might be having a heart attack." Moses grabbed her shoulders. "Somebody call—"

"No!" Anya snarled and grabbed Moses's face with both hands, shoving his shaggy head toward the window. "I feel something that way!" She stabbed her finger toward the shadows again.

Ferenc followed her line of sight. They'd already spent days blindly heading '*that way*,' but now—looming in the flames and smoke—an enormous silhouette stepped into view.

The creature's hulking size threw the scale of everything else into question; even the flames behind it flickered like candlelight beside its massive frame.

"You don't think . . ." Moses trailed off.

Ferenc leaned forward, gaze fixed. "That's the Keeper?" he finished for him. "I don't know. What else could it be?"

Moses didn't miss a beat. "'We could really use your resources and expertise,' they said. Funny—I don't remember *encounters with skyscraper-sized monsters* being in the contract!"

Charging straight toward something that size wouldn't have been Ferenc's first choice either. But choices had started running thin, and time even thinner.

"All right," Olivia chimed in, determined. "Our goal is information, not to harm it."

"And to protect Alexis," Ferenc added, catching Dormouse's gaze as she fidgeted with the edge of her coat sleeve. He shifted his focus to Olivia in the mirror as he cracked open the door. "Help me get the car out of the snow."

The winter air hit him full-force, sharp as glass, as he stepped onto the road. Olivia joined him, the snow crunching beneath their boots, the only sound along the quiet road just beyond the sleeping village. With practiced ease, they aimed concentrated bursts beneath the car frame, wind slamming into the snowbank until packed ice cracked loose and sprayed out the other side.

Even Moses got out to help, tossing down the floor mats to create traction. He didn't say a word to Olivia, and she didn't acknowledge him either—but at least they worked as a team instead of tearing into each other. They freed the SUV in no time.

Cautious driving carried them toward the city's edge, where Ferenc slowed to a stop. The flames at the construction site had died down, leaving a scorched skeleton behind—and the creature had vanished with them.

In the back seat, Anya hunched forward, one hand continuing to rub her chest. "It's still nearby," she grit out.

"Good," Olivia said. Then, more gently, "I mean—hey, you're doing great." She reached forward, resting a glowing palm between Anya's shoulder blades. "Here. This might ease the discomfort a little."

Moses's focus remained on the burned-out site. "Where is everyone?"

"It's past working hours," Olivia snapped. "For anyone who doesn't earn a living by lugging a gun and a bad attitude around, it's—"

Ferenc's gaze snapped to the rearview mirror, and she shut her mouth.

"I know that," Moses growled back.

Olivia cleared her throat. "Sorry."

"I meant because of the fire," Moses added. "Where are the emergency crews? Where are the onlookers? The press? That blast was massive. This place should be crawling."

Ferenc scanned the site again. Burned tarps flapped weakly in the cold wind. Scorched beams stood like ribs in the dark. But not a single siren wailed in the distance. Ferenc didn't like it one bit.

Dormouse pointed toward the windshield. "There."

She spoke softly, barely above a murmur, but Ferenc caught her motion. Just beyond a stationary crane, something shifted—only a flicker, but enough.

"Looks like someone *is* there," he mused.

Dormouse drew back into her seat, tugging her coat tighter around her. "So what do we do?"

"You stay here with Olivia and Anya," Ferenc said. "Moses and I will go check it out."

Moses sighed, unbuckling. "So, this is *our* circus, then."

Ferenc opened the door with a nod. "I guess so. And somewhere out there is our monkey." He scanned the site again, noting the angles and cover points—every tarp, beam, and rusted machine. He then turned to Dormouse one last time, voice quiet but firm.

"I'll keep you safe. You know that, right?"

"I know."

The words came soft, nearly lost under the hush of the wind, warming him. She still trusted him. Even after everything, she still believed he could keep her safe as her guardian.

He just hoped he could make good on his promise this time. He'd sworn to protect her before, then turned around and stormed off to face Richard alone. He'd left her in Olivia's capable hands, but Olivia had been outnumbered and almost killed—all because he hadn't stayed. That responsibility should've never been hers. It had always been *his*.

He'd never let go of that guilt. Not after Richard had hurt her or the way he'd forced her elemental transformation. Ferenc had tried so hard to give her something close to a normal life, even when Olivia called him out for sheltering her too much. Maybe she'd been right. But he'd done it anyway.

He nodded once and stepped out. "Come on," he said to Moses.

They didn't have much time. He didn't want to cross paths with the blond man again.

Or Amy.

CHAPTER 23
Ferenc

Ferenc made his way toward the thinning smoke, eyes and cheeks stinging with cold as he treaded carefully through the crusted terrain. Half-built structures loomed like silent sentinels above the churned drifts, their skeletal frames casting long shadows. Dozens of footprints pressed into the snow, none revealing how recently they'd been made.

Only the crunch of their boots broke the silence. The Keeper of the Realms remained elusive.

Moses's footsteps shifted behind him, veering off toward something in the dark. Ferenc glanced over his shoulder, tracking the sound, then slowed to a stop. An idea popped into his head.

He shut his eyes and tuned in to the subtle currents in the air— the ones that brushed over his skin and whispered between the beams. With a soft exhale, he cast arcs of wind forward like sonar. Like ripples on a pond, each gust skimmed across steel, coiled wires, tarps, and open scaffolding.

His mind mapped out the landscape before him, discerning the shapes and shadows hidden from view. Through his echolocation, a shift occurred in the pattern—a tremor in the airflow.

Ferenc turned toward the subtle movement betraying positions in the darkness, and his eyes snapped open. He moved again, steady and sure. "Hello?"

Each time he changed direction, he sent out another burst of wind to fill in the unseen in his mind. At last, a flicker of orange danced ahead. As he neared the source, muffled words cut off.

"Hello?" he tried again. "We mean no harm."

Three figures stood around a flaming metal drum. One, with short, spiky red hair, pivoted with a sneer. The other two straightened in place.

Ferenc raised his hands, palms open, signaling peace. "Do you speak English?"

Moses, not far behind, echoed the question in his own language. Ferenc only caught one word—*"Farsi"*—just enough to guess he'd asked the same thing.

The redhead responded fast and cold with words Ferenc didn't recognize. He glanced at Moses for confirmation.

Moses gave a shrug. He clearly hadn't caught it either.

The tall woman in layers of flannel and fleece squared her shoulders and cracked her knuckles. The wiry man beside her tugged his fur-trimmed hood tighter, but his stance said he'd drop someone in a heartbeat if needed.

Ferenc kept still, watching the group. Their posture, the cold glint in the redhead's eyes—it all pointed to trouble. He steadied himself, forcing his distrust to quiet.

"We're just passing through," Moses said, firm and unapologetic.

Ferenc kept his tone measured. "We're looking for someone. *Something.* Then we'll be on our way."

"*Ja?*" The redhead stepped forward. "And who or *what* would that be?"

Ferenc's mind raced. Telling the truth would confuse them, but lying would provoke suspicion. He took a deep intake of breath before finally answering. "A creature. A *large* creature. It appeared after the explosion."

"You won't find it here," the redhead said flatly.

Moses stepped forward. "Is that so?"

Ferenc held out a hand, stopping him with the same quiet authority Kamran might've used.

"It is," the redhead answered, taking a few more menacing steps. The others fell in behind him. "So I suggest you leave."

"Ferenc!"

His stomach dropped at the sound of Olivia's voice cutting through the cold. More footsteps followed, crunching over the snow. But he didn't turn.

The tall woman and the wiry man shifted, watching the newcomers approach. The redhead didn't move. His eyes stayed locked on Ferenc.

"I thought I told you to stay in the—"

"It's here," Anya blurted, cutting Ferenc off. "It's one of them."

Moses took a step forward, eyes on the tall woman now snarling like something feral. "So, which one of you's the Keeper?"

The redhead narrowed his eyes. "I said you won't find anything here. You need to leave."

"Please!" Olivia interjected. "We need the Keeper of the Realms. Someone's trying to—"

"I said *leave!*"

The woman cracked her knuckles. The wiry man snatched a crooked pipe from beside the flaming drum. Ferenc swallowed hard and took a step back. Then the redhead slipped a hand into his coat and drew a small blade.

A gunshot echoed into the night. The switchblade flew into the air, and the bullet ricocheted into the tall woman's shoulder before Ferenc's body even finished tensing up.

She howled in pain. The others glared at Moses, who stood with his weapon drawn and absolutely no apology in his stance. He'd fired so fast—faster than instinct, like he'd moved before the threat had even fully formed. No hesitation. No wasted motion. Just an eerie, unnatural precision that made Ferenc's stomach tighten.

The redhead snarled and threw his arms up. The ground trembled. Large spikes of stone burst skyward from beneath their feet, threatening to impale them.

Olivia dodged and swept her arm across her body, slicing the air with sharp currents like a Frisbee. Ferenc rushed to Dormouse, who'd dropped to her knees and curled her arms over her head. He waved his arm, throwing up a wind shield to protect her and Anya from any more of Moses's deflected bullets.

"Don't hurt them!" he shouted as he sent short, controlled bursts toward the redhead's group—just enough to slow, not injure. "We need their help!"

Nearby, Moses fired again, each shot designed to disarm, not kill. At least, Ferenc hoped so.

"They attacked first!" Olivia countered through gritted teeth as she pulled back.

Before he could reply, the ground split beneath him. He plunged down, the air ripped from his lungs as the earth opened like a mouth. Dormouse's scream echoed through the chaos as she reached down for him with her fingers stretched wide, but she missed.

He didn't panic. Falling never scared him. But instead of sky, collapsed dirt and stone boxed him in, pressing close.

Then the walls shifted. He caught the movement in the packed earth, ready to crush him. Ferenc flicked both wrists, wind coiling at his back like a spring. He fired upward in a tight spiral just as the pit clamped shut.

Rocks and snow blasted outward as he broke the surface, and Dormouse screamed. His boots slammed down as he landed, knees buckling from the impact. He stumbled, coughing, vision blurred by dust as he searched for Dormouse. He flung out a gust, clearing the debris. Relief washed over him as he caught sight of Dormouse and Anya huddled behind the barrier of wind he'd previously cast, shaken but safe.

He turned back to the one with earth abilities. "Stop! We just want to talk!"

"And I warned you to leave!" the redhead snapped.

The man slammed his foot into the ground. A shockwave of energy rippled outward, cracking the frozen soil. Ferenc braced, knees bent and stance wide as the packed snow shuddered beneath him; he raised his arms to shield his face as the blast buffeted him head-on. His boots scraped backward through the snow, heels digging in, but he held the line.

Another barrage came—shards of stone ripped from the earth, hurled like knives with deadly precision. Ferenc swung his arms, conjuring gusts to deflect most of the projectiles. The rest sliced around him, one nicking his coat.

Enough.

This fight had to end. Ferenc and his crew hadn't come as enemies. He didn't want to hurt anyone—but he needed to shut it down.

The redhead gathered more power. Another stomp. Ferenc braced himself again and looked up at the sky. The man hurled more debris, and Ferenc waved his arm, protecting himself behind a shield as a flash cracked through the clouds.

Lightning speared the night when the redhead raised his foot for the third time.

The bolt struck Ferenc with a flash so bright it lit the skeletal buildings like day.

The thunderclap that followed split the air wide open. The force hurled the redhead—and everyone else—to the ground. Ferenc staggered, knees nearly giving, ears ringing. His heart raced faster than he could ever remember. Static snapped along his arms and neck, leaving trails of heat across his skin.

He started to turn, ready to check on Dormouse—but froze. A new figure stepped into view.

The resemblance to the redhead hit him first—the same sharp jaw, same angular structure—but the similarities ended there. This one had dark-red hair spilling past his shoulders, nothing like the other man's short, spiky cut, the color of a lit match. His skin, paler and almost translucent in the glow, differed to the other's ruddy pink. And where the first one slouched, this one stood straight and still—like stone.

"Leave," the newcomer said. The word barely cut through the high-pitched whine still ringing in Ferenc's ears.

Olivia scrambled upright before anyone else, already taking charge. "We're looking for the Keeper of the Realms," she said firmly. "They're the only way to wake the others."

Moses grasped Anya's forearm and helped her up, steadying her against his side with a hand at her waist. "Trust us. We're not the bad guys here."

Anya clutched at her chest, her breath ragged, her face screwed in pain. "I feel—"

"I will say it one more time," the newcomer interrupted. His voice cut like ice. "Leave. Now."

Moses didn't move, one arm still braced around Anya. "Or what?" The words came edged with irritation.

The redhead, back on his feet and still glaring at Ferenc, extended a fist to the side, and the newcomer met it with his own. The satisfied smirk that followed sent shivers down Ferenc's spine.

The newcomer's skin darkened, his milky complexion shifting to a dense, stony gray. His frame expanded—broader, taller—until he loomed several stories high. Stone ground against stone as he moved, shoulders cracking into place, legs flexing under his new weight.

Crystal spikes jutted from the redhead's joints—shoulders, elbows, knees—and his pinkish flesh turned clear and glittering like quartz.

Ferenc took a few steps back. Beside him, Olivia gawked. "Whoa, there are *two* Keepers?!"

"You're making a mistake!" he called out to them. "We're not your enemy. The universe is in danger!"

The rock golem growled low in reply, like a landslide in slow motion. The crystal figure clicked its needle-sharp fingers together. The ground quivered beneath their feet.

"Right." Moses yanked a second gun from his holster. "Guardian, protect the elemental." The command rolled out, steady and controlled. "You take rocks-for-brains," he added, nodding at Olivia. "I'll take the pixie."

Before anyone moved, the crystal golem blurred forward and slammed into Moses, sending him flying.

Movement blocked the firelight—massive and slow, shifting across the site like a wall of stone.

"Move!" Ferenc swept his arm out, summoning a swirling vortex that coiled around Anya and Dormouse. The wind gripped them hard, yanking them off their feet and hurling them backward—just beyond the reach of the descending stone fist. It slammed down where they'd stood moments earlier. Much slower than the crystal golem, it still shattered the asphalt and sent chunks flying.

Ferenc rushed over to Dormouse and dropped down beside her. She clung to him, eyes wide, but nodded wordlessly. No injuries.

"What do we do?" Anya asked, her voice tight but clearer than before.

Ferenc turned his attention to her, eyes scanning her face. She'd stopped clutching her chest, breath still shallow but no longer panicked. The worst of it had passed. "Can you move?"

She nodded, even as her knees wobbled beneath her as she slowly stood up.

He got to his feet, Dormouse pulled close, and reached out, steadying her with his other arm.

"Hold on to me—both of you."

Wind curled beneath his feet, building fast. With one deep breath, he launched into motion. Snow kicked up around their legs as he guided them away from the worst of the fight, eyes locked on the nearest cover.

The wind settled as Ferenc guided them down behind a shipping container. He released Anya first, steadying her with a hand at her elbow.

"You good?"

She nodded, still catching her breath, but her legs held under her own weight.

"Stay out of harm's way," he instructed, eyes already darting back to the chaos. "Keep her safe." Dormouse clung to him for a second longer before easing her grip. Ferenc's jaw tightened. "They're going to need my help," he added, nodding toward Olivia and Moses. "So I'll stay and fight."

He turned his attention to Dormouse, his hand steady at her waist. He let his touch linger some before gently shifting, lifting his hand to cup her cheek. Dormouse met his gaze and gave a small nod, steady despite the fear in her eyes. She'd be okay.

He turned away at last, wind already stirring at his feet. A twister trailed him as he shot toward the fight.

Olivia dove aside as the golem's fist slammed down again. "I can't find a weakness!" she shouted.

Ferenc ducked beneath another heavy swing and lashed out with sharp gusts. The blasts barely scratched the surface of the towering stone monster. Olivia had been right—air clashed hard against stone, offering no clear advantage.

Fighting earth creatures made the battle with Richard look easy.

"While you two are dancing," Moses grunted, flat on his back with the crystal golem straddling his chest, "mind helping me out?" Its bladed arms pressed closer, crossed at his neck like a pair of shears. His muscles strained just to keep them apart. One slip, and he'd lose his head.

Olivia loosed a volley of air blades. "I thought you had it covered?" she snapped.

213

The gusts shredded into harmless streams, barely grazing the crystal surface. But the attack distracted the creature long enough to break the creature's focus. It lifted an arm reflexively, as if brushing away a swarm of gnats. That brief shift gave Moses his opening.

Moses's hand found the butt of his pistol. He jammed the weapon upward into the golem's side and fired. The crystal beast reeled, and Moses scrambled free, breathing hard.

The rock golem clasped its massive hands, stone grinding against stone as it shaped a boulder between them—one nearly as wide as its torso. It then drove both fists into the ground with earth-splitting force.

The shockwave thundered out in every direction. Ferenc dropped to one knee, bracing as the tremor tore through the ground. Olivia and Moses collapsed as well, caught in the quake.

Olivia screamed something, but he couldn't make out the words through the cacophony as the skeletal frame from the nearest building collapsed straight down on top of him.

CHAPTER 24
Ferenc

It happened fast—too fast for Ferenc to react.

The screech of tearing metal filled the air, deafening and immediate. A beam crashed down from above, slamming into his side as it toppled. The impact knocked the wind from his lungs and drove him to the ground. Pain flared across his ribs, raw and stabbing, as he landed face down. All around him, metal rained down in a shrieking storm. Steel clanged against steel and dust choked the air, clouding his vision and disorienting him in the chaos.

The beams pinned him in place. He couldn't move. Each breath came shallow and quick, the dust clawing at his lungs like fire. A bitter, metallic tang spread across his tongue: blood. Somewhere, something bled. Whether the source came from inside his body or out, he couldn't tell.

Flashes struck like static—Olivia. Moses. Anya. Dormouse. Each one spun his mind faster. Adrenaline shot through his system as he focused on Dormouse. He had to move, had to get out—had to find her and make sure nothing happened to her . . .

But first, he needed to stop the bleeding.

Ferenc forced an inhale through clenched teeth and blew a shuddered breath into the dirt and snow. The healing wind threaded through the grounded particles, stirring the energy at his skin where they touched, knitting tissue back together and numbing the ache in his ribs, settling the worst of it. His next inhale came deeper—not fixed, but functional.

"Olivia!" he called out. "Alexis!"

He held his breath, straining to hear past the pulse thrashing in his ears. But only a low whine answered him—a rising rumble, steady and wrong. Like a jet engine winding up. Or a train rushing past. Neither of which had been nearby.

His gut instincts screamed.

Ferenc clenched his jaw and forced a blast sideways through the twisted metal pinning him. Steel shrieked and shifted, but instead of scattering, the beams lifted—all of them. They spiraled upward, dragged into a cyclone he hadn't summoned.

It must've come from Olivia.

He stretched for a buried pipe within reach and clamped his fingers around the cold metal. Wind screamed past as the cyclone above spun tighter, pulling air and steel with it. Then the twister hurled its payload.

The bent framework that had pinned him moments ago shot outward like shrapnel toward the rock golem.

The stone creature twisted. One massive arm lifted, swinging slow and wide to swat them aside. A few deflected, spinning off into the dark like jagged missiles. But most slammed into him with a chorus of metallic thuds. Ferenc shielded his head with his free arm, pulse hammering. In the chaos, he couldn't tell where the stray beams had landed. He only hoped none curved back toward Dormouse and Anya.

Above, the cyclone cracked open. Limbs unfurled in an instant, vapor coiling into shape: a figure swift and glowing, form fog-colored and fluid, barely tethered to the ground. A sylph—Dormouse's elemental form.

Before the golem could fully right itself, she lunged.

"Alexis, no!"

Dormouse's sylph form—wild, towering, and dangerous—ripped through the chaos with terrifying speed. The form she feared. The one Richard had forced on her. Now she stood alone against the golem, and he hadn't been there to stop her from shifting. To protect her.

"Ferenc!"

Olivia appeared beside him, bruised and dirt-smudged, a twister dissipating around her feet. She summoned a dome around them, muting Dormouse's storm long enough for him to breathe.

"Can you get up?" She extended a hand.

Ferenc clasped it with a nod and a wince. "Where's—"

"Anya and Moses are fine—you're bleeding!" She dropped to her knees beside him, peeled back his coat, and tugged up the hem of his shirt. Her breath hitched. "Hold still." Then she leaned in and blew a stream of wind directly over the torn skin.

Ferenc didn't move, jaw tight. His own healing had patched what it could—enough to function, but not enough to ignore. The sharp throb beneath her breath reminded him just how close he'd come to being crushed. But he had no time to dwell.

He scanned the site, eyes catching on Dormouse's whirlwind form. Each strike from her wind drove the rock golem farther back across the clearing.

"Where's the crystal one?" he asked.

Olivia took a breath. "I don't know, but he's in rough shape. Dormouse did her shriek thing, and it messed him up pretty good."

A thunderous explosion went off nearby. Both of them flinched. Olivia straightened.

"We have to get her to stop," he said, voice tight.

"How?"

"I can get through to her."

Olivia shook her head. "Not if you can't get near her without getting sucked in."

Dormouse had spun into a tornado again. With a single heave, she hurled the rock golem through the air—farther than Ferenc had ever seen anything thrown. It crashed into the frigid sea with a thunderous splash. She shifted back to her sylph form midair and drifted toward the water like mist in the wind.

Ferenc inhaled and exhaled, slow and full. "I can get through to her," he repeated. He had to.

Olivia dropped the protective dome. "Be careful."

He turned, readying a gust beneath his feet, only to jerk to a halt when a figure stumbled into view. Dark splotches bled through his coat at the arms, irregular and spreading. But his face fared worse—

skin split at the cheekbone, and a deep crack sliced through his eyebrow and temple like a fracture in glass. The crystal golem.

"Stop her!" the man rasped. "He'll drown!"

Ferenc threw out an arm, shielding Olivia, but the man didn't attack. Instead, he extended a shaking, bloodied hand and summoned the earth beneath him, gliding atop a jagged swell of rock in the stone golem's direction.

Ferenc bolted. Wind curled at his ankles as he shot upward to meet Dormouse eye to eye.

"Stop!" he called out. She swatted at him, quick and forceful like swatting at a fly. He barely dodged the gust that clipped past his shoulder. "Alexis!" he tried again, more urgent. "It's me!"

Their gazes locked. Her form stilled.

She shrank back down to normal size, drifting gently until she hovered in full sylph form. A wraith made of clouds and shaped like a human, every motion left a trail of vapor, like breath fogging cold air. He followed, landing beside her.

"Hey . . ." he gently started, unsure if a touch would ground her or pass straight through.

Boots thundered behind him. He turned fast, stance already wide, protective instinct flaring—then softened at the sight of Moses and Anya.

"Stay with her," he said, gesturing to Dormouse. "I need to help Olivia." He launched forward, a twister churning at his feet.

Wind howled in his ears as he neared the shore. Olivia, in soaked winter gear, steered herself across the surf with a focused blast of air, the human form of the stone elemental clutched in her arms. She burst from the frigid water and hauled him across the snow-packed ground as he hacked up seawater, his long dark-red hair plastered to his face and neck. Behind her, the crystal man scrambled on hands and knees.

"Get away from him!" he snapped, shoving her.

Ferenc arrived and caught Olivia before she hit the ground. "Please, let us help—"

"You've done enough damage," the man spat. "Leave us!"

"I can warm him up," Olivia said, shivering. Her teeth clattered, but she pulled away from Ferenc and reached for the stone man again.

"I said leave!"

A snarl cut through the air; Moses, storming in from behind. "She saved him!"

Ferenc's body tensed. He jumped to intercept, gripping Moses's shoulders to hold him firm. "Let it go," he said, voice low, scanning for Dormouse. She and Anya hadn't followed.

But Moses shoved forward. "Your friend dropped a building on us, and she *still* saved his drowning ass! You already owe us your attention—so let her fucking help!"

"Let it *go*." Ferenc's grip tightened.

"No," the crystal shifter said, his voice frayed with fatigue as he trembled violently. "Not with her." His bloodied hand waved in Dormouse's general direction. "Not ever."

"You attacked first," Moses spat.

The crystal shifter growled. "You wouldn't leave. We were defending ourselves."

Steam hissed around Olivia's body, engulfing her in a cloud of heat before vanishing into the cold night air, leaving her dry. "At least tell me why," she demanded.

The stone shifter—now slumped and shivering—ran his fingers through the tangled, icy strands of hair plastered across his face. "With power like this," he rasped, "people either worship or fear you. And people always want what they fear destroyed."

"We don't need your help," the crystal one said with a wince, arms cinched tight around his ribs. "We've survived just fine without it. Fear keeps people back. That's the only kind of safety we trust."

The other's mouth twisted, bitter. "You saw it: no police. No neighbors. Not even a scream. People around here know what lives on this stretch of coast—and they stay away. But then you showed up. And that *storm* you brought? She was ready to kill."

"If we wanted you dead, we would have let her finish the job, because she was doing a damn *good* job at it," Moses snarled.

"We're on your side," Olivia insisted.

The stone shifter threw her a look—harsh and unflinching. "Your friend's actions say otherwise."

Ferenc's stomach tightened. They had it all wrong—about Dormouse, about everything. He released Moses's shoulders and spun, a twister already spiraling beneath his feet as he launched back the way he came.

Dormouse stood in the same spot he left her in. Dark blue eyes stared out across nothing in particular, unblinking and distant, her sylph form drifting faintly in the air.

221

"She hasn't moved or spoken," Anya said softly as Ferenc came to a halt at a careful distance.

He nodded once, swallowing the knot rising in his throat. The way she stared ahead, hollow and unmoving, something deeper must be churning inside. Shock. Guilt. Fear. Shame.

He slowly approached, his boots crunching softly against the packed snow. She didn't flinch or turn; she just kept staring at nothing.

He stopped in front of her. "Hey," he said, voice low. "Everything's okay."

It hadn't been—not even close—but nothing else came to him. He just wanted to pull her close and apologize for failing her.

He reached out and carefully slid his hand into hers. Her fingers closed around his, cold but real—not the mist they appeared to be. Her gaze dropped to their hands. A small victory.

"Everything's okay," he repeated, quieter this time. He lifted his free hand and gently cupped her cheek, thumb brushing the cool edge of her jaw. Her eyes, uncertain but present, finally found his.

He pressed a kiss to her temple—soft, reverent.

"Alexis," he whispered. He swallowed down the thickness in his throat. It burned. "I'm sorry." He'd let her down too many times before. But this time, it had broken something in her. "I'm so, *so* sorry."

Dormouse's skin warmed under his lips, and she exhaled a long, trembling breath. When he pulled back, she'd shifted back into the form he knew and loved. Her face crumpled, and tears slid freely down her cheeks. He brushed one away with his thumb, still cradling her face.

Her hand slipped free of his, and she gripped his coat instead—right where blood had soaked through. "I just panicked," she squeaked. "When the building came down . . . I thought I lost you."

His throat bobbed, and he pulled her into his arms. She collapsed into him, sobbing.

"I'm right here," he murmured. "It'll take more than that to keep me from coming back to you."

But as he held her, something twisted deep in his chest. She'd struck out because she'd thought he'd died. In that moment, she'd reached for the power she'd spent the last few months trying to avoid. Not because she wanted it—but because she'd been desperate. And now she'd have to live with what it had made her do.

"You did some pretty amazing things back there," he added, quieter now. "Are you okay?"

Her sobs slowed to hiccups. She eventually nodded, but the tension in her shoulders didn't ease. He kept her close.

Movement out of the corner of his eye caught his attention. Olivia and Moses approached without a word. The shifters hadn't followed.

Olivia reached out, gently rubbing Dormouse's back. "Let's find a hotel for the night," she said. "We'll talk about our next plan."

"How badly did I hurt them?" Dormouse asked, voice still thick with tears.

Olivia hesitated. Her eyes flicked to Ferenc, silently asking him to offer something—anything—to make this easier.

But he had nothing.

"They . . ." Olivia exhaled, her voice quieter now. "They'll live. But they weren't who we came for."

Dormouse's breath hitched. "I'm sorry," she choked out, her sobs muffled in Ferenc's coat. "It's all my fault."

"No, wait—" Olivia rubbed her back more firmly now. "You didn't—"

"None of this is your fault," Ferenc said, tightening his hold, voice firm despite the chaos pressing down on them. "They warned us. We didn't back off. That choice was ours, not yours."

"I hurt them. I almost killed them. I—"

"Frankly, they had it coming," Moses drawled, arms crossing tight over his coat. Anya jabbed an elbow into his ribs, and he raised his hands as if conveying his innocence. "What? It's true."

"You did what you had to," Olivia said, her tone softer now. She leveled a glare at Moses, then turned her attention back to Dormouse. "None of us blame you. We'd have done the same."

A distant wail broke through the darkness. Ferenc tensed. The rising pitch of sirens grew sharper by the second.

"Guess they *really* want us gone. Time to move," Olivia muttered, scanning the horizon, eyes narrowed against the night.

She turned and pulled away, Anya close behind. Ferenc scooped Dormouse into his arms but paused when he caught Moses staring not at the road, but up into the sky. Ferenc followed his gaze. The moon glowed steady above the shimmer of northern lights—nothing more.

"What is it?"

Moses lingered, eyes narrowed on the sky a moment longer, then shook his head and followed after the others. Ferenc trailed behind, his stomach churning at the entire situation.

They reached the vehicle as the sirens grew louder with each passing moment. Olivia opened the back door while Ferenc helped Dormouse inside. Moses climbed into the front without a word.

Ferenc then slipped into the driver's seat, engine roaring to life. He eased onto the road, careful not to draw attention, though his focus stayed locked on the wreckage shrinking in the rearview mirror. Behind them, silence reclaimed the shore.

They hadn't found the Keeper. Just two angry shifters and some hostile followers. The earth responded to those shifters with raw force—enough to suggest they might be earth elementals. But two? That didn't add up.

Still, Anya had felt something. As the Gatekeeper, her connection should've ran deeper than the rest of them combined. She'd led them there for a reason. Once they returned to the hotel, he'd bring it up. They needed answers, not just guesses, and as soon as possible—before the trail to Kamran vanished for good.

His gaze shifted to the back seat. Dormouse stayed curled in her seat, shoulders hunched, as Olivia and Anya comforted her. She didn't meet his eyes. Maybe she couldn't. And after everything, maybe she *shouldn't*. He'd failed her again.

His cigarette craving kicked in. He latched onto it, letting it smother the guilt clawing at his ribs.

The night dragged on with no end in sight.

225

CHAPTER 25
Shikki

Of all the powers in the universe, Shikki didn't understand how such a tiny, neutral territory held so much influence—how the marble planet became *the* place for exile out of all the realms.

Perched on the crumbling temple steps, dust flaking beneath him, he gazed out at Gaea in silence. His master hadn't been one of those exiled, but he'd gone willingly, blending in among the Gaians for years while nursing his revenge like an ember in the dark.

It must've been so *boring*.

His own revenge wouldn't drag out like that. He didn't need to walk Gaea's surface to make the air elemental's guardian pay for nearly killing the only person who'd ever truly seen him. From the moment Alican had staggered toward him through the dim hall, half-burned and barely breathing, reeking of scorched flesh, charred hair, rubbery clothing, and clotted blood, Shikki had vowed to make the guardian's life a living hell.

But he wouldn't stop there. Being passed over as the fire elemental's guardian still stung. Fixing that would be impossible to ignore. Everyone would remember—and fear—his name.

Faint commotion on the dark surface of the moon swelled, the restless stirrings of something volatile. Shikki's eyes drifted from the marbled planet to the sea of red eyes glowing in the shadows—lunanites, roused and waiting. Here lay the key to his revenge. Adrenaline sparked beneath his skin. Every time he remembered Alican would give the plan his blessing, his pulse kicked harder, faster.

It'd been Shikki's task to drain the obsessive desire for influence, control, and power from the Gaians Alican had recruited and grant them dark lunar abilities in exchange. That craving filled a deep reserve—nearly bottomless—mixing and fusing with the energies of the dark side of the moon . . . until Alican had been defeated. Without volunteers, the supply dwindled, and the well began to run dry.

But Shikki didn't stop. While he nursed his master back to health, he ran experiments on the side. He refused to let Alican's hard work go to waste and rot in the dark. The results of those experiments stirred now, anxious to be used.

"Is the army ready?" Alican's voice drifted from within the temple, weak but steady.

Shikki spun toward the sound, heart skipping a beat in his excitement. "Master! I restored this bench—come, rest here."

He rushed to help, careful with every step as he guided Alican down to sit against the weathered stone wall. The damage to his

227

form since draining the prince had returned, leaving him thinner, slower. Too much so.

"Thank you, Shikki."

An unsettling sensation floated at the bottom of his stomach. He hated asking again, but the words pushed out anyway. "Master, please let me drain the prince for you, I beg you. I fear for your life. You need strength."

Alican gave him a faint smile. "I appreciate your concern. But we wait for the lunanites. Just a little longer."

Shikki's lips pressed into a thin line. Each time the prince lost strength, the moon decayed further—a dulled surface, collapsed temples, dust where marble once gleamed. As much as he hated it, draining Lomos again too soon might push the realm past the brink. As long as Lomos lived, the moon held its shape. They needed him alive—for now. With no heir, the kingdom—barebones as it had become—still retained the power to vote in a successor. And Shikki fully intended that vote to go to Alican.

"Of course," he finally said with a bow. "But perhaps it would be easier to view the strike from the scrying sphere?"

A similar sphere—carved from selenite—kept the high priests connected across temples in other realms. When Shikki and Alican built the underground palace on the dark side of the moon, he'd presented Alican with a labradorite one. A gift for the next era. For Alican's rise. It ran through similar invisible channels and had already served them well—for watching, tracking, learning. And now, it could show them the assault on Gaea in real time.

"Nonsense," Alican rasped after a coughing fit rattled in his chest. "I couldn't sit idly on a throne while my best pupil puts his plan into action."

Shikki had winced at the cough, hollow and strained, but pride surged at Alican's words, instantly scattering the worry. To have Alican there beside him cast the moment in stark importance. "I'm honored by your presence, Master."

He turned back to face the marbled orb with renewed resolve. The guardian would pay. The universe would remember his name. And Alican would become the new lunar prince. Shikki drew a long breath, and the chaos quieted. The lunanites stilled, silence rippling out across the dark terrain. Through his exhale, he roared—

"*Attack!*"

A unified howl rose from the shadows as the lunanites charged. They clambered over each other, forming a living chain toward Gaea. Alican's skeletal hand settled on Shikki's shoulder, grounding and cold. A dark, flickering satisfaction rose in him, his grin stretching wide. Five days until impact. The Gaians wouldn't know what hit them.

Alican stood beside him now, frail but upright, shoulders drawn back with firm resolve. Even in his state, he'd risen for this moment. Shikki moved without hesitation, careful to match his master's pace. "Allow me to escort you back to the throne room," he said softly, almost a vow.

Out of the corner of his eye, he caught Kamran standing tall atop the crumbled temple steps—shoulders squared, posture stiff with formality, like some self-important noble about to announce his lineage. Shikki's jaw clenched. This moment had taken too long to build to tolerate an interruption. Especially not from a recruit barely finished crawling out of the shadows.

He usually lashed out at interruptions. Should have put Kamran in his place. But instead, he turned, steadying Alican's arm as they made their slow climb to the top.

"Master," Kamran called down, voice dipped in humble submission and respect as he bowed low at the waist.

Shikki opened his mouth to shut him down.

"They have found the earth elementals."

Adrenaline ripped through his body. His nostrils flared, breath catching at the edge of a growl. He swallowed down the explosion threatening to escape.

Taking their tracker should've derailed the air guardian's group entirely—or at least thrown them off-course long enough for the rest of his plan to unfold. But now the seams frayed faster than he could pull them tight.

Alican's hand clapped his shoulder when they reached the landing, a gesture meant to be grounding. But Shikki didn't feel reassured. Rage still surged, roiling under the surface. Kamran—the so-called mercenary with special abilities—should deliver results, not bad news. And yet Alican simply continued forward, slow and steady, as if the plan hadn't just tilted sideways.

Alican shifted his weight against the cane, steadying himself before lifting a bony finger toward Kamran. "Chin up, Shikki. He's still bowing. There's a 'but' in there somewhere."

Kamran held the bow. "However," he said, voice calm, "you will be happy to know—we have captured the guardian of water."

"Excellent," Alican called back, his voice never wavering as he moved toward the throne room, each step measured, echoing off broken stone.

If Alican didn't call it a failure, then Shikki wouldn't either. The volcano inside him rumbled low, sliding back into a temporarily dormant state. He drew a slow breath to keep it that way. "Where's the guardian now?"

"General Deon is locking her up as we speak."

His next breath came easier. "Good work, Kamran." He used the name deliberately—just as Alican always had with him. "Now move on to the next target."

"Yes, Master."

Kamran straightened, footsteps soft as he turned down the corridor. Ahead, Alican reached out—slow, unsteady. Kamran eased his pace, offering his forearm without a word. Alican took it, steadying himself as they moved on together.

Shikki turned back to the chain of lunanites outside the temple—limbs locked, bodies stacked, eyes glowing red as they clambered through the void of space toward Gaea. A satisfied grin curled back into place, measured and unshakable. Despite the setbacks, the pieces still aligned. His defining moment lay just ahead.

This marked the perfect opportunity to make things even more chaotic. Shikki slipped a moonstone from his robe pocket, the edges cool in his palm. He angled it slightly—a travel secret stolen from the lunar princess, thanks to a few lunanite spies—and it caught the cold light that scraped over the lunar surface.

The stone glinted, brief and pale, then he vanished.

The moment his boots hit the ground, the weight of Gaea's gravity tugged heavier than he liked. The musty stench hit harder—even muted by the blanket of snow. He gagged and jerked his sleeve up to his nose, already regretting the trip. Alican had spoken about Gaea with clinical interest—facts, patterns, weaknesses—never once mentioning the smell. No one warned him it would reek of dampness and something half-dead beneath it.

The cold followed. It carved straight through his silk robes and sank deep, fast, and merciless, impossible to ignore. His teeth chattered. The moon never cut like this. Wind never whipped across its surface. No damp chill clung to skin. And nothing ever crept beneath the flesh the way Gaea's winter did. No wonder exile here felt like punishment. He'd never felt it firsthand as Alican had kept him close, protected, spared from the same fate as the others.

He grit his teeth and straightened. The underground palace called to him, comfortable and familiar, but he shoved the thought aside. He had work to do.

Shikki forced himself to focus. His body, already numb from the cold, twitched under the effort. Then warmth gathered at his fingertips—first a flicker, then a surge—as dark lunar energy coiled into being. It rose like smoke, curling around him like an aura.

He raised both hands. From his palms, tendrils of shadow spilled upward, thin as thread at first, then thickening into strands that writhed and snaked like smoke. They unfurled through the

232

frozen air, weaving through the sky. The aurora borealis twisted and warped. Green veered into violet, then sank into the night's darkness. Like poisoned ink, the dark lunar energy streaked overhead, tainting the stars, one plume at a time.

When the last trace of power left him, Shikki dropped his arms. Cold clawed deep into his bones, and the drain of magic left his joints hollow and unsteady. With stiff fingers, he reached for the moonstone and fumbled, nearly dropping it. Then he cackled as the stone's magic took hold.

And just like that, he vanished.

CHAPTER 26
Deon

Deon marched the guardian of the water elemental down the dim corridor, her flats silent against the cold stone. She hadn't struggled or fought against them. She hadn't even screamed in fear or pleaded to be let go. Kamran's ability had led them straight to the massage parlor. They caught her mid-shift, dark hands still slick with oil, the air thick with lavender, eucalyptus, and the salt of nearby tide. Maybe her powers hadn't awakened yet, or maybe she simply knew better than to resist. Either way, she hadn't even lifted a finger to stop them.

Still, he hadn't let his guard down. Two lunanites flanked her, silent and hulking, all gangly limbs and curled, bone-spiked backs. Their claws twitched with anticipation, ready for any excuse to strike. She moved with eerie calm, head high, jaw set, but pride wouldn't earn her leniency. At least she kept her mouth shut.

Unlike the lunar prince.

"I demand you release us this instant!" Lomos snapped the moment the thick door groaned open.

Deon didn't answer. He never did. Only Shikki had the power to release the prince, and if he hadn't listened the first time Lomos protested, he wouldn't listen now.

Deon pressed his hand to the lock. Deep inside, the metal tumbled and clicked, rearranged by his will. With a muffled grind, the latch gave way. He pulled the door open. "Get in," he said. The guardian stepped in without hesitation.

As always, his gaze found her first—the small and fragile fire elemental in the corner, curled in on herself with her knees hugged tight. She barely moved, stringy red hair hanging limp over her face. Her tiny shoulders trembled with each silent breath. His stomach twisted.

Lomos sat chained to the floor, shackles tight at his wrists, ankles, and neck, each length of iron bolted to a heavy anchoring ring embedded in the stone. His glare seared straight through Deon. "This isn't who you are," the prince said. "I've seen how you look at my niece—how you care for her."

Deon's gaze flicked back toward the far corner, to the timid fire elemental—Lomos's niece.

The prince hadn't lied. Deon's eyes always found her first when he entered, and they always rested on her longer than normal. Something about her pulled at him. He couldn't place it—just like everything else. Every time he tried to remember more than the orders in his head, he ran into the same brick wall, the same disorienting fog that swallowed the edges of his thoughts.

But her . . .

235

She never flinched. Never cowered. Not even when he brought her to Shikki to drain her essence—when she should have feared him most. Maybe that quiet trust explained the strange pull toward her. He needed to understand. And that need made him gentler than he should've been. More careful than he meant to be.

"Please," Lomos begged, voice quieter now. "If you won't free me, then let her go."

Deon tore his gaze from the girl and swatted his hand. All five of the prince's shackles clanged down, the metal drawn tight to the stone floor as if magnetized. Lomos cried out at the sudden pull, his limbs and throat yanked into an awkward sprawl.

He stepped into the cell and approached the water guardian. Her stance tensed, but she didn't resist. He reached for the shackles.

"You lock up a child?" The guardian's Caribbean accent cut through the clatter—low and furious.

Deon didn't look at her. "Silence," he said, snapping the metal closed around her wrists.

"She is a child." Her voice didn't waver. "And you are a monster."

A tremor built beneath his boots. The walls groaned. Chains rattled. He finally looked up. The guardian's glare met his, steady and unshaken.

From the corner, a small sob slipped out.

Deon shut his eyes, and the tremor faded. He hadn't meant to scare the phoenix. No monster lurked beneath his skin. Only duty and orders given by a man he couldn't recall ever choosing to serve.

Chains ground together. His head snapped up.

The guardian pulled hard against her restraints, arms stretched as far as they would go, wrists twisting in the iron cuffs. She desperately reached for the girl huddled in the corner. But no matter how she shifted or leaned, the chains kept her just out of arm's length. She let out a low hiss, jaw clenched.

Deon's fingers twitched. With a sigh, he waved his hand. The anchoring ring scraped across the floor, dragging closer to the fire elemental.

The guardian stumbled in surprise, then dropped to her knees. She pulled the girl into her arms without hesitation, curling around her as sobs shook the child's frame. One hand cradled the back of her head. The other stayed firm around her shoulders, steady and protective.

Something raw clawed behind Deon's ribs as he watched.

He still didn't know why he cared for the child, why the sight of her crying chipped at something buried deep, something tender he hadn't known still lived inside him. Without her, he might not even know what having a heart felt like.

He tried to remember. He pushed through the fog that always met him halfway. And then a flicker—something too fast to catch. A memory, maybe. A feeling. Her voice, her tears . . . something that mattered. Something buried too deep.

His hand gripped a cell bar. His breath stalled in his chest. He clenched his jaw tight enough to ache, and his shoulders locked, motionless.

"Orders, General?"

Kamran's voice cut through the haze. Steady. Calm. Present.

Deon blinked hard. The cell spun slightly before grounding itself again. He looked at the girl one last time, still held tight in the guardian's arms. Then he stepped out, sealed the lock, and turned. He brushed past Kamran without meeting his gaze.

"On to the next target."

CHAPTER 27
Ferenc

Ferenc jolted awake, his chest heaving, heart pounding against his ribcage as he stared at the hotel room ceiling. Dormouse had been an actual mouse in his dream, and she'd been flung from a spinning carousel, squeaking in terror. The panicked, high-pitched cries still rang in his ears, too vivid to have come from the dream. A rustle followed, then a rugged gasp. The sound and movement pulled his attention toward the bed beside his.

"Alexis!"

He flung the covers back and bolted to her side, flicking the bedside lamp on. Soft, dim light filled the room, enough to catch her tangled in the sheets. Dormouse writhed, her back arched, fingers clawing at the fabric. She gasped for air, each breath jagged and uneven.

Olivia sat up beside Dormouse, blinking rapidly and rubbing her face like she'd been startled awake. "What's going on?"

Dormouse's eyes flew open, but she stared through him as if he didn't exist. She gulped for air, her chest heaving in uneven bursts like she'd been drowning. She then curled in on herself without warning, breath hitching once before it broke into hoarse, relentless weeping.

Olivia said something again—maybe a question—but Ferenc didn't register it. His focus locked on Dormouse: her pale face, her body curled in tight, breath stuttering through sobs.

If this had been a seizure, he had no idea what to do. She had the medical background, not him.

"Alexis, look at me."

She didn't. She just curled tighter, her nails still digging into the sheets as she continued to sob. No better words came to him. His mind locked up, frozen stiff—just like the Norwegian ground they'd crossed. The helplessness clawed at him, useless and bitter.

He eased himself onto the edge of the bed. When he reached to rub her back, Dormouse flinched, her body stiffening at his touch. She'd done it before—it felt so long ago now—and it hit harder than it should've, but Ferenc stayed there, steady.

He lowered his voice. "You're safe. It's just me."

"It's just us," corrected another whisper.

His tunnel vision cracked open, and the hotel room filled in again—dim walls, tousled sheets, Olivia on the other side of Dormouse. Her hand rested on Dormouse's shoulder as she gave it a light squeeze. When he looked up, her green eyes met his, brimming with that unmistakable mama-bear concern; the fierce, protective, and deeply present kind Olivia never voiced but couldn't mask.

"Me and Olivia," Ferenc agreed softly. "We're right here."

The moment afterward stretched too long. Then her grip on the sheets loosened, and her sobs eased into hiccups. He pulled her into him, one arm wrapping across her back, the other cradling her head against his chest. She didn't resist. Her breath snagged once, then eased. He held her there, steadying her weight with his body. He didn't know if it helped, but he just knew he couldn't let go.

"What happened?" he whispered.

Her voice broke against his chest. "I couldn't breathe."

Olivia slid closer and closed her hand over Dormouse's. "Was it because of yesterday?"

No answer.

Ferenc's throat tightened. This hadn't happened when Richard forced her to shift. But then again, she hadn't pushed herself then like she had yesterday. Not to that extent.

A sudden knock rattled the door, fast and urgent.

"Hey," came Moses's muffled voice. "Open up. Quick."

Ferenc and Olivia exchanged a shared look of reluctance. Rumpled sweats clung to their bodies, hair disheveled from sleep—not exactly the way people liked to look when they answered the door. But when Moses started to pound the door again, Dormouse flinching with every knock, he gave them no choice. Olivia let out a quiet groan and slid away to answer it.

Moses pushed past her without hesitation, his hands landing on her shoulders as he redirected her out of his way. He beelined straight for the TV.

"Hey!" Olivia snapped, spinning after him; her eyes sparked with warning, and her posture shifted as if ready to hurl some air attacks in his direction. But Anya slipped in behind Moses and caught Olivia's wrist before she could act, shaking her head.

Moses grabbed the remote and pressed a button. The TV screen flared to life.

"What the hell is your prob—" Olivia cut off as her gaze landed on the broadcast, her hand lifting to cover her mouth. "Oh my God . . ."

Ferenc raised a brow and turned to the television. The news-caster spoke rapid-fire Norwegian—none of which he understood—but the video didn't need translating. The footage jittered, likely filmed on a phone, too close and shaky as if the person behind it hadn't stopped moving. The moon hung dim and brown in the sky . . . and near its lower edge, a black mass drooped from it, like a drop of ink stretched thin against the dark blue hue of twilight.

He didn't know how the moon could possibly cry, but ever since Olivia came crashing into his life—and especially after literally standing on the moon's surface—he'd learned not everything could be explained with logic.

"What's going on?" Dormouse asked, her voice soft but focused.

She'd straightened in his lap at some point during the broad-cast. Then she slipped from his arms without a word, crawling across the bed toward the edge. Her knees sank into the mattress, hands braced as she leaned in like the news report might make more sense up close. Though her posture still curled inward, her gaze didn't waver.

"What is that?" she then asked.

"I don't know," Ferenc said. "But I'll bet anything Richard's behind it."

For the longest time, Richard had been a thorn in Ferenc's side. As Amy's boyfriend—or fiancé, as she'd argue—and a lawyer with an annoying knack for sniffing out every legal gray area, Richard never missed an opportunity to bleed Ferenc dry. Of all the people Amy could've chosen to date after him, she had to pick the one who didn't even register as human.

He glanced back at Dormouse, who continued to stare at the TV. She'd been the most affected by Richard—both physically and mentally. Her fingers crept to her mouth again, chewing her nails in distracted silence.

Olivia crossed her arms as she watched, her expression hardening. "My guess is that tear's made of the same stuff as those lunanites. Same texture. Same look."

"And what happens when it gets here?" Moses asked.

Ferenc didn't know, but the knot in his stomach said enough. His gaze returned to the screen, to the black shape suspended in the sky like a threat.

"Nothing good," he finally said.

The moon sat hundreds of thousands of miles away, yet they could still clearly see the tear. Anything visible from that far couldn't be anything small. Their side only counted five: a guardian, a general, an elemental nearly drained by Richard's hands, a mercenary, and a Gatekeeper. Barely a squad against whatever that thing turned out to be.

Olivia let out a breath. "What I want to know is why he's doing this."

"With everything he put me through as Amy's lawyer, revenge wouldn't surprise me," Ferenc replied. "I did beat him pretty badly."

Moses looked over. "So, what's our next move?"

Ferenc inhaled deeply, then let it out slow. They'd come halfway across the world for help, only to be turned away. They could wait, watching the thing drift closer, but waiting could take days—a luxury they didn't have.

He dragged a hand through his disheveled hair. The pressure sat heavy on his shoulders, too heavy to think straight without his morning coffee and smoke. And everyone watched him, expecting a plan.

"I'll be right back," he muttered.

He didn't wait for a word from anyone. Ferenc grabbed his silver case and room key from the nightstand, shrugged on his coat, and slipped into the hall. The door clicked softly behind him.

The hotel's yellow glow battled the washed-out blue that spilled across the sky just before dawn. He leaned against the rough stone wall, hurrying to slide a cigarette free before the cold could stiffen his fingers. The flick of his red lighter cut through the silence, and the first deep drag scorched his throat in the best way—the familiar burn of nicotine grounding him, if only for a moment.

He let the smoke spill from his mouth in a long, slow exhale and watched it curl into the chilled air. His gaze wandered upward, drawn to the sky he loved so much—a place that usually calmed him, even on the worst days. What he wouldn't give to be up there now, far from all of this.

The aurora borealis had vanished with the first signs of dawn, but something else caught his eye in the fading twilight: dark, serpentine trails snaked across the heavens like vapor left in a jet's wake—their blackness stark, even as the night surrendered to morning light.

He squinted. Contrails didn't look like that.

The chill crawling down his spine had nothing to do with the cold. None of this felt natural—same as the brown dimness of the moon, same as that black teardrop.

This reeked of Richard.

He stamped out the cigarette and rushed back inside, practically throwing the door out of his way.

Ferenc never panicked, but his steps quickened down the hallway anyway. The carpet muted his boots, the overhead fluorescents buzzing just loud enough to scrape against his thoughts. He needed more time. More data. More than whatever the hell that sky had just shown him.

He reached the door and swiped his key card. The indicator lit red. He swiped again, slower this time, as if patience might earn him compliance. Another red light blinked back at him, the lock remaining stubborn.

He frowned and glanced up at the plaque to double-check the number. The room matched. His jaw tightened as he lifted the key card to swipe a third time—

But the door opened. Olivia stood on the other side, blinking.

"That was quick," she said. Then, "What's wrong?"

He didn't answer right away. Instead, he slipped past everyone, a hand brushing against Anya's arm as he moved to the window. He tore the curtains open and pointed outside.

"That," he said.

Anya and Moses blinked, neither quite understanding. Anya's brow then furrowed, gaze flicking between Ferenc and the sky. Moses leaned toward the window slightly, suspicion brewing in his eyes.

Olivia stepped closer, eyes narrowed as she followed the direction of his finger. "Okay . . . what am I looking at?"

Anya hovered behind her, squinting. "The clouds?"

"Those are a little dark to be what I think they are," Moses added. "Did you smell anything?"

"I don't think so," Ferenc said. He hadn't even checked—he'd been too locked in on the sky. "I think it's connected to the moon's tear."

"What the hell is Richard doing?" Olivia hissed.

Ferenc didn't respond. Dormouse had distracted him.

She'd risen from the bed without a word and padded across the room, each barefoot step measured and careful. She moved past the others and stopped beside him, closer to the window than anyone else dared stand. Her arms stayed tight at her sides, fists clenched in the folds of her oversized sleeves.

Ferenc studied her. He'd seen her quiet before—shoulders hunched, fingernails chewed to the quick—but something about the way she stood now, so still, so focused, carried a weight he couldn't explain.

Maybe it stemmed from her seizure-like episode from earlier. Maybe exhaustion. Or shock. Still, something about it unsettled him more than he wanted to admit.

"Hey," he said softly, keeping his voice low as he slowly reached for her hand. She'd already been through enough—he didn't want to push. "Everything'll be okay. I'll keep you safe. I promise."

She nodded, but her eyes stayed fixed on the window. He didn't know if she'd even heard him.

Olivia turned away from the scene, her expression hard. "We can't just sit here. We need to figure out how to stop it."

"We don't even know what *it* is," Moses drawled, his attention back on the TV. "I haven't seen any mention of it in the news yet."

Dormouse slowly uncurled her fist in Ferenc's grasp and squeezed his hand. His pulse picked up as concern washed over him.

"Talk to me," he whispered.

Her gaze finally flicked to him, focus sharpening. "I can stop it," she said, her voice barely above a breath. Her words trembled at the edges, but underneath, something steadier began to rise. "With help from those pixie things."

Ferenc stiffened. "No."

Back in Florida, while Olivia had gone head-to-head with one of Richard's masked goons, he'd attempted to summon a creature of his own—a match for their lunanites. What had started as a

247

shapeless blob, formless and slow, had split apart into dozens of wind-like pixie creatures that broke free like a swarm.

He still remembered the sound of Dormouse's scream as they circled her. She'd dropped to her knees, hands clamped over her head, but they hadn't touched her. They'd surrounded her, protected her, turning on the enemy instead.

He hadn't forgotten the way they'd nearly devoured that woman.

"Absolutely not," he added, just for good measure.

Dormouse's eyes held more resolve than he'd seen in her before, but he couldn't ignore the dread roiling inside him. "That cloud stuff is spreading. I can at least clear the sky with them before the tear gets here. I have to try."

"You couldn't breathe just a few minutes ago," he pointed out.

Dormouse didn't answer right away. Her silence drew out, long enough to make something coil tight inside him. He'd gotten used to seeing her nervous, seeing her shy—seeing her so stoic now terrified him in a new way.

When she squeezed his hands again, he knew something bad sat behind her silence. He knew whatever came next, he'd be powerless to stop it.

"I think . . ." Her gaze drifted back to the window, back to the sky and those unnatural streaks. "I think that's the reason I couldn't breathe. It's affecting the air, and I'm—"

She shut her eyes, inhaled slowly, and exhaled slower.

"I'm the air elemental," she finished, looking back at him.

Ferenc's heart skipped a beat. She hadn't trained for this. She hadn't *wanted* this. And now she stood there, willing. Asking for it. Choosing it. She'd barely caught her breath earlier, poisoned by whatever tainted the sky. And now she wanted to leap back into it.

But his fear ran deeper.

The shift in her eyes terrified him. The way she volunteered. No panic, no rage, no Richard forcing her hand. She chose this. She'd never done that before.

Before now, she'd never come close.

She'd resisted the truth of her past life from the start. She avoided training, flinching whenever someone mentioned her true form. He'd thought shielding her from it would help. Maybe it had. Until now.

Now, she stood ready to throw herself into the sky. And he hadn't been prepared for that.

He could protect her on the ground, as a human within his reach. But once she transformed into that elemental again, that creature of clouds and air, she'd slip out of his grasp. She'd become something he didn't know how to shield, to save.

And without that, the title of guardian rang hollow. He swallowed hard. "I can't ask this of you. We'll find another way."

"Ferenc." Dormouse said his name so softly, he almost drowned in the desperation of his protective instincts. "I know you wouldn't ask me to. But you're not asking—I'm choosing. The decision's mine."

She rose to her toes and leaned in, pressing a kiss to his chin— gentle and final. He wanted to return it. Hell, he'd wanted to for so long. But not like this. Not when it carried more farewell than feeling.

Dread pressed down on him. "Wait . . ."

His grip tightened, but her hands had already started to change, her skin dissolving into wisps of cloud.

"Wait!" He frantically tried to hang on to her, but she kept slipping through his fingers. "I can't—I can't protect you when you're up there—"

He couldn't finish. The look in her eyes stopped him cold. She turned translucent right in front of him, and he couldn't fight that kind of resolve.

"Oh," Moses muttered. "We're doing this here and now?"

Ferenc didn't look at him. He couldn't. Chills ran down his spine as he watched Dormouse float before him, no longer flesh and blood but a figure spun from cirrus clouds—already drifting out of reach.

And he couldn't follow. Not even as her guardian.

"Please." His voice cracked.

She shot for the room's entrance faster than he could blink, trailing wisps like vapor as she slipped through the crack beneath the door.

Ferenc lunged forward and flung the door open. The hallway outside stood empty, like she'd never been there at all.

"Ferenc." Moses tilted his head toward the window.

He shut the door behind him, the click too quiet in the silence she'd left behind. He made his way over, squeezing between Olivia and Anya.

Outside, a black-stained sky greeted him. And through the trails moved a single, giant sylph—her body all cirrus and grace—devouring the poison with a dancer's precision and a storm's hunger.

And Ferenc stood there, powerless, as understanding wove through him in slow, careful stitches, binding him to the truth he couldn't bear.

CHAPTER 28
Olivia

O livia found herself running before learning how to crawl.

She had no idea what being a general entailed, but with Ferenc distracted and helping Dormouse, someone needed to take charge—and she sure as hell couldn't let it be Moses.

Behind her, the television droned in Norwegian with the same emergency footage it had played for the past hour. Packed hospitals. Black trails in the sky. The images had already seared into her memory—all the same information she'd already read in English on her phone.

Moses stood just off to the side of the TV, scowling at the screen. "Why bother poisoning us if those moon things are just gonna crash through the sky? Feels like overkill. Literally."

She turned toward him, her jaw aching with grim tension as she scrolled through the article. "Hospitals are already filling up. They think it's some kind of respiratory infection, but . . . this is strategic." She finally looked up. "They're telling people to stay indoors."

He scoffed. "Like that's gonna help." He then leaned against the wall, arms crossed in that careless, maddening way she hated. "I still don't like your plan," he added.

Of course he didn't. Moses didn't like anything. She rolled her eyes. "We have no other option. Someone has to go with Anya."

"You're not thinking this through."

"I'm thinking more than you are," she snapped, before catching herself. She exhaled slowly as Ferenc's words cut through her memory—how she'd been on Moses's case since Siberia, doing nothing but criticizing him. "Sorry. It's just—I need to help Anya with feeling this out."

"You need to help Ferenc," Moses countered, tone low and firm. "I'll go with her."

Olivia narrowed her eyes. "And what makes you think you're the better choice? You can't feel these people. And you don't have elemental abilities. You can't help if things go sideways."

Moses pushed off the wall, shoulders bristling with tension. "That's exactly why I'm the better choice! *You* have powers. *You* can help with whatever the hell he's doing." He stepped closer, jabbing a finger toward the window. Toward Ferenc. "Don't forget I'm damn good at what I do—and I do it *without* abilities. I'm also the one with the connections, so I can get her what she needs. Fast." His voice steadied. "Let me do what I'm good at."

She opened her mouth to argue, but his logic stopped her. She hated that he had a point. As much as she despised admitting it, Moses had already proven himself more resourceful in a pinch. He'd gotten what they needed when it counted.

Out the window, Ferenc continued summoning the pixie-like creatures, each gesture slower than the last, every motion lagging with exhaustion. Only Olivia could replicate his work and offer him a break he hadn't asked for but so clearly needed.

She turned to Anya, who'd yet to say a word—only to find her gaze already on her, gentle but resolute. Anya nodded once. "He needs you." A small, reassuring smile followed. "I'll be okay. I'll keep him in check."

Olivia's shoulders dropped as she drew in a deep breath, her resolve locking into place. Dormouse had bought them a chance of survival, but it wouldn't last. Time continued to sprint forward, however, and if they could get to the other elementals before Richard's people did, that mattered more than comfort. More than safety.

She didn't like splitting up. Not now. Not with poison in the air and that tear from the moon looming overhead. But Ferenc needed her. So Anya had to go without her.

"Okay," she said quietly. "Okay. But be careful."

"You too," Anya replied as Moses grabbed the rental keys, tossing a hand up in a lazy farewell without so much as a glance back.

The moment the door clicked shut behind them, her chest went tight. She didn't have time to grieve the decision, but the guilt still gnawed at her. Anya headed off to follow a feeling she barely understood, and Olivia should've been the one guiding her. But Moses, for once, had it right—Ferenc needed her more.

She grabbed her coat, hat, and mittens from the closet and charged down to the lobby, her thoughts spinning in a storm of worry and determination. The murmurs of concerned onlookers in the lobby barely registered as she pushed through the crowd of hotel guests toward the doors.

Outside, the silence hit first—eerie and heavy, with no birdsong, no wind, and police cars gliding by without sirens, like ghosts on patrol. Her own footsteps crunched against the snow, far louder than they had any right to be in the hush.

She pulled her coat tighter against the cold, but the chill bit through her layers.

Then she saw them, and her breath caught in her throat.

Hundreds of tiny, lifeless bodies dotted the snow—the fallen pixie-like creatures. Their delicate forms, once wispy and bright, lay dull and crumpled.

Olivia's heart ached with every step around the fallen bodies. The sheer number of casualties sent a shiver down her spine. She quickened her pace, then swept herself off the ground with a twist of wind—just enough to clear the ground without disturbing the fallen pixies. She guided the current carefully, setting herself down with precision beside Ferenc, her feet finding clean space between the fallen.

Worn to the bone, hunched, and pale with exhaustion, he coaxed another swarm of pixies into being. Each motion dragged, stiff and labored, powered by sheer will alone.

"What the hell happened?"

"She can't do this on her own," he said hoarsely.

"I know," she replied, confused.

He hadn't really answered her. He just kept working, lost in that quiet, frantic urgency.

She tore off a mitten and caught his hand, his skin ice-cold and stiff in her palm. He paused, but his eyes never left Dormouse in the sky.

"Jesus, Ferenc, you're gonna lose something to frostbite." Olivia adjusted her grip, clasping his fingers as she heated the air around them, coaxing warmth into skin that barely responded to touch. "I'm here to help. You need a break. Let me take over."

He shook his head, jaw tight in stubborn determination. "I can't. She needs me. I have to—"

She released his hand and tore off her other mitten, cupping his ears to warm them as she tilted his head down, forcing his eyes to meet hers. "You're so exhausted, you're not even making sense," she countered. "Look around. We can't afford to lose you too."

He blinked slowly, as if registering her presence for the first time. His eyes darted across the snow in a quiet double-take, then swept over the pixie bodies scattered like fallen embers. His expression shifted—shame softening the lines in his face, mouth drawing downward. He exhaled and closed his eyes. "I didn't realize . . ."

"It's not your fault," Olivia said, quieter now. "But you need to rest. Let me handle this for a while. You've done more than enough."

His eyes flicked back to the sky. "I want to be up there with her."

She lowered her hands from his ears with care. "I know. But the best thing you can do is be here when she comes back down."

He hesitated. A flicker of conflict passed through his eyes before he finally nodded. His shoulders sagged, the last of his strength seeming to go with it. "Okay," he whispered.

She squared her stance, arms lifted in front of her, energy already pulsing beneath her fingers. "So what happened?"

The first time Ferenc had summoned the pixies, it hadn't been pretty. But whatever he'd figured out since then, he'd clearly refined. She'd watched him pull them from the air—clean, deliberate, practiced—and she needed to do the same.

Ferenc took a cautious step back and reached into his coat pocket, pulling out his silver case with digits too frigid to bend properly. His frozen fingers fumbled with the lighter—once, twice, three times—before a flame finally caught, and he inhaled like it might be the first real breath he'd taken all day. The smoke curled upward, blending with the cold air before dissipating.

"I don't know," he said at last. "Whatever that stuff is up there they're eating, it's killing them. I tried to get her to come down, but she won't. So all I can do is keep summoning these things like . . . like some sort of sick sacrifice."

Olivia winced. That image didn't sit right in her mind.

She looked up. Thick trails still streaked the sky, but some bore jagged gaps—chunks carved out by Dormouse, like bites from a giant's meal. Around them, smaller portions sparked and flickered, like steel wool catching flame as pixies sank their teeth in.

Ferenc had it all wrong. No one forced the pixies into this. They made the choice. Not for ritual or for praise. They rose with

Dormouse, fully aware of the cost. And that truth held more power than anything else.

She took a breath and focused, eyes closing slowly. The cold stilled around her as she tuned in to the air. A subtle, familiar tingle met her fingertips—like breath against skin. Olivia reached with both hands, feeling for tension in the space around her. Then she pulled.

The air gave way, like unveiling a gem beneath silk. Wisps spilled out—fluttering, human-like forms no bigger than her palm, delicate and pale as cirrus clouds. Their wings unfurled, shimmering softly in the air around her.

"Come on," she murmured, coaxing more to life. "We need all the help we can get."

They gathered, spinning tighter around her, until she raised her arms to the sky and sent them upward. In a burst of motion, they rose together—glimmering and swift—streaking toward Dormouse.

But with each group she sent up, more dulled forms drifted down, landing softly in the snow, their brief lives snuffed out. No swirl of mist. No puff of air. Just stillness.

Olivia continued, every ounce of her will focused on pushing through. The fight hadn't ended. Not yet. Even now, smoke thinned overhead, gapped and ragged in places, nibbled thin by the pixies. Progress crept forward, slow but real. One breath of clean air against miles of poison.

Ferenc gasped beside her.

She turned in time to catch him toss his cigarette aside and thrust a hand toward the ground. A twister surged beneath him, lifting him into the air in a blur of wind and motion. Her gaze followed instinctively—

—and her stomach lurched.

Dormouse plummeted from the sky.

Olivia stepped forward, flicking her wrists to follow, but a guttural growl behind her froze everything.

Then came the screams. Muffled, frantic—from inside the hotel.

As if they didn't have enough problems already.

She spun toward the threat. Her blood turned to ice.

Two lunanites flanked a masked figure, gnarled bodies hunched low, muscles drawn tight, vibrating with restrained violence. Snarls curled from their throats in ragged plumes as they bared their fangs, glowing red eyes fixed on her with feral intent.

The masked figure—Amy—stepped forward, grinding a lifeless pixie beneath her boot with slow, deliberate pressure.

The sick display twisted something deep inside Olivia. She clenched her fists, ready to unleash her fury. "You bitch."

Ferenc landed beside her in a gust, Dormouse limp in his arms.

"Take her. Get her out of here," Ferenc said, voice strained but resigned, his glare fixed on Amy.

"What? No! I can help—"

"Now, Liv." His tone left no room for argument.

Once the protector in her kicked in, backing down had never been in her nature. She wanted to fight, wanted Amy to feel every inch of what she'd put Ferenc through—and the rest of them by extension. But Ferenc didn't give her a choice; he passed Dormouse into her arms with the kind of care that spoke volumes.

"I've got this," he said, quieter. "I only trust you with her."

Olivia lowered her gaze. Dormouse lay limp and cold, her breath thin, her color leached away. Life hadn't left her yet, but it toyed with making an exit.

"Please," he whispered. "Keep her safe."

Of course it had to be him. She couldn't imagine anyone else seeing this through. Ferenc had earned that right. Olivia's rage cooled to resolve, and she tightened her hold around Dormouse, taking a slow step back.

Be careful," she whispered before turning.

Wind spun beneath her feet. A twister pulled them skyward, toward the hotel. And behind her, everything unraveled.

CHAPTER 29
Ferenc

W hat do you want, Amy?"

Richard had control of her again. Not fully—she hadn't become the hollow, feral creature he'd twisted her into before—but Ferenc recognized the echo of it in the two lunanites flanking her, coiled and snarling, as if extensions of her will. He couldn't decide if that made it better or worse. He stood his ground, each breath spilling in pale clouds that vanished fast in the frigid air.

"You mean you don't know?"

The playful purr in her voice nearly paralyzed him, stirring memories he'd only just managed to quiet. That same tone had once been soft, teasing, threaded through laughter that mingled with sunlight and the clatter of breakfast dishes on the day he didn't have to travel. He could almost smell the rich coffee between them as she leaned over the table to kiss him. For a heartbeat, everything came rushing back—the warmth, the way she'd brightened the world, the way her laughter followed him like sunlight through clouds.

261

It pulled at him—a quiet undertow he refused to let take hold. He forced himself to step back from that edge. Dormouse needed him, and he couldn't help her if he let Amy back inside his head.

"You can't have her," he said. "I won't let you."

Amy threw her head back in laughter. Thick curls flew wild, catching the pale morning light as her joy warped into something cruel.

"You still don't get it, do you?" she said, voice rising behind the mask. "You really think this is about your *girlfriend*?"

He let the jab pass. She always did that—spat the word like poison. But something in her tone tugged at a loose thread in his thoughts.

The random ambushes. The timing of it all. The remote village after Kamran disappeared—the one place Richard shouldn't have known about.

The pattern aligned, every piece snapping into place.

She hadn't been attacking to win. She'd been keeping them distracted, scattering their focus so Richard could hunt the others first.

So *Kamran* could find them first.

A bitter taste filled his mouth. He almost pitied her for being so blinded by devotion she mistook her invisible leash for love.

He wanted to tell her again—that Richard had used her, that he'd never loved her—but she wouldn't hear it. Not now. Least of all when she wore the mask of his followers and wielded the power he'd given her.

He exhaled, steadying himself. Dormouse needed him.

"I won't fight you," he said.

Amy's voice hardened behind the mask. "I know. But I'll fight you."

She flung out her arm. The lunanites lunged.

Muffled screams flared from the hotel. In his periphery, bodies pressed to the glass—phones raised, faces pale—before the beasts rushed in.

Ferenc braced. One creature's claws flashed midair as it descended. He sidestepped, twisting with the motion, and sent a gust of wind slamming into its chest. The blast hurled it into a pine; it hit the ground hard, limbs splayed.

The second hit the ground in a snarl and sprang again. He raised an air shield, its shimmer catching the cold light as teeth scraped against it. The impact rippled through Ferenc's defenses, resonance trembling through the barrier. He drove one hand forward, turning defense into force. A vortex burst from the shield's surface, hurling the creature into the snow.

Both lunanites staggered to their feet, shaking off the hit. Then they attacked in unison—one from the left, the other from the right.

Ferenc caught their rhythm, fending them off with quick bursts of wind and shifting defense.

Still they recovered, almost in sync—circling him with animal precision and unnerving resilience, every step a measured pattern meant to wear him down.

His mind raced. He needed to end this. Fast.

Ferenc lifted his hands to the sky. The air thickened. Static crawled along his arms beneath his coat. He drew a slow breath and braced himself—then released a shout that cut through the charged silence.

Lightning tore from the sky itself, born from nothing and striking him dead on. Blinding light swallowed everything for a breathless moment. The instant thunderclap shattered the air, sending the hotel onlookers ducking behind the glass. Ferenc caught the current and flung his arms outward. Two arcs split away and struck the lunanites, searing them into drifting plumes of smoke.

Silence held for a heartbeat. Then movement behind the glass—phones lifting as the crowd slowly rose in the pale morning light.

Ferenc lowered his arms and turned back to Amy, heart still hammering from the surge. "I don't want to fight you," he said, forcing steadiness into his voice. "I know the real you is still in there. So I'm going to save you. *Again.*"

Amy moved with an otherworldly grace, her dark lunar magic swirling around her like a living entity. Ferenc braced and summoned an air shield as her first strike hit—dark energy meeting light in a crackle that stung the air.

"Fight it, Amy! You're stronger than this!"

She answered with another wave of dark energy that shattered his barrier and sent him skidding through the snow. He dropped to one knee, breath fogging the air. The cold clawed at him, but the deeper chill came from within, draining and hollowing. His legs wobbled as he pushed himself upright, locking his knees, refusing to stay down.

Amy thrust both hands forward. Tendrils of inky black energy coiled from her palms, writhing through the air like living serpents.

He swept his arm wide, a sharp gust scattering them. Snow lifted in sheets, swirling between them as the pressure shifted.

Her attacks came faster—fiercer—each one carrying the edge of resentment. She hurled a bolt of dark lunar energy; he countered with a vortex that devoured the impact. Another burst followed. He ducked, the wind from the blast biting at his neck. A third tore past, splitting the ground at his feet, the air warping where it struck.

Her assault never broke. Every strike drew her closer to frenzy. He couldn't keep deflecting forever. If he wanted to help her—to reach her—he needed to get close enough to touch her.

"Amy, stop—"

A seething blast caught him in the side. A sharp, burning pain flared beneath his ribs, stealing his breath. He staggered, clutching his side, vision blurring. Ferenc blinked hard, forcing his vision clear again.

Amy's stance turned rigid, every motion precise and measured. Every movement confirmed it—her will had been tuned to another's rhythm.

Healing her lunanite form had been easy by comparison. But she hadn't changed form this time, which meant healing her would take something different—something he hadn't figured out yet. But he had to try. Anything beat doing nothing.

He lunged forward anyway.

A soft glow flared across his hands, running up his arms in branching trails until it engulfed him whole. Amy raised her arm to strike, but he caught her wrist, spun her, and locked his arms around her to pin her in place.

Amy went rigid, then thrashed in his hold. Her elbow drove into his ribs; pain surged through the fresh injury, hot and immediate. He tightened his grip anyway. She clawed at his sleeves, fabric tearing under her nails.

"Let go of me!"

Her voice struck with the same fury, the same words she'd screamed when the blond man pulled her through the portal. He'd thought he could save her then too. He'd been so damn worried for her—never realizing Richard had his hold on her once again.

Tendrils of lunar magic lashed out, coiling around his legs, tightening until his muscles trembled from the strain. He ground his teeth against the pain, refusing to release her.

Smoke-like substance gathered at their feet, shaping into two familiar beasts clawing their way into being. The tendrils locked him in place, every muscle straining against their pull. Still she summoned, ready to strike while he stood helpless.

He gritted his teeth. If he wanted to break Richard's hold, he needed to do it now.

He focused on the warmth building in his hands, willing every ounce of healing energy into her. The glow around his body pulsed brighter, eating through the tendrils that bound him. They dissolved into drifting flecks of luminescence.

Amy thrashed harder. Her heel slammed into his shin, but he held firm.

"Fight it, Amy. Come back."

The lunanites she'd summoned finished taking form—red eyes glowing, teeth bared. The light from his hands brightened, spilling over Amy's clothes, her skin, her hair. Her body arched against him, a raw scream tearing through the air as his healing light met her darkness.

"You're stronger than this. Fight him!"

She gasped, and the mask burst apart with a sound like breaking glass. Shards hit the snow around his boots, and he glimpsed the pallid curve of her cheek before she sagged in his arms, her sobs shaking against him. The tendrils recoiled as the lunanites dissolved, leaving only flecks of light suspended in the cold air between them.

Ferenc held her close. "It's over. You're safe."

Her head snapped up. With a guttural sound, she wrenched herself free and twisted out of his grasp. "Get away from me!" She staggered forward, clutching her temples, her breath jagged.

He reached out instinctively. "Amy—"

"I said get away!"

She stumbled ahead, boots sliding out from under her. Ferenc flinched as she hit the ground, the impact dull against the snow. He moved to her side in an instant, hand outstretched. She glared at him through the jagged remains of her mask, eyes blazing with fury.

"I'm not the bad guy," he said quietly. "Richard used you. You know that."

She bared her teeth in a vicious hiss. "I'll never forgive you."

Her words stung, but only for a moment before the old numbness crept back in—the same cold detachment he'd felt on the moon when she'd refused his hand after he'd changed her back from her lunanite form, after he'd saved her. His hand dropped to his side, his mind blank, refusing to form a single thought.

She turned away with a pained scowl. Then she ran, vanishing around the hotel's corner, her footprints scattering snow in her wake.

Ferenc shuddered through a sigh. He ran a hand through his hair, then flinched as his ribs protested. He needed a cigarette. A long drag and maybe ten more after that. But first, he had to deal with his ribs.

And Dormouse.

CHAPTER 30
Olivia

Olivia had no idea how Ferenc fared against Amy, and the uncertainty gnawed at her. But she couldn't leave Dormouse to find out.

She'd tried forcing her concern into purpose, pouring it into the act of healing, but it only made the anxiety bubbling inside worse. She'd tried everything she could think of—from gentle wind healing to sharp bursts of electrical stimulation—but Dormouse's skin stayed dull and ashen from the trails she'd swallowed, her breaths shallow, her sleep tormented by feverish dreams.

"Stay with me," she said, draping a cool cloth across the girl's forehead. "Ferenc will be back. He'll think of something. He'll . . ."

The rest caught in her throat.

Every instinct screamed at her to move, to fight, to do something. But Ferenc had ordered her to keep Dormouse safe. And with Richard still out there, she couldn't risk leaving her alone. She hated feeling trapped, unable to protect both of them at once. The tension inside her built like a storm pressing against its own winds. If only she could see Ferenc from the window. If only she could help. Her fists tightened and released. She wanted to hit something. Instead, she paced, hands on her hips, trying to bleed the energy off.

A whimper pulled her back. Dormouse.

"I'm here," she murmured, running her fingers through the girl's thin black hair. "Just hang in there, okay?"

The door handle rattled. Olivia's breath caught. She rose, ready to strike—then froze when Ferenc stepped inside.

"Oh my God," she said on a breath of relief, lunging at him for a hug.

He stiffened, groaning in pain before he managed a faint squeeze in return.

"What happened?" she asked, pulling back. Her eyes darted to where his hand clutched his ribs. "You're hurt."

"It's healing," he said with a wince. "Slowly."

"Here—take your coat off, let me—"

"How is she?"

Olivia blinked as he brushed past her, his focus already locked on Dormouse. Ferenc checked her pulse, then eased down on the edge of the bed beside her with a grunt, taking her small hand in his. Olivia's chest tightened at the sight—half worry, half reluctant admiration. Each motion betrayed his pain, yet his gaze never left Dormouse.

"She's been in and out," Olivia said. "I've tried everything I can think of, but she's not improving."

"Describe 'everything.'"

"Well . . . healing wind, electric pulses, vibration, temperature control . . ." She trailed off, frustration edging into her tone. "I even tried increasing her oxygen levels and using air currents to help circulation. Nothing's working. I feel useless."

Ferenc nodded slowly, as if weighing her words. Then, silent, he leaned closer to Dormouse, cupped her cheeks, and pressed his lips to hers.

Olivia froze. She'd never experienced romantic or sexual attraction—it had simply never been part of her—but even she knew this moment left no room for confessions of feeling. Before she could say anything, he drew back a fraction, still hovering over Dormouse. A faint thread of black vapor unspooled between their mouths. Olivia's confusion tipped into understanding. He hadn't kissed her; he'd drawn the poison from her lungs.

She crossed her arms, watching, quietly impressed. It hadn't even occurred to her to extract the toxins instead of neutralizing them. Ferenc always thought better under pressure—well, most of the time. But as the dark mist funneled from Dormouse into him, a cold thought settled in her stomach.

He was transferring whatever she'd swallowed into his own lungs.

"Ferenc," she tried, reaching toward him just as he pulled away.

He tipped his head back and blew the black substance out with the practiced ease of a smoker. But it refused to behave like smoke. It spread fast, curling through the room in ribbons that clung to the air, thickening into a dark, sulfuric fog.

The acrid sting hit Olivia's nose; the scorched bitterness clung to her tongue. She swept her arm, pulling the haze into a vacuum of compressed air.

"Ugh, that stuff's nasty!" Ferenc rasped before breaking into a cough.

He bent, hacking into his elbow. Black specks splattered against his sleeve. Olivia's heart skipped a beat. At first, she thought he'd hacked up blood—but the specks rippled across the fabric, spreading and swelling as if trying to take form.

"What the hell is that?" She lurched back, but he tore off his coat and flung it aside, throwing up an air shield around it.

He didn't answer. His body trembled as his gaze shot to Dormouse, still feverish and unmoving. He didn't have to say it; she saw the same realization in his eyes. If the stuff spread like that on his sleeve, it could be doing worse inside Dormouse.

The substance on his coat erupted like a fog machine gone rogue, filling the air dome until it deepened to midnight black. She swept her arm, and the shield swirled. The darkness spiraled inward, vanishing like vapor into a vacuum until only his coat remained.

Ferenc bent over Dormouse again, intent on pulling more from her. "Ferenc, wait!" Olivia blurted. "You can't—"

He turned his head toward her, eyes red-rimmed but voice calm. "It's okay."

"It's really not," she shot back. "You can't both go down on my watch."

"I have to do this," he said. "I can take it. Trust me."

She shook her head, frustration and fear colliding inside her entire being. "There has to be another way."

He lifted from Dormouse's side and reached out, his hand settling on Olivia's shoulder—gentle despite the tremor in his fingers. "I know you're scared. So am I. But right now, she needs me. And you're strong enough to handle what comes next. You always have been."

She wanted to argue, to find another way, but every counterpoint died before it reached her lips. A shaky breath left her like a quiet sigh of surrender. "Okay. Just be careful."

Ferenc managed a faint smile before turning back to Dormouse. He leaned in again, lips brushing hers before he drew another slow pull of the black poison.

Olivia's pulse pounded. She controlled the air around them, drawing in each wisp of darkness the moment it left his lungs. The tension in her muscles burned, every nerve on alert. She stayed poised, ready to move the instant something went wrong.

They worked together until Ferenc collapsed to the floor, hacking up more of the black gunk. Olivia dropped beside him, hands shaking as she dispersed the substance. Dormouse's breathing had evened out—but Ferenc's had gone shallow, strained. He sagged against the bed, eyes closed, his skin pale beneath the sweat.

"I shouldn't have let her go up there," he breathed, voice thin. "It was a mistake. I failed her."

Olivia's heart clenched at his words. "You didn't fail her. It was her choice. She knew the risks and wanted to help. You have to respect that."

273

He opened his eyes, wincing as he shifted to look at Dormouse's still form. His hand went to his ribs.

"All right," Olivia said softly. "Let me see your injury."

Ferenc lifted his shirt, revealing bruises the color of storm clouds and a gash still raw around the edges, skin drawn tight where it struggled to mend. She frowned but steadied herself. "So what happened with Amy? Is she . . .?"

"She ran off." He tensed as she exhaled a steady breath over the wound, then released his own—rough, shaky, but edged with relief. "I don't know if I got through to her or not."

The edges of the gash knitted together, slow but steady. Olivia finally drew a full breath after holding it through the worst of it. She laid a palm over the bruise next, sending subtle vibrations through the muscle to ease the strain. The motion steadied her focus, but not her thoughts. Not knowing what had become of Amy gnawed at her; she'd caused enough chaos already. They didn't need more.

After a few minutes, she lifted her hands, satisfied with the progress.

"How does that feel?"

Ferenc inhaled deeply and released it through his nose. "Better. Much better. Thank you."

A small smile tugged at her mouth. "No more heroics for a bit, m'kay?"

He chuckled, but it caught halfway and turned into a cough. "I'll try my best."

Olivia shifted and sank beside him, her back finding the edge of the bed frame. After a moment, she let her head rest against his shoulder with a sigh.

She hoped Anya and Moses fared better than the two of them. With the lunanite teardrop looming closer and Amy's fate uncertain, they could use one piece of good news—just one.

CHAPTER 31
Ferenc

Ferenc had tried everything over the last two days, but he couldn't get the flavor of dark lunar poison out of his mouth. He set his Styrofoam cup down and scrunched his nose. Even his coffee couldn't wash the taste clean.

The bathroom door opened, and Olivia peeked out at him, expectant, her long blonde hair fluffy from the blow-dryer.

"Nothing yet," he confirmed. She sighed and stormed toward the landline phone on the small table between both beds, picking up the receiver and dialing a number. "Hey," he tried. "Don't work yourself up again."

After a few seconds, she slammed the receiver down. "Why won't he answer?" she hissed.

They'd both been on edge, taking turns steadying each other. Olivia had tried calling Moses on his satellite phone again—same ring, same *silence*—since sending him and Anya to track down the other elementals before Richard could find them first. Ferenc had finally convinced her to shower, hoping the heat might ground her.

But even he'd started running out of reassurances. He could only tell her the others remained safe so many times before he stopped believing it himself.

His gaze drifted to Dormouse. He and Olivia shared another burden between them: he'd kept drawing the poison out to blow into the air, and she'd kept pulling it into that whirlwind void of hers. Dormouse had seemed to improve after the first attempt, but her condition had worsened overnight. Whatever still lingered inside her spread fast and without mercy.

He needed air. Room to think. A cigarette, though it barely helped when every breath still burned with the sulfuric bitterness of toxin. When Olivia returned to the bathroom to soak the cloth for Dormouse's forehead again, he grabbed his coat and slipped out. No one at the hotel asked questions anymore—not after the pixies, the lunanites, the lightning flash and thunderclap. Yet the lobby always fell too quiet when he passed through for another cigarette.

The Norwegian air bit cold but no longer completely clean. He almost gagged as the acrid smell mingled with the lingering poison on his tongue. He lifted his gaze to the sky. The lunar teardrop hung lower now—too close to Earth. By his calculations, they had hours left before it touched down. Maybe minutes. The odds sat stacked against them, but he refused to yield.

He lit his cigarette and shoved his hands into his coat pockets, striding toward a bare patch of ground between skeletal trees—a small circle of exposed earth he'd used for his rituals. The snow around the hotel held the remains of fallen pixies, dark traces of poison staining the drifts where they'd fallen. Too many of them had given their lives to help Dormouse clear the trails in the sky. He owed them at least the return of their essence to the air he'd taken them from.

He crouched beside one, scooping the delicate form from the snow. Its wings crumbled like ash against his fingers. He carried it to the circle of trampled grass and laid it down gently.

"Thank you for your service."

He bowed his head and waved a hand over the pixie. The tiny body disintegrated, shimmering dust rising like faint sparks before vanishing into the cold. He'd done this hundreds of times, yet thousands still waited. He turned, scanning the snow for more—

—and froze when a low crash rolled through the air like surf slamming a breakwater.

Water spilled across the ground, spreading fast as it darkened the snow. Ferenc jumped to his feet and spun toward the noise, heart hammering, instincts ready to defend.

A red blur surged from the churning torrent.

Moses.

The mercenary coughed and wheezed for breath, lunging toward a blonde figure still tumbling through the water. The wave broke around them, scattering pale froth across the snow as she slipped from his grasp.

Then another shape strode through the portal—dry, furious, the air around her still rippling from the passage. Anya.

She barely reached the bank before slamming into Moses, knocking him onto his back.

"You made me open a portal!" she shrieked, swatting at him with wild, frantic precision.

Moses threw his arms up, blocking a few hits to his head. "What the fuck are you *hitting* me for?" He caught her wrist but froze when she yanked his gun from its holster. The barrel came up fast—aimed between his eyes.

A jolt of adrenaline hit hard, stealing Ferenc's breath before he lunged forward. "Anya!"

Moses released her and raised his hands beside his head.

"You made me open a portal!" she repeated, voice icy with pure wrath.

Ferenc launched a quick, controlled burst at her hands. It struck with enough force to knock the gun from her grip, sending it spinning harmlessly into the snow. He seized Anya's wrist and pulled her away from Moses's chest. She fought him hard, straining to get back to the man as he sat up in the slush.

"You *made me* open a portal!" she screamed again.

"Enough!" Ferenc's voice cracked through the air, louder than he meant it to.

Anya froze mid-struggle, chest heaving. But her glare stayed fixed on Moses, who rose unsteadily, scooped up his gun, and holstered it with a clatter. "I didn't *make you* do anything."

A soft sound broke through the tension—a small, frightened whimper. Ferenc turned toward it.

The blonde girl Moses had tried to grab from the wave stood several feet away, soaked and shivering, eyes wide in horror. Her limbs jerked as if her body had forgotten how to move.

279

Moses staggered toward her. "Give her your coat," he called over his shoulder.

Ferenc blinked, his focus shifting to the girl instead of the order. Then he released Anya and crossed the slick ground, unzipping his coat as he went. Moses reached the girl first, touching her arm gently—but she flinched back, startled, and nearly slipped.

She couldn't have been more than twenty. Pale hair clung to her face, and soaked fabric pressed to her skin, heavy with brine. She turned to run, but Moses caught her wrist. He pulled her in hard enough to stop her, steadying her by the shoulders and the back of her head.

She thrashed, kicking and clawing until Ferenc laid his coat over her shoulders. The moment it touched her, she froze—rigid for a breath, then sagging against Moses's chest.

"What the hell happened?" Ferenc demanded. "Who's she?" The girl trembled in Moses's hold, her breath hitching. He softened his tone. "Are you all right?"

"She can't hear you," Moses answered through chattering teeth. His soaked shirt had frozen stiff, his hair and chin beard hung in icy clumps. "She's deaf."

Ferenc exhaled, his questions falling away with the breath. The poor girl had just witnessed something unnatural. Her fear and confusion must've gone beyond anyone else's. He placed a hand on both their shoulders and focused on warming the air around them—just enough to get them moving toward the hotel lobby.

"Anya." He motioned her closer with a quick lift of his chin. "Let me warm you up too."

Her gaze flicked to Moses. She crossed her arms, lips pressed thin, and looked away. Ferenc almost rolled his eyes. Moses could rile anyone, but Anya's brand of stubbornness came with more feeling than sense.

"Anya," he tried again, firmer. "Come on."

"Let her be a wretched little *brat*," Moses said through clenched teeth, fighting the tremors.

Ferenc sighed, more at him than her. At least Anya had remained dry. He opened his mouth to tell them all to head inside but stopped when the girl suddenly clutched Moses's shirt and buried her face against him. Her shoulders shook.

Moses didn't move—he just kept her close while she cried, his hand cradling her head. Ferenc had only ever seen him that gentle with Kamran.

"What happened here?" Anya asked at last. Her tone had cooled but her eyes flicked around the snow. "What are those things?"

Ferenc followed her gaze to the tiny dark forms scattered over the ground, wilted and still. "They're . . . pixies," he said quietly. "They helped clear the trails in the sky."

Anya frowned. "If this is what happened to them . . ."

". . . Then where's your charge?" Moses finished.

The bitterness of poison flooded Ferenc's mouth again. "She's very ill," he said. "Olivia's with her."

The blonde girl lifted her head, red-eyed, her breathing uneven but calmer now.

"All right, let's get inside," Ferenc said, steady but firm. "Then you can tell me what the hell happened."

He caught the girl's eye and gestured toward the hotel. She hesitated, studying him as if weighing her safety, then nodded and stepped away from Moses's hold.

"Come on, Gatekeeper," Moses said, trudging after.

"You—" Anya started, voice hoarse.

Moses spun around, pointing at her with a shaking finger. "*You*! *You* opened a portal. That was *your* choice. You very well could've let us drown."

Ferenc, an arm around the girl beneath his coat, paused—ready to step in if they started again.

"I'll have you know, though," Moses said, his teeth clattering so hard Ferenc half-expected them to splinter, "that your portal worked. It didn't open into a fiery world. No demon leaped out to eat us."

Anya flinched at that.

"Here we are," he went on, "back in Norway—alive and in one piece. All thanks to you. So get over it."

Ferenc couldn't wait to hear what had actually happened, but right now, he needed Anya calm enough to follow them inside.

"He's right," he said. The truth came harder than he liked. "You're all alive, and we have another piece to our puzzle." He inclined his head toward the girl. "That's what matters now."

She kept her glare fixed on Moses, her mouth a hard, silent line. Then she turned and walked toward the hotel without a word.

Moses exhaled through his nose, irritation cutting through his exhaustion, and trudged after her.

Ferenc needed another cigarette—but he pushed the thought aside and tightened his grip around the girl instead, guiding her toward the lobby. Warmth first. Answers later.

CHAPTER 32
Ferenc

Ferenc wrung out the cloth and wiped the fever from Dormouse's brow. Her skin burned hotter each hour. He hated the helplessness clawing at him. His gaze shifted to the newcomer on the other bed beside Olivia. "Are you sure she's one of us?"

"She is," Anya said. "I feel it."

He nodded. He trusted her instincts. After all, she'd led them all the way to Norway, where they'd found the stone and crystal golems. And she'd been trained by Olivia, whose own gut had led her to find him.

But this girl struck him as untouched by their world, much like he'd once been. No elemental sense, no training, no way to defend herself. She hadn't yet faced Richard's masked crew or their lunanites—thankfully—and she couldn't possibly help Olivia find the Keeper of the Realms.

The girl—Laine—scribbled something on the hotel notepad before passing it to Olivia. Notes and online Estonian-to-English translators had kept them communicating since the start. Estonian sign language and American sign language diverged as much as their spoken counterparts. Or, as Moses put it— "One man's thumbs-up could mean another man's middle finger."

Ferenc adjusted the blankets around Dormouse once more, then straightened. "So which one of you is going to tell me what happened?" He crossed his arms and looked between Anya and Moses.

Moses had been a little testy since his return. He barely looked away from the TV, where the news cycled between live shots of the approaching teardrop and shaky clips from the hotel—caught through windows and doors by hotel guests' phones—of the pixies falling and a familiar battle with Amy and the lunanites. *Ferenc's* battle.

"There's nothing to tell. The kid fled, I followed, we almost drowned." He waved a dismissive hand. "You know the rest."

He'd get nothing more from Moses; that tone said enough. Kamran might've gotten a full report, but he wouldn't. So he turned to Anya. "Why'd she run?"

Anya lifted her chin. "She's a teenager, and he's terrifying. I don't blame her; I'd have run too."

Moses finally turned from the screen. "Say that again. I dare you."

Anya moved directly in front of him and leaned in, her face inches away from his scowl. Ferenc's stomach tightened as he prepared to step between them.

"You're a big, scary man," she said, dragging out each word. "And stubborn. And aggressive. And *always* angry."

Moses growled low in his throat.

Anya straightened, hands on her hips. "You're proving me right."

He hissed through his teeth and swatted her away, conceding. "Get out of my face."

She backed off with a satisfied smirk. Olivia mirrored it before schooling her expression when Ferenc caught her eye.

He sighed, running a hand through his hair. "And what about the almost-drowning part?"

"She dove straight into the bay." Anya mimicked the dive with her hand. "Clothes and all. And he followed, like an idiot."

"I thought she might drown!" Moses snapped. "How was I supposed to know she swims like a fucking fish!"

"But then this whirlpool came out of nowhere," Anya added. "And that's why—I couldn't just—I had to—" Her expression flickered through fear, pain, panic, and finally rage. "You made me open a portal!"

Ferenc jumped between her and Moses as she launched at him. "Okay." His hands caught her shoulders—steady, firm. "Take it easy. A *whirlpool* appeared out of nowhere, you said?"

She huffed at Moses over Ferenc's shoulder, glare still fixed on him, before stepping back with a curt nod. "Yes."

"Right after she dove in?" Olivia asked. "Definitely sounds like a guardian or elemental."

"That's what I was thinking," Ferenc mused, turning his attention back to Laine, who sat rigidly on the bed, eyes fixed on the TV. On the screen, the teardrop sank through the poisonous haze—a vast column of black matter twisting as it descended. Red glints flickered within the mass, moving in restless swarms. Not light. *Eyes.* Thousands of them.

Moses pushed to his feet. "We've got company."

Dormouse's breathing hitched, and Ferenc rushed to her side, wiping sweat from her clammy gray skin. Her pulse fluttered beneath his fingers, too fast, too weak. He didn't want to leave her—but he had to do something about the lunanites. Anything. Even if it meant losing against impossible odds.

He looked up to find all eyes on him.

"Anya, can I count on you to watch over Alexis and Laine?"

She nodded, even as uncertainty flickered in her eyes. "I'll try my best."

"Let's go," he said to Olivia and Moses, then turned back to Dormouse. "I'll be back. Hang in there. Don't you dare leave me."

With one last lingering look, he grabbed his coat and followed them out the door.

The hotel halls roared—shouts, pounding feet, doors slamming in quick succession. Outside, chaos churned through the streets. People scattered in every direction, faces bloodless, voices cracking into cries and half-formed prayers as they ignored the calls to stay inside. Somewhere beyond the square, sirens wailed, rising until even that had been swallowed by the crowd's panic.

Overhead, the monstrous black mass of gangly creatures oozed in the sky, growing closer by the second. The ground trembled beneath the pressure of it—a low, mounting rumble that made the windows quake in their frames as if the city itself braced for impact.

Olivia vaulted upward, wind spiraling beneath her boots, and hurtled toward the teardrop. Ferenc turned to Moses, his words slicing through the roar.

"Shoot any creature that touches down."

Moses's eyes widened, but he said nothing as he reached for the weapons hidden beneath his coat and drew them, one in each hand. He nodded once, jaw set. "On it. Just don't get yourself killed up there."

Ferenc managed a grim smile. "I'll do my best. Stay sharp."

Moses gave a quick salute, and Ferenc launched into the air to join Olivia.

She unleashed wind blades and vortexes, the air splitting with each desperate strike. Ferenc swept in beside her, hurling gusts and air missiles between her attacks.

Hundreds of lunanites spilled from the sky. Thousands. Maybe millions. Their numbers climbed by the second, forming a living ladder from above. Ferenc couldn't fathom how so many existed on the moon. It made no sense. They had to be coming from somewhere deeper—like an endless factory churning in the dark.

He shifted from offense to defense, targeting the lunanites that slipped past Olivia's attacks. But each beast he struck down gave way to another, their ranks endless. Soon, the overflow from the onslaught above spilled around him.

"There are too many!" he shouted to Olivia above the chaos.

Her answer came ragged, strained. "We can't let them reach the ground!" The desperation in her voice cut through the roar.

Ferenc's chest heaved, breath slicing cold through his throat and lungs. Every motion burned—each twist, each strike, each desperate blast of air. But he couldn't afford to let them destroy the world. And he couldn't fail Dormouse. With a raw cry, he summoned a massive bolt of lightning that tore through the swarm, vaporizing a wide cluster of lunanites in the blast.

Despite everything, the tide pressed harder. Every kill vanished into the swarm. And the truth settled in, quiet and absolute: they couldn't win.

The moment his focus faltered, the swarm broke through. They hit like a collapsing tide, the world reduced to claws and teeth and the burn of poisoned air. He fought blind, fending off the maws that snapped too close until Olivia's voice cut through the noise.

"Hold on!"

She snatched Ferenc's wrist and pulled him into her protective cyclone. The wind whipped around them, forming a barrier against the onslaught as Olivia directed it toward the ground at near-breakneck speed.

They hit the street hard. Ferenc dropped to his knees as Olivia released the cyclone, both gasping for breath. Before they could steady themselves, the torrent struck.

Olivia pitched forward into him, and they threw their arms up to shield their heads. But instead of the swarm crashing down, the creatures burst, dissolving into a fine black dust that poured over them in sheets. The teardrop collapsed above, breaking apart midair until nothing remained but the drift—miles of it.

Ferenc lifted his head. The snow around them had vanished beneath a thick, dark layer, and the air shimmered faintly, particles suspended where they shouldn't be.

Moses stood a few feet away, coated in lunanite dust—like everything else. He shook his shaggy head, black flecks scattering like fine sand. Chest heaving, he looked up at the brown moon hanging dead in the sky after it bled.

Olivia peeked past her arms, her voice a rasp in the stillness that followed. "What just happened?"

Ferenc dragged a hand through his hair, then glanced at his palm as if expecting it to come away streaked. "I don't know," he said after a beat. "But I don't like it."

As the finer haze settled, the silence held, dense and expectant. Then, far off, a snarl. A single scream. Silence.

Ferenc turned toward the sound, scanning the empty street. Dust drifted in thin veils through the air, blurring distance. Another noise—a gasp this time, followed by a muffled cry—snapped his gaze in the opposite direction. Nothing. Just haze and movement that might've been wind.

Then a shape broke through. A figure ran—human, panicked—before something dark pulled itself from the dust behind it. The creature lunged. Both vanished without a sound, the air swallowing everything that followed.

Ferenc stiffened as Olivia gasped beside him, a hand clamped over her mouth. Moses cursed under his breath, guns rising instinctively.

"They're forming on their own!" Olivia breathed.

The silence pressed in again, heavier this time. Then—so close it vibrated through his chest—a snarl.

The dust beside them rippled. A shape rose to life—half-formed, gleaming red eyes and jagged limbs—before a gunshot cracked through the air, and it disintegrated mid-scream.

Ferenc blinked through the new haze, ears ringing. Moses already had both guns raised, scanning the street for movement—faster than seemed possible. Ferenc caught it again, that uncanny reflex, but the thought vanished as the next snarl broke through the dust.

Ferenc's heart stuttered. He met Olivia's gaze—wide, mirroring his own. "Run."

Olivia jumped to her feet before he finished. Another snarl tore through the air as four shapes flickered to life. Ferenc flung a gust wide, slicing two lunanites back into the particles they rose from, while Olivia and Moses took the other two.

They ran. The ground shifted underfoot, slick with fine black powder. A lunanite rose on their left—Olivia hurled a blade of air through its torso, and it burst apart. Two more followed. Moses dropped them with quick, precise shots, his movements tight and sure.

The hotel loomed ahead, half-shrouded in drifting black. When they shoved through the entrance, the noise struck like impact—shouting, doors slamming, people crying—chaos pressing close from every side.

Moses stopped just inside, shoulders tight. He dragged a sleeve of his winter coat across his face, scattering faint remnants of dust, then pushed past the crowd toward the hall.

"Where are you going?" Ferenc demanded over the din.

Moses didn't slow. "Getting Anya," he threw back. "She needs to open a damn portal—now."

Ferenc and Olivia exchanged a glance with no words needed. Moses's tone said enough. He drew a slow breath and motioned for her to follow. "Let's go before he makes it worse."

They pushed into the corridor, the roar of the lobby thinning but never vanishing, blending into the sharper edge of an oncoming argument ahead.

CHAPTER 33
Ferenc

The room pulsed with leftover noise—the kind that lingered after shouting stopped. Ferenc stood near the door, counting the breaths between them, waiting for the next spark to catch.

Moses lingered near the window, the thin daylight cutting across the faint grit still clinging to the glass, his eyes fixed on Anya like a man daring her to blink first. "Open it," he said, low and hard. "Now, Anya."

She stood by the TV, arms folded across her chest, shoulders squared and chin lifted just enough to make defiance look deliberate. "I told you. I'm not opening another portal."

"You don't get to pick and choose when the world ends," Moses shot back.

"That's not what I'm doing!" Her voice climbed, raw with frustration. "You don't understand—"

"I understand you're wasting time!" he snapped.

Olivia stood beside the dresser, shoulders squared in that stubborn way that always came before a retort. "You think shouting will change her mind?"

"Liv." Ferenc kept his voice low, steady enough to slice through the tension without adding to it.

Moses turned to Olivia, his glare cutting clean across the space between them. "Every minute she stands here shaking her head, people die out there." He jabbed a finger toward the window, toward the lunanite dust swallowing people whole. "Maybe you're okay with that, but I'm not—because you know who's next when they're all gone? Us. Stay here long enough, and it's as good as suicide."

"You think I don't want to help?" Anya shot back. "You think I'm the problem—but you have no idea what you're asking me to do."

"Enough," Ferenc cut in before Moses could fire back, his tone low but edged with warning. "She's not wrong to hesitate. Caution isn't the enemy—but hesitation will cost us time. So will arguing."

Silence tightened between them—Anya pulling inward again, that familiar retreat; Moses refusing to yield. A sudden shift cut through the tension—Laine lurched forward on the bed, hands flying to Dormouse's shoulder. The movement jolted Ferenc; she'd been small and quiet in the background until now. A low, broken sound escaped her, frantic enough to pull every gaze toward her. She didn't need words; her panic said enough.

Ferenc moved before thought caught up. His body knew what his mind didn't want to confirm. He crossed the space in two strides, dropped to his knees beside the bed, and pressed the back of his hand to Dormouse's clammy forehead.

Her body jerked, an involuntary tremor rolling through her. Heat radiated off her skin in waves—hotter than any natural fever. Her lips had lost all color; her breathing had gone shallow. The air around her warped slightly, as if the space itself couldn't decide whether to hold her or let her go.

His heartbeat thundered in his ears as he leaned closer, the rest of the room falling away in a wash of muted sound. He sealed his mouth over hers and drew more poison from her lungs, the bitter taste of it burning down his throat.

"Ferenc. Ferenc, please."

Someone grabbed his shoulders and pulled him back. He coughed bursts of black smoke as the poison burned its way out of his throat. Olivia dropped to her knees beside him, summoning her vortex shield. The air warped, then funneled tight, drawing the dark haze into itself until nothing remained. Ferenc wiped his mouth, lungs spasming, and scrambled toward Dormouse again. "I need to do something," he rasped. "I can't lose her."

"You won't do her any good by being dead," Moses said, his tone dry.

He didn't answer. His attention had narrowed to Dormouse's feverish face. At the edge of his vision, Laine reappeared beside her with a damp cloth. Ferenc hadn't even noticed her leave. She pressed it into his hand, eyes gleaming with worry.

Olivia pushed to her feet, her shadow shifting across the bed. "We need help." Her voice angled toward the other side of the room.

"What about the other elementals and guardians? Can you feel anyone else?"

"Other than the two golems, I can't feel others," Anya replied.

"Well, try harder," Moses snapped.

Ferenc laid the cloth across Dormouse's forehead and ran a shaking hand through her hair. His lungs still burned, his muscles screamed, and whatever energy he'd had left to stop another argument had drained away. He didn't even have the strength to think up a plan.

"I can't feel anybody else," Anya repeated, a huff slipping through her words. "It's like they disappeared."

Olivia's voice cut through, steady but curious. "Disappeared how?"

Even through the ache, he caught enough of their voices to track the argument. Anya couldn't feel the others. She'd tried. That left one explanation.

"Richard probably got to them first." The words slipped out before he could stop them. He shifted on the floor, bracing a hand against the bed to steady himself as he turned. The motion left his arms trembling, but he kept going. "Amy implied something like that. We need to get back to the golems."

"In case you don't recall," Moses said flatly, "they weren't exactly willing to come with us the first time. And they made it perfectly clear we weren't welcome back."

He knew this. But they had no other choice. "We have to try."

"What if we get the solar king's help?" Olivia turned to him, composure masking uncertainty. He knew that look—the one that came when she'd already accepted a risk. "He has just as much to lose as we do. We need to meet with him."

"And how do you suggest we do that?" Moses shot back. "You already said you don't even know if we can use the sunstone to reach out."

Olivia's gaze shifted to Anya, who tensed under it.

"No." Anya's eyes flicked between them, hands trembling at her sides—the motion too tight to be hesitation. "No. I don't know why you keep making me say it."

Moses exhaled hard and turned toward the window, where the dull brown moon hung low against the daylight. "Not this again."

"We're out of options," Olivia said quietly, stepping closer. "If we don't do this, Dormouse won't make it. And after what we just saw out there, I doubt the world will last much longer either."

Anya's jaw tightened, her eyes glistening. "You don't understand. I can't . . . I can't."

Moses pushed away from the window and crossed to her, his expression softening. He placed a hand on her shoulder. "Hey. You faced your fears before, and you can face them again."

Her eyes flashed, fury sparking through tears. "You made me open a portal!" she snapped, striking at his chest. "You gave me no choice, you *made me—*"

Moses caught her wrist, gently but firmly pushing her backward until she landed in the armchair in the corner. Laine, curled up against the headboard beside Dormouse, flinched and gasped. Olivia moved to her side, a hand raised in comfort.

"If lying to yourself makes you feel better, fine," Moses said lowly. "But the truth is, nothing bad happened to us. That portal you made saved my life, and making another one will save more. And they're not even asking you to do this alone this time."

Anya glared at him, shoulders rising and falling too fast. Ferenc pushed himself off the floor. The effort scraped through every muscle, but he forced his body upright and crossed the space. He set a hand on Moses's shoulder and pulled him back a fraction.

"Easy," he said under his breath. Then, "Anya, look at me."

Her gaze flicked to him, the turmoil surfacing in her eyes before she could hide it. He dropped to one knee beside her, steadying himself on the chair's arm. He forced his voice even, the back of his throat still raw from the poison.

"You're not alone," he said. "We're all here with you. We trust you. And we need you to trust yourself."

He turned his head toward the bed. Dormouse lay still, her skin too hot, her breathing uneven. Each shallow rise of her chest came slower than the last, and the flush beneath her skin had darkened. The poison continued working its way through her.

"She needs you," he continued, voice low. He looked back at Anya. "We all need you."

She shook her head and pushed to her feet, backing away, tears bright in her eyes. "I can't. I can't go through that again. You don't understand what it's like to watch your brother be—" Her voice broke; her chin trembled.

Laine rose from beside Dormouse, a notepad clutched in her hand. The sudden movement pulled Ferenc's gaze. Her eyes found

Anya—wide, uncertain, edged with dread—as she crossed the space and held the page out for her to read.

Anya blinked, her eyes darting over the page in quick, uneven passes. Confusion tugged at her brow, and she looked up at Laine.

Laine pointed to one spot on the page, her hand trembling a little, the gesture urgent.

After a beat, Anya gave a small, hesitant nod.

The confusion in Laine's eyes broke, replaced by stark, unmistakable fear. Her lips parted. A few urgent syllables spilled out as her hands flew through signs—uncoordinated, desperate. Then she turned, darted to Olivia, and snatched the phone from her hand. Her fingers flew across the screen.

She bounded back toward Anya and thrust the phone forward, the translator's glow washing her face in pale light.

"What does it say?" Moses asked.

Anya's expression wavered, the fight in her eyes faltering. She looked up at Laine, apology trembling in her voice. "She says she doesn't want to die."

Laine glanced down at the phone again, her eyes darting over the word as if memorizing its shape. Her lips moved once, twice—silent practice—before sound forced its way out.

"Please," she managed in halting English. "Please."

Anya's breath hitched. "No, I—" she began, but Laine reached up, wrapping her hands around Anya's throat—not to hurt, but to *show*.

Ferenc's heart skipped a beat. He shot to his feet and reached out to stop her, but Moses lifted a hand, holding him back for once.

"Wait," Moses murmured. "Just watch."

Laine didn't strangle her. Her fingers pressed lightly at Anya's vocal cords—a guide rather than a restraint.

"Please," she tried again.

"I can't," Anya whispered, shaking her head.

Laine drew one hand back to her own throat and she shaped the word with careful lips, the sound halting, broken. "Hh . . . elp. Please. Help."

Moses's grin cut sideways. "Well, damn." He jerked his chin toward Laine, rough pride running beneath the words. "Took the kid to do what the rest of us couldn't. Best do as she says."

Moses hadn't stopped Ferenc from stepping in to help Anya just to keep order. He'd known exactly how this would play out. The precision in Laine's touch meant it couldn't be the first time she'd done this. Moses had probably witnessed the same act before—maybe before he'd jumped in the bay after her.

The air stilled around them. Anya's composure trembled, then fractured. Tears slipped down her cheeks, cutting through the composure that still held her upright in the chair. Laine's eyes stayed on Anya—wide and wet, pleading through the fear that quivered just beneath them.

"Please," Laine whispered again.

Anya abruptly rose from the chair, shouldering past Moses as she moved. She paused by the window, hands flexing restlessly at her sides as she squeezed her eyes shut. When she let go, her voice came out rough, thin with strain.

"What if it doesn't work?"

"What if it does?" Moses countered, tone firm but stripped of its bite.

"Either way, we're here for you," Olivia said softly. "We've got your back."

Anya crossed the room toward the door, each step measured, the distance shrinking too slowly. She stopped with her fingers hovering over the knob, tension drawn tight across her shoulders. Her head dipped, a small, shaky breath escaping her. One by one, her fingers curled around the metal, trembling until her knuckles whitened. She didn't move.

Olivia drew a careful breath. "It's okay," she said gently. "Just focus before you open it. Like you do when trying to find the elementals. Think of the sun—its warmth, its pull. That's your direction."

"Oh, because opening a portal to the molten surface of the sun is *so* much better . . ." Moses drawled.

Anya flinched, a faint sound catching in her throat.

Olivia's head snapped toward him, eyes narrowing into a glare that could stop a heartbeat. "Moses," she said through clenched teeth, every word measured and low. "Not. Helping." The silence that followed sat utterly still, like the air itself waited for her permission to move again. Then she exhaled, gaze softening as she turned back to Anya. "Ignore him—he's an idiot. You're not reaching for the sun itself. Just, uh, its *echo*. The place where its light settles."

The tremor in Anya's hand didn't ease. Fear thickened in the air, tilting the balance toward failure. They'd lose her if someone didn't ground her now.

Ferenc crouched beside Olivia's bag, rummaging through it, fingers brushing until they closed around the sunstone. The faint warmth pulsed against his palm as he brought it to Anya.

"Here," he said quietly. "If it helps, don't think about the sun. Think about the one who gave Olivia this. Let it guide you to *them*."

"Yes!" Olivia's eyes brightened. "It should take you to Eeolas. He's Ariol's adviser."

Anya turned slightly, hesitating before taking the stone. Her shoulders trembled once before she shut her eyes and stilled.

Then she turned the handle, and the room held its breath.

CHAPTER 34
Deon

Deon shoved the fire guardian down onto the cold floor of the energy room. She cried out as her knees struck the surface. Strands of dark-red hair clung to her face, the rest twisted half-loose from a ruined braid. A mix of defiance and fear flashed in her hazel eyes as she turned to him, shouting words he couldn't understand— Dutch, probably, given where they'd found her. She pushed herself up again, toned frame tense with the same stubborn will that had carried her through the kitchen fight, when she'd turned every sharp, hard, and scorching thing within reach into a weapon. Even the staff had tried to protect their chef—but only long enough for Deon to drop them with a violent tremor.

She'd fought bravely, but in the end, he'd subdued her.

Shikki had wanted her last. Deon didn't understand why, but he never questioned orders. Questions meant disloyalty. Still, lately they surfaced uninvited—slow, splintering thoughts drifting through the fog that dulled his mind: Why he'd work for a madman. Why only a handful of them carried abilities no one else seemed to have. And many other disconnected thoughts. Something in them refused to add up.

The fire guardian forced herself up again, swaying but steady enough to strike. Her persistence might have earned respect once. Now it only grated.

"Stand down," he said, but she lunged anyway.

He sensed the vibrations before she moved. The floor spoke first—weight shifting, tension gathering. His body answered, muscles tightening to counter. But she never reached him. Two lunanites materialized beside him, snarling as they pounced, driving her hard into the floor. Her cry of defiance broke into a scream.

"Come now," Shikki said, stepping past Deon toward the woman. "That's no way to treat your hosts."

As the creatures drew back, still circling and snarling, Deon caught the collar of her shirt and hauled her upright with ease. He shoved her toward Shikki, then drove a kick behind her knee, forcing her down onto one leg. Her cry of pain echoed through the chamber.

Shikki crouched beside her, his eyes glinting with dark satisfaction. "Do you remember me, Esmée?" Her glare faltered, widening when he spoke her name. He tilted his head. "Take a good look. Think *real* hard."

When she didn't answer, fury twisted his features. He seized her chin, his fingers digging hard enough to leave her skin caved beneath them. She whimpered, one hand clawing at his wrist, the other raking down his arm in a desperate attempt to make him let go.

"I asked you a question." His calm tone betrayed the fury etched across his face.

She managed the smallest shake of her head. His breath hissed out through his teeth. "Of course you don't." His words dripped with venom. He shoved her face aside and stood. She rubbed her jaw, and the motion hadn't even finished when his boot struck, snapping her head back.

Blood splattered across the dark stone. She gasped—a sound caught between a choke and a sob—then pushed herself up to spit a mouthful of red onto the floor. Deon's fists clenched. For an instant, something behind the fog recoiled—revulsion, maybe guilt—but it slipped away before he could grasp it. Watching her bleed stirred something he couldn't reach.

Shikki seized the braid at the base of her skull and yanked. The motion jerked her head back, her cry fracturing against the stone. She clawed at his hands, nails raking his skin.

"Do you know what it feels like to be forgotten?" he hissed through clenched teeth. "To be invisible?"

Then he slammed her head into the floor.

His muscles locked, the fog in his head rippling like disturbed water. For a moment, the detachment slipped, leaving only a raw edge he couldn't name.

"It cuts like a knife!" Shikki roared, the words splitting through Deon's thoughts like shrapnel, tearing at the fog that dulled his mind.

The lunanites that had been circling pounced at Shikki's signal. Esmée's shrieks ricocheted off the stone walls as the beasts tore through her arms where she tried to shield her face and throat.

"And you being chosen over me cut deepest of all!" Shikki's voice struck like a whip. "Do you at least remember *that*? *I* was supposed to be the guardian—not *you*!"

Humiliation. Jealousy. They bled through every word, emotions so raw they thrummed against Deon's own pulse. But whether that fury carried truth, he couldn't tell. He sank inward, through the fog that sealed his thoughts, the world outside dimming to Esmée's screams and the sick rip of flesh beneath claws. He needed to remember how he'd come to serve this man. Why he obeyed.

The haze thickened the deeper he pressed, threatening to drown him. But he continued on until his hands found the wall—cold, brick-solid, rough beneath his palms. The barrier that had always stopped him.

Esmée's screams carried through him like a second heartbeat. His muscles stayed locked, but something deeper fought to move—to stop this. Inside, he clawed at that mental barrier, feeling along its edges, trying to find a way through, over, or under. The wall went on endlessly, vanishing into the fog, no opening, no end. It stood, silent and absolute.

He struck it once in his frustration. Then again. Each blow sent dust through the fog, grit stinging his skin. He hit harder, desperate now, fear clawing at his chest.

Cracks spread beneath his knuckles, faint but real. The sound startled him—a brittle snap, like stone giving way. He froze, breath ragged. Something had shifted. But before he could reach for it, a voice pierced through the haze.

"Master, I have some urgent news."

Deon hadn't registered Kamran's entrance. His words hit like a drop of cold water. Panic surged through him, instant and electric. He tried to warn him of the danger of interrupting Shikki—to move, to speak—but the fog clung tight. His body lagged behind his mind, too slow. Too late.

Shikki's head snapped toward the voice, fury sparking wild behind his eyes. The air around him pulsed once—then he lifted a hand, dismissing the lunanites in a blink. Their growls cut off, and Esmée trembled on the floor in the brutal silence, her limbs jerking weakly, eyes fluttering as she fought to stay conscious. Each breath rasped out from her throat, thin and broken.

"This had better be as urgent as you claim," Shikki said through his teeth, "or you'll share her fate."

Kamran dropped to one knee, head bowed low. "Master, the air elemental's crew failed to recruit the twins."

A pause. Then a glimmer lit behind Shikki's eyes—first thought, then calculation. His brow knit, then the corner of his mouth twitched, not yet a grin, but the threat of one. He nudged Esmée's bloodied cheek with the tip of his boot. She barely stirred.

"You're lucky," he said. His tone had gone cold again, precise. "I was going to leave you to my pets, but I might have use for you yet." His gaze cut to Deon and Kamran. "Fetch them. *Now*."

"Yes, Master," they said in unison.

Deon bowed low while Kamran pushed to his feet beside him. Together, they turned toward the door. But before Deon stepped through the threshold, he risked one last glance back. Shikki loomed over Esmée's broken form, a grin spreading slow and deliberate across his face.

A chill slid down Deon's spine. The unease had shape now, faint but real—like something inside him had shifted out of place. He reached for the memory of how he'd come to serve this man once more, but the fog closed in before he could touch it. He forced the thought aside. He had orders.

He always had orders.

CHAPTER 35
Olivia

It worked. It actually worked.

Olivia's heart pounded as she stared at the portal—a vortex of black, white, and gray, pulsing with otherworldly energy. What had been the hotel room door seconds ago now swirled and breathed like wind caught in a current.

Anya had done it. No fire. No demons. Just the mesmerizing spin of light and shadow.

Relief mingled with pride. Progress, at last.

She glanced at Anya, whose hands trembled faintly at her sides, her breath shallow and uneven as she stared into the still-churning void. Olivia placed a hand on her shoulder, the muscles beneath drawn tight, like a rubber band about to snap. Despite the success, a haunted look lingered in Anya's eyes—a fear Olivia recognized all too well.

"Hey," she said softly. "You did great."

Anya blinked, as if her mind needed a moment to catch up. She managed a small nod, though her gaze stayed distant.

"Right then," Moses said, eyeing the portal with suspicion. "Who goes first?"

Olivia turned to him. "Sounds like you just volunteered yourself."

He studied them, his expression unreadable. After a beat, he sighed, resolve sliding back into his posture. He checked the chamber of his gun, then stepped past them and through the portal without another word.

Ferenc scooped Dormouse into his arms and turned to Laine, motioning his head toward the swirling door. "Come on."

Laine took a step back, breath catching as she shook her head.

Her fear made sense; she'd asked for this, but that didn't mean she trusted it. Olivia couldn't fault her for that.

"Go," Olivia told Ferenc, already moving to Laine's side.

"Be careful," he said. He took one last look at her before stepping into the swirling light.

Olivia slid her hand into Laine's. The girl's wide, frightened eyes tore from the portal to meet hers. She squeezed gently, slow and steady, her thumb tracing a grounding line back and forth across Laine's skin. She brought their joined hands to her chest and drew in a deep, deliberate breath. The motion said what words couldn't: *you're safe, follow me, I've got you.*

"I know this is terrifying," Olivia said to both her and Anya, even if Laine couldn't hear. "But we're going to get through it together. You're not alone."

A faint nod came from Anya, hesitation still flickering in her gaze. Laine's eyes darted between Olivia and the portal, fear tugging at every breath.

"Hold my hand." She extended her other hand to Anya. "We'll go together."

Anya hesitated another second before swallowing hard, gathering herself. With a shaky breath, she clasped Olivia's hand.

Olivia smiled with quiet certainty. "That's it," she murmured. "We're in this together."

She stepped backward toward the portal. Predictably, both resisted, their grips tightening. Her own pulse thudded against her ribs, but she forced calm into her breath. She had to be the steady one.

"Eyes on me," she said, giving Laine's hand a small upward tug until the girl looked up. "That's it," she added as they both relented.

The air near the portal shimmered and swirled. She'd stepped through many lately—including via moonstone and sunstone—but this one carried a weight all its own.

With Anya's abilities still developing, their destination remained uncertain. For all they knew, it could open straight into the realm of fire—a risk they couldn't afford to ignore.

She drew in one last breath and stepped forward, pulling both girls with her as the world dissolved into motion.

Big mistake.

Heat scorched her skin, and Olivia clamped her eyes shut against the blinding firelight. Anya and Laine's panicked shrieks tore through the heat, pure and jagged, feeding the surge of dread already clawing its way up her insides. For one breathless instant, she believed they'd stepped straight into the inferno.

Then awareness caught up. Her skin didn't burn. The air ran hotter than a California summer, but not deadly. They hadn't burned alive; every inch of skin proved they'd made it through intact and still breathing.

She risked a glance, squinting against the glare. The landscape rippled ahead of them, the air bending and trembling with waves of heat. Her stomach dropped. She'd promised Anya they'd be safe, yet here they stood—fire all around, heat in every direction.

Anxiety twisted in her gut as Moses rushed to grip Anya's shoulders, his voice cutting through the noise—"It's not your fault, it's not your fault,"—fierce, stern, but not unkind. Laine had collapsed beside them, arms locked around her knees, rocking in silent terror.

Olivia released her hold on both girls and moved, scanning the scene for threats or bearings. Ferenc sat nearby with Dormouse cradled in his lap, concern furrowing his usually composed features.

Her breath caught. Behind them, a palace loomed—golden, radiant, every wall gleaming like King Ariol's armor or Eeolas's spaulder. Relief flooded through her. The Solar Palace.

"We made it," she whispered, blinking fast, as if the sight might vanish. Then louder, with disbelief cracking through: "We made it!" She turned back, pushing past Moses. "Anya, it's okay! Listen to me—you did it!"

"Did what?" Moses asked, blinking against the heat.

Anya didn't act like they'd spoken at all; she kept struggling in Moses's grip, her screams tearing through the air like knives.

Olivia quickly cupped Anya's face in her hands, shaking her lightly. "Anya! It's all right. This isn't what you think—we're at the Solar Palace. We're safe."

Hysteria had too tight a grip on Anya. Her eyes stayed unfocused, her body locked tight with fear, breath coming too fast, trembling as if she still expected a fire demon. Olivia couldn't blame her, but Anya had slipped too far to talk down.

Olivia drew a slow breath, fingers flexing as current gathered beneath her skin. The charge traveled through her hands into Anya's shoulders. A soft pulse shivered outward; Anya's body slackened, eyes fluttering shut as she slumped forward into Olivia's arms, silent at last.

"What did you do?" Moses hissed.

"I sedated her."

"Oh, like you did to me?" He rubbed the back of his neck with a low huff. "That shit hurts, you know."

"No, I used a low-frequency pulse on her. She's getting actual rest. You, I flat-out electrocuted at the base of your skull. Big difference. Now are you going to help or not?"

His expression hardened into a glare. He grumbled something under his breath, then scooped Anya into his arms. Olivia ignored his complaints, her focus already shifting to Laine. The girl's shoulders trembled, her face buried in her knees, muffled sobs shaking through her frame.

Her chest filled with a tender ache, the kind that came from seeing someone hurt and knowing she could only offer her presence. She kneeled beside her, resting a gentle hand on her back. Laine flinched, then looked up—eyes swollen and wet, confusion clouding the fear. Olivia pointed toward the palace. The girl followed the motion; wonder slowly replaced panic.

Olivia rose and extended a hand, nodding once. She mouthed the words carefully—*We're going to be okay*—then pressed her free hand over her heart so Laine would feel the intent, not just see it. Laine hesitated, then reached for her, allowing herself to be pulled upright.

Keeping Laine's hand in hers, Olivia moved toward Ferenc. "Ariol and Eeolas know me—someone should let us in."

Ferenc gathered Dormouse again and stood. "Then let's go."

She led them toward the golden doors, Laine at her side. The palace loomed larger with each step, radiant and solid, stirring a fragile spark of hope within her. At the entrance, she raised her fist and knocked hard. The sound cracked through the stagnant, superheated air.

"King Ariol! Eeolas! Please, let us in—it's urgent!" She struck again, knuckles rapping against the smooth surface until pain shot through her hand. For a moment she feared she'd shatter bone before anyone answered.

Only one of the golden doors moved beneath the Gothic arch, hinges groaning softly as a guard peered through. The tension in Olivia's chest loosened a fraction.

"State your names and business," the guard demanded.

"I—we—" Olivia stammered before forcing her composure back into place. "The elementals and guardians are here, by the king's request."

The guard's suspicious gaze drifted over them, pausing on Dormouse and Anya's limp forms. Olivia held back the retort on her tongue, trying to steady herself.

"Please." The word came out rough instead. "The air elemental and the Gatekeeper need medical attention. Earth has been—"

The door slammed shut.

She stared at the gilded surface, mind stumbling to catch up. Shock bled into sorrow, then anger. They couldn't be turned away now—not after everything. She raised her fist to pound again, but before it landed, the same door cracked open wider.

The first guard stood aside, and another appeared behind him, posture crisp. "Follow me," the new guard said.

They moved through an intricate corridor, familiar in design to the Lunar Palace but steeped in shiny gold instead of glimmering silver. Every surface gleamed, throwing back distorted flashes of their weary faces like the worst-timed funhouse mirrors in history. Warm air pressed against her skin as the guard led them into a grand chamber lined with plush sofas and gilded chairs. Ferenc and Moses eased Dormouse and Anya onto the nearest couches.

"Where's the king?" Moses asked, boot tapping too loudly against the floor as he took everything in. Standing in a palace on the *sun,* and he still had to be the biggest jerk in the room.

"Hopefully on his way," Ferenc replied, the calm in his voice belying the frenzy of worry in his eyes as he idly rested a hand on Dormouse's forehead.

Laine perched beside Dormouse, her trembling fingers combing through her tangled black hair. Moses started pacing, the rhythmic thud of his boots against the polished floor drilling into Olivia's nerves—until she realized her own steps had become an echo to his, the two of them pacing parallel to each other.

"His Royal Highness, King Ariol," boomed a guard's voice, "and his trusted adviser, Eeolas."

Olivia turned as Ariol and Eeolas entered. Their faces, alight at first, faltered at the sight before them. Olivia swallowed the lump in her throat, trying to steady her racing heart.

"Majesty," she said softly.

Eeolas scanned the group, his tone edged with urgency. "Where . . . where are the others?"

Olivia found Ariol's gaze, the weight of his expectation pressing down. "I have bad news," she said, her voice catching.

Ariol closed his eyes, and in the stillness, she recognized the same dread that had lodged in her chest.

"Earth—er, Gaea—has been covered in what I can only describe as . . . lunanite dust," she continued. "From the moon. And other than two golems we encountered on the way, the Gatekeeper can't sense the others. We think Alican reached them before us."

The words hung heavy, pulling the room into silence. Olivia's mind flashed back to the poison, the moon tear, the lunanites that burst into dust as they fell. She clenched her fists. They needed a plan—and fast.

Ariol's eyes snapped open. He turned to his guard. "Send a detachment to Gaea. Investigate the disturbance and report back immediately."

"Yes, Majesty." The guard bowed and hurried from the room.

Ariol turned back to Olivia. "You mentioned the twins."

"Twins?" Moses asked, voicing the same confusion that flared through her.

"The earth elementals," Ariol explained. "The golems."

Olivia lifted a brow. "I thought you said there could only be one elemental per element."

"Typically, yes. But the earth elementals are a rare occurrence." He turned to Eeolas. "We need to return for them immediately. We must ensure—"

"We need your help," Ferenc cut in, his voice thick with urgency. He then shifted under Eeolas's steady, assessing stare. "With all due respect, of course, Majesty. But Alexis—the air elemental—she tried to stop the trails, and she—"

The brittle, pleading crack in his unfinished sentence nearly broke her. Fear tightened around his eyes, his calm held together by duty—and by the love he tried not to show. Guardian first, and a man in love second. His strength stretched thin, the break inevitable.

"Prep the infirmary," Ariol ordered. As Eeolas inclined his head and left at once, the king turned to Ferenc. "Follow me."

Ferenc and Moses hurried after him, with Dormouse and Anya in their arms. In the flurry of movement, Olivia reached for Laine's hand, keeping her close as they followed the others. Her heartbeat thundered in her ears, every step blurring into the next as fragments of the past hours swirled repeatedly in her mind.

They entered a wide chamber alive with motion. Gold-trimmed uniforms moved through the blur—medical staff weaving around

317

one another with efficiency, voices low but brisk. One medic motioned for Ferenc and Moses to place Dormouse and Anya on adjoining beds. Sigils brightened beneath them as diagnostics began.

Two attendants crossed toward the rest of them. One reached for Moses, who waved him off with a growl. Olivia ignored the medic who approached her, her focus locked on Ferenc instead. Amid the chaos, he stood rooted like a tree growing along a flooded riverbank—steady, precise, every answer clipped clean as his gaze stayed fixed on Dormouse.

Gradually, the room settled. The hum of conversation softened, though the undercurrent of activity remained. Ariol stayed close, overseeing it all, his presence filling the room like sunlight through glass. Eeolas returned a moment later and leaned toward him, whispering something in his ear. The king's expression darkened, the gold in his eyes dimming. He said something back, and the two turned, disappearing down the corridor.

Olivia groaned, her back finding the wall behind her. The thought pressed in before she could stop it—Earth might already be gone. She closed her eyes, fighting the images clawing their way in her mind: cities collapsing under black dust, lunanites devouring everyone, silence where life should have been. The thoughts wouldn't stop. She pressed her palms to her temples, trying to hold back the rush of everything she couldn't fix. And she hated that she couldn't think of anything else.

CHAPTER 36
Ferenc

Ferenc had lost track of time in the Solar Kingdom. Minutes, hours, days—he couldn't tell anymore. The only constants: Dormouse still hadn't woken, and he could've smoked an entire carton by now.

He sat hunched forward in a plush chair beside her bed, elbows braced on his knees, fingers knotted in his hair. Some guardian he made. He never should've let her go up there. There had to have been another way—something safer, smarter. Every outcome circled back to him.

A light touch brushed his back, and he jolted upright, heart hammering.

"Whoa, hey, it's just me," Olivia said, snatching her hand back.

"Sorry." He sank back into place, guilt pressing down until his spine curved with it.

"How ya making out?" she asked quietly.

He didn't answer. She already knew. Olivia always knew. She understood the dark pit of self-reproach he wallowed in—the one thought kept feeding. She didn't need him to spell it out; she could read the silence for him.

After a pause, her hand returned, tracing slow circles against his back while he berated himself in silence. The faint tingle of current followed her movement, subtle but familiar. He frowned and shifted, turning just enough to catch her wrist, grip firm despite the exhaustion.

"Don't," he muttered, releasing her with a sigh.

Electrical stimulation. Of course she'd try that. She hadn't pulled her hand back that time—probably expecting him to catch on.

"Hey, at least *you* get a choice." Olivia slid down the wall beside him, crossing her legs. "She'll wake up. She's stronger than she looks."

Ferenc nodded absently, mind drifting to the first time he'd lost her—when he'd tried to save her through lightning travel and *killed* her instead. Dormouse hadn't yet learned to shield herself; the current had hit them both, but her life had ended in his arms. Panic and guilt followed, crushing and absolute. Then came the miracle— her breath returning, and, eventually, her eyes opening.

He wanted nothing more than for her to open them again.

"Anya's doing better," Olivia said softly, as if coaxing him back. "The healers had me perform some kind of . . . electroconvulsive therapy. It sends electrical impulses to the brain. I was terrified of hurting her, you know? Like, using electricity on an arm or chest is one thing, but straight to the brain? It could've gone so wrong."

Ferenc's stomach clenched. He knew that fear. When he'd re-vived Dormouse, he'd acted as a defibrillator, unsure if the current had been too strong or not strong enough. That uncertainty still gnawed at him—right up until his brain snagged on something else entirely.

"Wait. Did that thought even cross your mind when you zapped Moses at the base of his skull? Because from what I saw, you had no hesitation at all." The edge of a smile tugged at his mouth before he could stop it.

Olivia let out a dramatic groan. "Oh, come on—he deserved it!" she whined. "I can't stand that guy."

His mouth twitched again. "We still need him, though."

She wrinkled her nose, and the sound that escaped him startled him—a chuckle, a real one he didn't have to force. Olivia grinned up at him, winked, and patted his arm before rising to stretch. Without another word, she headed down the hall.

He watched her go, quiet gratitude tugging at his chest. She'd never know how much he appreciated her steadiness, how her in-stinct met his reason and somehow made it all work. They shouldn't have balanced as well as they did, but somehow they always did—guardian and general, *again.*

He sighed and turned back to Dormouse's still form. He hoped they'd get answers soon. No one deserved them more than Olivia.

A sudden, harsh cough from Dormouse shattered the quiet. Ferenc shot up from his chair before thought could catch up. She'd curled in on herself, body racked with violent spasms as she hacked up the last of the poison clinging to her lungs.

He leaned close, brushing the damp hair from her face with shaking fingers. "I'm here."

A medic's hand caught his shoulder, firm but careful, steering him back toward the chair as others moved in. Ferenc sank into the plush cushion. He couldn't do anything, and the familiar sting of helplessness cut deeper than any physical wound.

Her weak cry of his name cut through the chaos, and he moved before thinking—back at her side, healers be damned.

He shoved his way through until he broke against her bedside, searching until he found—

There they were.

"Hey," he murmured, forcing a steadiness he didn't feel as he gazed into her eyes. Her open, awake, beautiful eyes. "How're you holding up?"

"My lungs burn," she rasped, another fit overtaking her.

"You look better, though." A ghost of a smile crossed his face. "A little less green."

She tried to laugh, but it collapsed into another cough. His chest tightened in response. "Well, that's a relief," she managed between breaths.

His faint smile faded. He leaned in, pressing a tender kiss to her forehead—grateful for each breath she drew, even as guilt refused to let go.

She blinked up at him, voice barely a whisper. "Did I save the world?"

Ferenc bit down hard on his tongue to keep the flood back. Her question struck deep—his disbelief slamming into pride, pride splintering into heartbreak. The way she'd eaten most of the poison, swallowing it into herself to stop the spread . . .

He didn't know whether to cry, laugh, or scream. His throat burned for the taste of smoke, anything to steady his hands. More than anything, he wanted to hold her and never let go, for however long *forever* meant to a guardian.

Finally, he nodded. "You did."

The strain eased from her face. She exhaled a trembling breath and closed her eyes. "Good."

A healer stepped forward. "I'm afraid I must insist—Her Eminence needs rest," they said, calm but unyielding.

Ferenc nodded and started to step back, but Dormouse opened her eyes with a soft whimper, fear dull but clear beneath her exhaustion. He managed a crooked grin. "Don't worry, *Your Eminence*— I'm not going far."

He pointed to the chair he'd occupied for what felt like ages. When she gave a faint nod, he caught her hand and brushed his lips across her knuckles, adding a quick wink to ease the heaviness between them. A small, breathy laugh slipped out of her—half giggle, half wheeze—before the coughing took over. She turned on her side, huddling into the blankets as the fit racked her frame.

The sound of her laughter, albeit brief, left something raw and aching in his chest. He stepped back, letting the healers move in.

His gaze drifted to the doorway, where King Ariol stood watching, unreadable. Ferenc bowed his head in respect but didn't move from his post. If the king wanted words, he'd have to come closer.

Ferenc had promised Dormouse he'd stay, and no one—royal or otherwise—would tear him away.

Ariol approached, posture regal and unyielding, his attention fixed on the bed. "You love her," he said. The words hung in the air, more verdict than question.

Ferenc's fingers tightened around the armrest. The truth needed no ceremony. "I do." The admission came low, steady, carrying all the weight he'd kept buried—fear, devotion, the fragile edge of hope.

"Relationships between elementals and guardians are not—"

"I'm not changing how I feel because of our titles," Ferenc cut in, voice flat and final.

Ariol shook his head. "I did not suggest it; I was merely stating a fact. Even my own relationship is . . . complicated."

"I'm sure it is," Ferenc muttered, eyes still on Dormouse. Two medics drifted away to tend to others, leaving one to fuss quietly over her. He didn't mean it as dismissive—just truth. From what he'd seen of royalty, on Earth or anywhere else, love and duty rarely fit cleanly together.

"My wife is . . . right there." Ariol gestured to the bed beside the one Anya had occupied before her recovery.

Ferenc followed the motion. A statue rested atop the covers, unnervingly lifelike. Veins of red light threaded through fine cracks across its form, faintly pulsing like molten lava trapped beneath stone.

Ariol's wife must have died. But a memorial statue in a medical ward made little sense—especially one laid out on a bed and tended by healers. Then the likeness shifted—so slight it could have been imagined. His breath caught.

"The previous elemental of fire was killed during the war between realms," Ariol said quietly. "That is why all realms were exiled to neutral territory. I married Kennia, queen of the Realm of Fire, as a political union. Her daughter Cirees, the new elemental, became my adoptive daughter. While Cirees was to be reborn on Gaea, Kennia was permitted to remain here in the Solar Kingdom—both part of the Central Realm—closer to her daughter than she would have been in her own sealed world, a plane apart."

Ferenc drew his eyes from the queen's unmoving form and back to Dormouse. He couldn't imagine living another life—one so far beyond memory, yet somehow his own. Olivia's visions had shown flashes of that war: flame, ruin, and loss that still echoed through them, even if they no longer remembered why.

"Kennia grieves her daughter's kidnapping," Ariol said, his tone thinned by sorrow. "Her health declines. Her fire has dimmed to embers. She hardens—fading more each day. Her only hope lies in holding her daughter—the phoenix—once more." His next words fell almost to a whisper. "My marriage to her was a mistake. I should never have taken her from her realm, from her world."

Ferenc studied the king in silence. The burden clung to him, heavy and visible in the stillness between his words—love bound by duty, regret hardened into something that no longer bled.

"You love her," he said at last, a careful echo of the king's own proclamation.

Ariol's jaw worked once before he nodded. "With all my heart. But she does not return it. She accepted my proposal out of necessity, not love. Her heart still belongs to the one she lost."

The words settled in Ferenc's mind like embers, faint but enduring. His gaze drifted to Dormouse again—her pale face, her shallow breaths—and something in him understood. Love didn't need to make sense. It only needed time.

"Be there for her," he said at last, shoulders lifting in a faint shrug. He didn't have more to give. "Show her." He'd always been there for Dormouse, even when he didn't completely know why. Words had never been his strong suit; his actions said far more.

Ariol's golden eyes softened. "Thank you," he said quietly. "I did not mean to unburden myself. What I came here for was to inform you that we're ready."

Ferenc's brows knit. "Ready for what?"

"To meet the Keeper of the Realms."

Ferenc's pulse picked up. The moment they'd waited for—fought for—arrived at last.

Ariol's voice lowered. "Not her physical form. Only her projection. The Gatekeeper's power *could* reach the Keeper's body—but her mind has not yet recovered enough to attempt it safely. Until she stabilizes, this is the only way."

Ferenc exhaled, slow and steady. Their journey hadn't ended, not yet. But for the first time in what felt like forever, answers waited ahead. Real ones.

SIGN UP FOR S.W. RAINE'S AUTHOR NEWSLETTER

Be the first to learn about S.W. Raine's new releases and receive exclusive content!

http://swraine.com

ALSO BY S.W. RAINE

Standalones

The Techno Mage

The Adventures of Captain Keenan

Rise of the Sky Pirate

The Elementals Trilogy

The Elemental's Guardian

Just call her Raine. S.W. Raine writes steampunk and urban fantasy adventures full of action, banter, and found-family vibes. A Canadian-born mischief-maker now living in Michigan, she's usually scheming new ways to put her characters through magical mayhem, adventuring with her family, or wrangling two cats who are probably plotting world domination. She's also a gamer and Marvel fangirl—especially when it comes to Loki and Bucky. Want more mischief and magic? Join her newsletter for sneak peeks and stories.

Connect with S.W. Raine
Website: http://swraine.com
Facebook: @swraine
Instagram: @s.w.raine

www.ingramcontent.com/pod-product-compliance
Lightning Source LLC
Chambersburg PA
CBHW031332020726
47499CB00005B/1232